MERLYN'S MAGIC

A sob caught in Merlyn's throat for the ravages this man's grief had made on his face, his eyes dull with his private pain.

A shudder racked his body as she looked at him. 'Rand . . . ?' She half ran to him, and then stopped, not knowing what he wanted her to do. *She* wanted to go to him, put her arms around him, and comfort him in any way that he would let her.

As he slowly stood up, the magnificence of his body bathed in the glow of firelight, she knew there was only one way she *could* comfort him, that mere words alone wouldn't be enough.

'I want your magic tonight, Merlyn. I *need* it.'

CAROLE MORTIMER
is also the author of

GYPSY

MERLYN'S MAGIC

BY
CAROLE MORTIMER

W🌐RLDWIDE ROMANCE
London ● Sydney ● Toronto

For my husband John,
and our sons
Matthew and Joshua.

CHAPTER ONE

'HE says he doesn't want you to be his wife, Merlyn,' the man seated across the restaurant table told her with barely concealed anger.

She had known when Christopher Drake took time away from the film he had almost finished directing to take her out for lunch that something had gone wrong with their plan to work together in six weeks' time. Christopher was already way behind deadline, a fact that was reputedly making him harder to work with—and *for*, according to the cast and crew. He was a veritable demon, and as both producer and director, who demanded nothing less than perfection one hundred per cent of the time from those who worked for him, he must have been hell to be with these last few weeks of production.

Merlyn knew a lot of people considered her insane to feel this way, but she was actually looking forward to working with him. She had no doubt that he would live up to his reputation, but she had taken on difficult directors before and lived to tell the tale, and she had liked Christopher's looks from the first. He was tall and slim, the latter maintained by his barely leashed energy, with over-long blond hair that he constantly pushed off his forehead in impatient movements. It was an endearing habit, and Merlyn found herself resisting the impulse to smooth back those wayward locks herself.

But if what he said was true, then she wasn't going to get the chance to know him better, the prospect of working with him apparently in jeopardy. And knowing who 'he' was, she knew why.

'Don't feel bad about it, Merlyn.' Christopher scowled, obviously not pleased with the development at all. 'You're the fourth he's turned down in almost a year.'

Tact and diplomacy didn't appear to be part of Christopher Drake's personality either, but after years of living and working with people in a profession full of affectations and insincerity, it was a refreshing change to meet someone so bluntly honest.

'Who was my competition?' she asked in an amused voice.

'Not competition,' Christopher dismissed disgustedly. 'Just your predecessors. None of them got any further than this stage either.'

'This stage?' she prompted, toying with the scampi on her plate.

'The film studio bought the screen rights to the book from the author but, unfortunately, she made the stipulation in the contract that her brother-in-law had to approve of the actress chosen to play the part of his wife.' Christopher's disparaging tone told her exactly what he thought of that clause.

Merlyn shrugged, the long swathe of her shimmering red hair rippling halfway down her spine to her waist. 'That seems only fair.'

Christopher's slender fingers tightened about

his wineglass. 'Not when he doesn't want the film made!' Blue eyes glowered his displeasure. 'Anne Benton forgot to mention that little fact when she signed the contract.'

Merlyn had read the book Anne Benton had written about her sister's short but eventful life, had been touched by the affectionate admiration the younger sister had for the elder. The book was poignantly tender, a fitting tribute to a warm and beautiful woman who had died too young. It must also be a heart-breaking reminder to Suzie Forrester's husband of his tragic loss.

'That's that, then,' she sighed, sitting back, her disappointment reflecting in the deep green of her slightly uptilting eyes. She had never met Suzie Forrester, but she had been attracted to portraying her as soon as she read the script, even more so since reading the book.

'Not necessarily,' Christopher said slowly.

She looked at him sharply. 'If Brandon Carmichael doesn't want me in the part——'

'How does he know what he wants?' the man opposite her dismissed impatiently. 'He's never seen you! He didn't see any of your predecessors either, he just turned them down flat. Now if he could just meet you, and we could convince him——'

'Don't you mean *I* could convince him?' Merlyn cut in hardly, easily able to guess the way his mind was working; he was far from the first completely ruthless man she had met in this profession. And she doubted he would be the last, either.

'Why not?' Christopher wasn't in the least abashed at the admission.

Merlyn gave him a pitying look. 'Brandon Carmichael hardly sounds the type to be swayed by a pretty face!'

'You aren't merely pretty, you're beautiful,' Christopher stated, as a man used to dealing in nameless beautiful faces rather than personalities. 'You're also a damned good actress,' he added, just as practically. 'Besides, there's only six weeks left until production starts, and I'm beginning to feel like Selznick looking for his Scarlett!'

Merlyn didn't like to disillusion him, was sure he believed that every film he made was a masterpiece, but she knew that however poignantly moving the film on Suzie Forrester was going to be, it was only Christopher's conceit that allowed him to in any way compare it to the legendary *Gone With the Wind*. He was hardly the enthralled producer David O. Selznick, and she certainly wasn't Vivian Leigh!

Christopher scowled at her sceptical expression. 'For God's sake, I'm not asking you to sleep with the man, just convince him that we aren't all "ghoulish bastards"!'

She ignored the reference he had made to her using bedroom tactics to get Brandon Carmichael to agree to her playing the part of his wife in the film, knowing Christopher Drake was quite capable of asking that of her if he thought it would get the result he wanted. She was equally as sure what her answer to him would be! 'Is that a direct quote?' she asked ruefully.

Those deep blue eyes narrowed angrily. 'That's one of the more repeatable remarks he's made about the film being shot,' he confirmed harshly. 'The man is so damned arrogant——'

'He did lose his wife, Christopher——'

'Two years ago,' he put in in a disgruntled voice. 'God knows she was a beautiful woman, but——'

'You knew her?' Merlyn asked with interest.

Christopher shrugged. 'I worked with her a couple of times. Any man would be upset at losing her, but it was *years* ago now.'

Merlyn's expression softened indulgently. It didn't take too much intelligence to know that in all of his thirty-six years Christopher Drake, for all that his intensity as a lover was as renowned as his ability as a director, had never been in love. She wasn't too familiar with the true emotion herself, but she had known enough of the *untrue* kind to appreciate that to have loved and lost must be infinitely more painful than never having known the emotion at all.

But Christopher saw this situation one-dimensional, could only see Brandon Carmichael as the man who stood in the way of his making his film and not as the man who had loved his wife so much her death had all but destroyed him. Time certainly hadn't lessened the man's pain.

'What *did* you have in mind by way of convincing him?' Merlyn arched auburn brows mockingly.

'Well, I did invite him down to London to see you at the theatre, but——'

'He refused,' she guessed dryly. 'I really don't

think seeing me play Kate would endear me to him!' she derided, her title role in *The Taming of the Shrew* nothing at all like the vivacious but warmly beautiful Suzie Forrester. If Brandon Carmichael had seen her as Kate he would definitely have refused to let her take his wife's role in the film of her life!

He had turned her down anyway.

But being reminded of the latest role she had played during her year at the theatre, she was also forced to realise that she had turned down the offer of another contract so that she could start work on *To Live a Little* . . . , that she only had another week to go before her replacement took over. Originally, she had planned to take a month off before work began on the film, now it looked as if she were about to join the more than lengthy queue of the unemployed, and for someone who had rarely been out of work the last five years, that was going to be difficult to adjust to. But she had effectively closed one door and now another was being slammed in her face.

'This is as important to you as it is to me.' Christopher was shrewd enough to realise this as he watched the changing expressions on her face.

'I want the part,' she nodded. 'And not just because I'm out of work without it,' she added ruefully. 'It really is something that appeals to me.'

'It appeals to me too,' Christopher grated. 'We could pick up a few Oscars with it.'

The fact that their reasons were so different didn't surprise Merlyn, and she knew that Christopher's more mercenary attitude would in no way detract from his ability to make a fantastic film. But she had spent so much time during the last few weeks in learning the script and doing the research she felt necessary to get an all-round picture of Suzie Forrester, that she felt an affinity with the other woman, almost as if she had known her as a friend, even though they had never met. She would feel as if she were losing that friend if she didn't play Suzie.

'I had in mind,' Christopher paused, watching her closely, 'your going to see Carmichael.'

'Why?' Merlyn frowned, getting ready to punch him on his arrogant nose if he so much as hinted again that she sleep with the other man. Although she didn't think he would, not after the way she had already reacted to the idea; Christopher certainly wasn't a stupid man.

'To talk to him, of course,' he said in exasperation. 'Once he's met you he's going to realise we aren't all "ghoulish bastards", that some of us are even quite decent.'

Merlyn looked sceptical. 'According to the book written by his sister-in-law, he never liked or approved of his wife's career, and he's shunned everything to do with that world since her death. A visit from a woman who, in his mind, intends to capitalise on her death, isn't likely to endear me to him!'

'Do we have any other choice?'

She knew that Christopher did, that he could shelve the film and just keep coming up with other Suzies until Brandon Carmichael accepted one out of desperation. On the other hand, *she* had no real choice, and Christopher knew that.

He turned to the waiter and nodded for their bill. 'Let's go back to my place and discuss this further,' he suggested, silkily soft, sure enough of his own attraction not to doubt her acquiescence.

Merlyn smiled as she answered him.

'Mad dogs and Englishmen . . .' Merlyn thought irritably. Only she was a woman, and it wasn't the 'midday sun' she had ventured out in but torrential rain. Nevertheless, the maxim seemed to apply.

Christopher had encouraged her to take this trip with a glowing description of the beauty of the Lake District, assuring her that even if her visit to Brandon Carmichael proved unsuccessful then at least she would have had an enjoyable break from the hectic pace her life had been lived at the last year while she had been appearing on stage.

Since leaving Manchester Airport in her hire-car over an hour ago, the rain hadn't stopped falling, and she was beginning to realise why it was called the 'Lake' District; lakes seemed to be forming everywhere, especially on the roads, several drivers having pulled off the road altogether as the driving conditions became more and more difficult.

The wettest English summer for years, the weathermen had cheerfully informed them. As if anyone needed telling that—summer this year having consisted of one week in early April!

Merlyn knew why she was feeling so irritable,

and it had nothing to do with the weather. When she had decided on this month off between jobs it had seemed like a good idea but, after years of working constantly, the inactivity had gotten to her after only three days. The flat only took one day to clean thoroughly, another day to restock her freezer, and then another day to sit about with absolutely nothing to do. She ruefully acknowledged that Christopher had seen her restlessness and taken advantage of it.

That wasn't quite true, she accepted. She had still wanted the part of Suzie, and it had taken hardly any encouragement on Christopher's part to persuade her to make this trip to see Brandon Carmichael.

Anne Benton had been all for it, too. Although the two women had never met, Anne busy with the hotel she and her husband ran, Merlyn had spoken to her on the telephone, feeling an instant rapport with the warm-voiced woman. She had jumped at the chance of being a guest at the hotel when Anne suggested it, her brother-in-law living only a few miles away.

But Merlyn hadn't expected the delay in her flight because of fog, or the torrential rain that had greeted her when she went outside to get in her hire-car. It had been so bad when she first set out, the windscreen wipers proving ineffective, that she had contemplated staying in Manchester overnight and continuing her journey in the morning when, she hoped, the weather would have cleared somewhat. A telephone call to Anne had assured her that they had only a light drizzle falling up there, and so she had decided to make the drive after all. Unfortunately, the heavy rain had followed her all the way up!

Lake Windermere, as she drove past, was no more than fog-enshrouded greyness, the small town of Windermere itself deserted, the day-boats that were usually for hire, from the signs Merlyn saw up, had long-since closed down for the day. Who would have believed it could be August!

Anne's instructions for the location of the hotel had been explicit, but she hadn't allowed for the fact that Merlyn was used to driving in London, and that when told to take the first turning on the right she did exactly that, regardless of the fact that what had begun as a road soon tapered off as someone's driveway!

After twice getting soaked when she had to run to the house to ask for fresh instructions, the second time splattering the owner of the house with mud from his own driveway when she got stuck turning around and he had to push her out, she was near to deciding that the Lake District didn't like her and she didn't like it!

And then she saw it, The Forresters, the wooden sign beside the wrought-iron gates clearly discernible through the rain. She decided then and there to mention to Anne that her hotel would look infinitely more welcoming if the gates were left standing open, getting wet a third time when she ran out into the rain to correct the omission.

All of eight feet high, the gates groaned and creaked as she swung them back, the sneeze she gave as she hurriedly climbed back inside the car boding ill for the next few days. Maybe a nice long soak in the bath would rid her of the chill that was even now making her teeth rattle.

She drove through the gateway, slowing down after doing so, looking reluctantly in her driving-mirror. The rain seemed to be coming down heavier than ever, and the thought of going out into it again didn't appeal to her one bit but, on the other hand, a little voice at the back of her head kept saying something about the 'country code' and 'always shutting gates after you'. A town girl born and bred, she must have read it somewhere, because in all of her twenty-six years the only time she had spent in the countryside had been when she was working in some provincial theatre, and then she hadn't had time to explore her surroundings. But that voice kept nagging, and besides, she couldn't get any wetter than she already was.

Water dripped down her neck and into her eyes as she turned back to the car, but for the first time she had a clear view of the hotel that stood at the end of the driveway. It only needed Edward Rochester to come thundering up behind her and the whole scene could have stepped straight out of *Jane Eyre*!

The shiver Merlyn gave as she once again climbed into the car wasn't completely one of damp and cold, and she chided herself for her imagination. It had been that imagination that had influenced her into seeking success in a career that her two doctor parents and lawyer brother had been scandalised about. Her mother still explained the insanity by telling people her daughter had received a concussion as a child!

Her poor mother had never recovered from the shock of finding herself pregnant again at thirty-seven, after deciding at the birth of her son eight years earlier that she wanted no more children, and had taken the necessary steps to ensure that. The interruption to the career she had entered only three years earlier, while she gave birth to Merlyn, had been a brief one—Merlyn, and Richard to a degree, cared for by a full-time nanny.

Nanny Sylvia had been kind, but she hadn't been their own mother, and the experience had left Merlyn with a desire to fill her own house with children if she married, and it wouldn't be the sort of house her parents had either, elegant but lacking warmth; she wanted a real home. Not that she was any closer to finding the man she wanted to share that with. After seeing Christopher for only a week, she knew he wasn't that man; she had known that after only a few minutes in his company. A wife and family would definitely not fit in with his lifestyle.

Still, he was fun to be with, and he really did want her to play Suzie Forrester. All she had to do was convince Brandon Carmichael into agreeing to it. All? Hah!

'Hotel and country club' Anne had described The Forest, and although there wasn't much sign of the country club at the moment the hotel looked to be very comfortable. Anne and Suzie had come from a wealthy family, and this had obviously once been the family home.

The service could use a little improving, though, the front door remaining firmly closed, no one outside to open her car door for her or to take in the luggage either, as there would have been at a London hotel. Well, she didn't mind opening her own door—she had done it enough already today for one more time not to count! —but someone would have to take in the large suitcase and vanity case she had in the boot of the car; she refused to get soaked again while she grappled with them.

She pressed on the car horn, looking expectantly at the huge oak doors at the side of her. The doors remained closed. Obviously they weren't expecting any guests in this downpour, but even so—! She hooted again, keeping her hand pressed down on it. It was an act guaranteed to make her unpopular, but she was feeling too cold and miserable to care.

Her hand faltered slightly as one of the doors swung open. She heard the crash as it hit the wall with force even with the doors and windows to her car closed and the sound of the rain falling. She had long since ceased pressing on the horn.

Her eyes widened with apprehension as a giant of a man filled the doorway, and she had the fleeting impression of immense power—and anger—before he strode out into the rain as if it were no more than a light drizzle falling. Merlyn caught only a glimpse of overlong black hair, an equally unkempt black beard, and the fiercest silver eyes she had ever seen, before he disappeared behind her car. She turned anxiously in her seat to see where he had gone, almost falling

out on to the driveway as her door was suddenly
wrenched open.

'Have you ever heard of just ringing the doorbell like other people do?' the man exploded.
'I happened to be on the telephone when you
arrived. What do you——?'

Merlyn barely registered what he was saying,
let alone the fact that he had broken off the tirade
so suddenly. Their gazes were locked, green
merging into silver, and where once there had
been a damp chill to her body there was now a
quivering heat that she had never known before.
She couldn't even see the man's face properly
beneath the beard and the overlong hair being
whipped about his features by the fierce wind.
She had always preferred slender elegance in a
man to the muscles she could see beneath the
thick black sweater and fitted cords he wore, and
yet as she gazed—drowned!—in those silvery
depths, she knew this man could have carried her
into the house and up to his bedroom without a
word of protest from her.

As she gazed into his eyes, Merlyn knew that
she wanted him. Now!

The man seemed to shake off the spell that had
been weaving about them, anger darkening his
eyes. 'What the hell do you think you're doing?'
he rasped harshly.

She still wanted him. Unless she was becoming
feverish already from the numerous soakings she
had received today! His next words seemed to say
she had to be.

'If you prefer to just sit there looking like a
drowned cat than answer me then you can damn

well do so!' He slammed the car door back in her face.

'No—please!' He had reached the front door by the time Merlyn had managed to open her door and scramble out of the car to talk to him. He stood on the step looking back at her, oblivious of the rain streaming on his hair, over his face and body. Maybe if you lived with this weather long enough it did that to you! 'I—Could you take my luggage inside—please?' she added hopefully, feeling as if she had walked on to the set of Fawlty Towers and encountered John Cleese in his classic role as Basil Fawlty!

A dark scowl settled over those curiously light-coloured eyes. 'Do I look like a porter?' he scorned.

Merlyn chewed on her bottom lip. He was like no other porter she had ever met, possessed too much arrogance and authority for the—Oh no, this wasn't Anne's husband, James, was it? If it was she had committed a double gaffe, that of assuming he was one of his own porters, and of finding herself attracted to a married man, her own hostess's husband.

'Well?' He arched mockingly arrogant brows at her lack of response to his question.

Merlyn moistened her lips. 'Er—I'm sorry if I made a mistake about your position here. I——'

'I would say that's the second mistake you've made in the last few minutes,' he derided, his teeth gleaming very white against the darkness of his beard as he grinned at her discomfort.

Merlyn was so bemused by the unexpectedness of that grin that for a moment she was too

mesmerised by the change it made in his appearance—his eyes a warm grey, deep grooves
etched into the leanness of his cheeks—to realise
exactly what he had said. But once she did realise,
her gaze became wary. Had she shown so clearly
the impact he had had on her? If she had she
would never be able to look Anne Benton in the
eye when they were introduced.

'Oh?' she queried with a casualness she was far
from feeling.

'You're looking for The Forest hotel, right?' he
drawled, arms folded confidently across the
power of his chest, his stance challenging.

She frowned. 'Yes . . .'

'Well, you didn't find it,' he seemed to take
great pleasure in informing her.

'Oh, but——' The sky seemed to open up at
that moment, blinding Merlyn in its deluge so
that she gave a start of surprise as lean fingers
closed about her arm.

'For God's sake,' the man at her side exclaimed,
'let's get inside where it's at least dry!'

It was 'at least' the most beautifully furnished
house Merlyn had ever seen, the whole of the
downstairs area that was visible from the entrance hall decorated in subtle greens, greys, and
off-white. Huge cut-glass chandeliers adorned
the high ceilings and the delicately ornate staircase in front of her was like something out of a
fairy-story—or a film-set, Hollywood-style, that
is; things weren't done as grandly in England.
What was clearly apparent was that it wasn't a
hotel but a family home!

Her dismay was obvious as her gaze returned

to her reluctant host. 'I'm sorry, I seem to have —Atishoo!' The force of the sneeze made her shake uncontrollably, her eyes starting to water.

'You *seem* to have caught pneumonia,' her host remarked wryly. 'Come on.' He took her arm and pulled her towards the staircase.

'Where are we going?' Merlyn voiced her alarm. After all, what did she know about this man? She had no way of telling if he had any more right to be here than she did; he could just be taking refuge from the storm too. He certainly didn't look wealthy enough to actually own this house! Unless he was the caretaker? That was quite possible. If she had a house like this she wouldn't want to leave it unattended. But the man facing her didn't look the type she would entrust her lovely home to either! Well, maybe *she* would. After all, she suspected she could entrust her heart to him without too much encouragement.

'Upstairs,' he murmured softly. 'Scared?'

The recipient of a lot of teasing from a much older brother, Merlyn had never liked to be mocked, her eyes sparkling challengingly. 'Of you?' she taunted in a derisive voice.

His mouth quirked. 'Why not? As soon as I get you upstairs I'm going to rip all your clothes off,' he stated calmly.

Merlyn stiffened, drawing herself up to all of her five feet five inches in height, aware even as she did so that the man seemed to tower over her by nearly a foot, and that he weighed at least a hundred and eighty pounds. As she had driven up she hadn't seen another house anywhere near this one, and she was well aware that she would stand little or no chance against his weight and size if he should decide to take advantage of her vulnerability.

Nevertheless, she stood her ground. 'I might have something to say about that,' she murmured.

Dark brows rose. 'Judo expert, are you?' he mocked.

'I could be,' she evaded determinedly.

'Do you usually make this much fuss about taking your clothes off for a shower?' he taunted.

'Shower?' she blinked. 'You——'

'Yes?' he teased softly.

There were two red spots of anger in her otherwise pale cheeks, her indignation apparent by the scathing look she was sending him, the whole effect ruined by the ignominious sneeze she suddenly gave.

'No more arguments,' he declared, pulling her up the stairs with little regard for her stumbling, pushing her into a bedroom and stripping her coat off her before she had time to stop him. She did manage to pull back as he began to unbutton her blouse. 'What is it?' He frowned at her modesty. 'I have seen the unclothed female body before,' he told her impatiently.

She didn't doubt it. There was a raw masculinity about him that bespoke an intimate knowledge with women and his power over them. But he hadn't seen *her* body before, and that was the one she was worried about. Her hands placed over his halted his movements. 'I don't even know your name,' said Merlyn in exasperation.

His brow cleared, the mockery back. 'You mean that if we had been formally introduced you would have let me take your clothes off without protest?' he drawled.

This time the twin spots of colour in her cheeks were from embarrassment. 'No, I——'

'You can call me Rand.' He sighed his impatience with her indignant anger. 'And if you won't let me undress you then at least have the good sense to do so yourself, and then get into a hot shower. I'll be downstairs making us some coffee.' He walked forcefully from the room.

Merlyn was left with the impression that she had just survived a whirlwind. She sank slowly down on to the bed behind her, until she realised her sodden clothes would be dampening the silky peach coverlet. She stood up to undress, her thoughts with the puzzling man downstairs.

Rand. It had a nice sound to it. Her glance fell to the bed beside her. How would it feel to be in that bed beside him, her body entwined with his, crying out his name as he possessed her? Because that man would possess, not merely make love. That warm tingling she had known when she first looked at him returned to her body as she envisaged his dark head next to her fiery one on the pillows. He——

'Here you are.' Rand walked back into the room without warning, carrying her suitcase and vanity now, his eyes narrowing on the nakedness of her flesh beneath the dark blue of her unfastened blouse. Merlyn didn't need to look down to know that her flesh looked like pale ivory against the dark material.

Again that feeling of time standing still possessed her, and she made no effort to conceal the rounded curve of her breasts from his gaze. Instead, she made a rather provocative movement which brought the barely concealed nipples into thrusting prominence against the silky caress of the material.

Rand turned away abruptly. 'I thought you might like a change of clothes,' he bit out. 'Come downstairs when you're ready. I'll be in the lounge.'

As the breath slowly released from her lungs, Merlyn became aware that she hadn't drawn a breath since the moment Rand had burst in with her cases. No man had *ever* had this effect on her, and she found the feeling very disquietening. She didn't go around thrusting her body at men she had just met either. But then, she had never wanted a man like this before! Something was definitely making her act out of character, because she came from a family that masked their emotions, that didn't make any overt shows of feeling. Thrusting herself at Rand had been positively blatant!

The hot shower she took soothed the chill from her bones, it also stopped her teeth from chattering, what it didn't do was dampen that inner heat she had known from the moment she set eyes on Rand, as if her body knew and recognised him.

It was so ridiculous, had to be part of some sort of fever. For the first time in her life she wished flu on herself—she certainly couldn't actually want to make love with a complete stranger.

Pointedly keeping her gaze averted from the bed that had given her such erotic thoughts a few minutes ago, she gratefully pulled on dry denims and a warm jumper, although in the centrally-heated house the latter would probably be too hot once she was thoroughly rid of the chill that still racked her body. Her hair was already part-way dry, and she brushed it loosely down her back, ruefully accepting that it would become a mass of thick curls without the use of her hair-dryer to style it. In a profession where appearances often counted for everything, she had forgotten the last time her hair had been allowed to dry in this wild way. Oh well, what was the point in worrying about that now, when there wasn't a thing she could do about it? And she couldn't possibly look any worse than she had when she arrived!

The door to the bedroom opposite hers stood open now and, her curiosity piqued, Merlyn couldn't resist a glance inside. Like the rest of the house it was a splendidly furnished room, very masculine, and obviously belonged to her reluctant host, the huge bed easily able to accommodate his large frame, the peach and brown décor warm but lacking any femininity. It was a man's room, and——

Merlyn felt as if the breath had been knocked from her body as she stared at the photograph on the table beside the bed. It was of a beautiful, dark-haired woman with laughing blue eyes, love glowing in those eyes for the person on the other side of the camera.

Merlyn was drawn like a magnet to the inscription in the bottom right-hand corner of the photograph. 'Darling, I love you'. It didn't say who darling was, but because it was Rand's bedroom it had to be him, there was no signature to the declaration, but there didn't need to be one; no one who had lived in England the last ten years could help but know the woman who had dominated both British screen and theatre for that time. Suzie Forrester . . .

He had said his name was Rand, but— *Brandon*? Was that man downstairs Brandon Carmichael, Suzie's husband?

It wasn't surprising Merlyn hadn't recognised him, the only photographs she had seen of him had him dressed like the millionaire businessman that he was; the man downstairs wore faded and old clothes, and he didn't look as if he had shaved or had his hair cut for years. Years? *Two* years? Since the death of his wife . . .

Suzie Forrester's illness and then tragic death had been a blow to everyone who had ever seen her act, but to her husband of eight years it had been a loss from which he was reported never to have recovered.

He was never going to believe that Merlyn's arrival here had been accidental. He was going to think the whole thing had been staged so that she could meet him!

CHAPTER TWO

SHE looked at her host with new eyes when she joined him in the lounge, able to see some remnants of styling left in the overlong dark hair, also able to see the grey among the black on closer inspection. She knew Brandon Carmichael, or *Rand* Carmichael as he seemed to prefer to be known by those he chose to admit into the intimacy of his friendship—and after the way she had blundered in here she doubted she would ever be admitted into that small circle—was thirty-nine years old and, despite the youthfully overlong hair and the lean muscularity of his body, he looked it!

He was watching her in return, those silver eyes narrowed speculatively as she eyed him nervously. 'You'll want to telephone the hotel,' he spoke with sudden impatience.

'Will I?' She blinked cat-like eyes, wondering where all her confidence had gone when she needed it so desperately. 'I mean, I will. Of course I will,' she dismissed, irritated with herself for acting like a bumbling idiot. 'Anne will be worried about me.'

Those silver eyes glinted warily now. 'You're a friend of hers?'

She wouldn't recognise the other woman if there were only the two of them in the same room together! But she didn't stand a chance of persuading this man into letting her play the part of his wife now, had ruined any chance of that the moment she struggled to open those iron gates and drove inside. She should have known a hotel wouldn't shut its gates in that way, and she probably would have done if she hadn't felt so wet and cold by that time that she just wanted to take shelter somewhere, anywhere. Christopher was going to be far from amused when she told him what she had done, she didn't find it all that amusing herself!

'Sort of,' she answered Rand evasively, avoiding going into the details of that acquaintance as she frowned up at him. 'Is the hotel far from here?'

He shrugged. 'A couple of miles. It's at the other end of the estate.'

Merlyn knew from her research on Suzie Forrester that the Forrester sisters had been the only children of wealthy land-owner John Forrester, and that his estate had been left jointly to his daughters on his death. As she had initially guessed, this was the main house, so Anne must have built her hotel on her half.

'Don't worry,' Rand mocked, positioned to the left of the fireplace, a cheery fire burning there in the chill of this mid-summer day. 'You're far from the first person to make this mistake, this house is called The Forresters, the hotel, The Forest.' He shrugged. 'They're too similar. Although usually the wall and gates keep people out of here,' he added dryly, seeming to imply as he did so that there was nothing 'usual' about her!

She was blushing more today than she had the

last eight years, and she felt incredibly stupid. 'I'm sorry,' she grimaced. 'I've driven up from Manchester, taken so many wrong turns that I must have added twenty miles on to my journey; I was just desperate to reach the hotel by the time I spotted your gates.'

He nodded. 'I'll pour the coffee while you call Anne. You aren't going to be able to make it there tonight, I'm afraid.'

'What?' she gasped, her horror reflected in her eyes. 'But you said it's only a couple of miles away.' She shook her head. 'I can leave straight after I've had my coffee.'

'Unfortunately not,' he drawled, pouring the coffee.

'Why not?' she attacked. She had driven up here, she could drive back out again!

'You remember the ford you crossed about half a mile from here?' He arched dark brows, down on his haunches beside the low table.

She had been so blinded by the rain by that time that she had been lucky to stay on the road, let alone remember crossing a ford; the whole road had looked like a river to her. But if he said there was a ford then she believed him; she doubted many people disbelieved what this man said. If they did they were fools.

'It's flooded.' Rand straightened, the silver eyes cold at her dismayed expression.

'You mean it's completely impassable?' she groaned, needing to have her worst fear confirmed rather than just imagined.

'Unless your car floats, yes.' He gave a mocking inclination of his head.

'Is there another hotel near here?' Merlyn could feel her panic rising at the thought of being stranded here and left dependent on this man. When she had to tell him who she was she would be lucky if he didn't throw her out into the rain again to take her chances!

'The ford is on the private road to this house,' Rand told her. 'There is no other way out. You're stuck here until the river goes down again.'

She winced at his obvious displeasure as the realisation of her enforced stay struck him too. 'And how long will that take?'

He pursed his lips thoughtfully. 'If the rain stops soon, probably tomorrow.'

Merlyn turned to look out of one of the long windows at the steadily pouring rain; it didn't look like it was *ever* going to stop!

'Oh, it will,' Rand assured her in an amused voice as she unwittingly spoke her dismay aloud. 'Some time,' he added mockingly, the expression in his eyes one of challenge.

She inwardly groaned her despair. Her feelings for this man had been bewildering enough before she knew who he was. Now that she knew he was the still-grieving widower of Suzie Forrester, they were absolutely ridiculous. And she only had to look at him to feel her temperature rise and her senses quiver into life in a way she had never known before.

'You can use the bedroom you used earlier, opposite mine,' he added softly, as if guessing her response to him was the reason for her dismay.

And why shouldn't he have realised how he affected her, her behaviour earlier had been rather obvious! 'That's very kind of you——'

'Kindness doesn't have a damned thing to do with it,' he rasped. 'I don't have a choice.'

Neither did she, by the sound of it. And she couldn't blame him for resenting her intrusion either, he didn't come over as the sort of man who enjoyed having to be polite to a woman who had been stupid enough to get herself lost the way that she had.

'I'll telephone Anne,' she said quickly.

'Do that,' he nodded tersely, standing up to restlessly pace the room.

Merlyn watched him as she dialled the hotel number. He was prowling about like a caged lion, as if impatient with the confines even this large house offered. Continuous rain often had that effect on her too, and yet she sensed there was more to it than that where Rand was concerned; he and Suzie had shared this house all of their married life, so he must be used to the weather here after all these years.

She was prevented further speculation about him as she was put through the switchboard to Anne Benton. 'It's Merlyn,' she explained, looking questioningly at Rand as she heard his snort of disbelief as he heard her name.

'Thank God.' Anne's relief at hearing from her distracted her attention back from Rand. 'I've been so worried about you; we expected you hours ago.'

'Yes. Well, I—I got lost.' She avoided Rand's mocking gaze at this understatement. 'A—a neighbour of yours has kindly offered me a bed for the night,' she added awkwardly.

'A neighbour? But we don't have—Brandon?' Anne realised suddenly. 'Are you with Brandon?'

'He says his name is Rand,' she confirmed with a casualness she was far from feeling, relieved the other woman had guessed who the neighbour was and she didn't have to go into the details of her stupidity in front of this broodingly quiet man.

'Oh dear,' Anne groaned.

'Yes,' she agreed wholeheartedly.

'What a mess,' the other woman muttered.

That had to be even more of an understatement than the one Merlyn had made seconds ago; it was a catastrophe! From what Anne had told her, and what she had read herself about Brandon Carmichael, he was never going to believe she hadn't planned this whole thing, right down to the rain!

'The ford is flooded, right?' Anne guessed heavily.

Merlyn glanced at Rand as he crossed the room to pour himself a glass of brandy. 'I'm afraid so,' she answered the other woman.

'Does Brandon—know, about you?' The grimace could be heard in Anne's voice.

'Not yet,' she sighed, wishing she could be long gone from here before he did.

Anne drew in a ragged breath. 'Do you want me to tell him?'

'God, no!' she protested; she had to spend the rest of the evening and the long night in the same house with this man!

'No, probably not,' Anne conceded ruefully.

'You'll come up to the hotel and see us before travelling back to London?'

There was no point in either of them pretending there was any reason to go through with the visit now, and Merlyn was grateful for the other woman's understanding. 'Yes,' she agreed heavily. 'I'll do that.'

'Does Brandon want to talk to me?' the other woman prompted with obvious reluctance.

Merlyn glanced across at him as he grimly swallowed down the contents of his glass. 'Rand?' She held out the receiver to him questioningly, shrugging as he shook his head. 'He —he's busy at the moment,' she excused his rudeness to his sister-in-law.

'I'll bet,' Anne said knowingly. 'Merlyn, go easy with him today. It's——' The line went dead.

'Anne? Anne!' she questioned worriedly, shaking the receiver, as if it were its fault that the call had been terminated so abruptly.

'The lines have gone down,' Rand informed her without concern, confirming her worst suspicions. 'I'm surprised it didn't happen before now in this weather,' he told her in a calm voice.

She was completely alone, cut off here, with a man who would have reason to hate her if he realised who she was! Although her name hadn't elicited the response she had been dreading, only a mocking scepticism. Christopher had said Rand turned down every actress he proposed. Maybe, by the time they got to her, the fourth in line, they hadn't even got as far as the relating-her-name stage!

'Merlyn?' Rand looked at her scornfully.

She frowned, putting down the telephone receiver now that it was no longer of any use to her, running her hands nervously down her denim-clad thighs as she felt their damp palms. 'Yes?'

'No, I meant—Merlyn?' He sceptically repeated her name.

The flush to her cheeks came from anger this time. 'That is my name, yes,' she challenged.

His mouth twisted, his eyes cold. 'And can you do magic?' he jeered.

'I don't know,' she answered. 'I've never tried!'

He gave a bitter laugh. 'There's no such thing as magic,' he dismissed in a hard voice. 'How on earth did you get a name like that?' he derided harshly.

'After the birth of my brother, my mother had herself sterilised,' Merlyn told him quietly. 'She was more than surprised to find herself pregnant again eight years later.'

'Magic!' acknowledged Rand hardly.

'Considering my parents rarely saw each other enough to make love, it was all the more of a shock,' Merlyn nodded. 'My father was the one sent for an operation this time.'

He gave a harsh laugh. 'Poor bastard!'

She shrugged. 'I don't think he was all that thrilled to find himself a father again at forty-six, either!'

Rand turned away. 'Would you like a drink?' he bit out, pouring himself another one while he waited for her answer.

'The coffee will be fine——'

'It will be cold by now,' he dismissed.

'I'll make some more,' she offered, picking up

the tray. The way he was knocking back the brandy he was going to be needing a lot of black coffee soon! Unless this was how he spent his days now—she knew that he left the running of his considerable businesses to a number of assistants.

'Could you manage to "conjure" up some dinner for both of us?' he prompted. 'The only household staff I have come up from the village each day,' he explained abruptly. 'And I gave them all the day off.'

Considering the weather, that had been a very wise decision; Rand might have ended up with a *houseful* of unwanted guests instead of just one! As far as Merlyn was concerned, that might not have been a bad thing. 'I'll see what I can find,' she nodded. Food might help to counteract the alcohol he had been consuming, too.

It was a delightful kitchen, obviously belonging to a time long-gone, with its huge open fireplace, copper pots and saucepans hanging from hooks along its ledge. But Merlyn quickly discovered that although the charm and character had been maintained in the room it was also filled with every modern convenience, from a dishwasher to an electric knife.

The freezer was stocked with already prepared meals that just had to be defrosted in the microwave and then heated in the oven, and Merlyn mentally thanked the absent cook as she placed the beef casserole in the oven to warm through, making the mixture for dumplings before dropping them into the already warming meal, its aroma mouthwatering.

The kitchen at her flat was adequate, but it was nothing like the luxury of this one, and Merlyn was humming softly to herself as she put an apple pie in the oven with the beef. The humming stopped abruptly as she straightened, her face flushed from the heat of the oven, to find Rand Carmichael leaning against the wall just inside the kitchen, watching her every movement.

'As I haven't seen you since you brought up the fresh coffee almost an hour ago, I thought perhaps you had made your escape out the back door while you had the chance,' he drawled.

Merlyn frowned a little as he made it sound as if she were a prisoner here, although considering the state of the roads and the broken telephone lines perhaps that was what she was! 'That would have been ungrateful of me,' she dismissed, with an effort at her usual confidence, although just knowing who he was made that difficult, if not impossible.

'But perhaps wise.' He straightened. 'I was near to being drunk.'

'Was?' She frowned at the past tense; he had seemed pretty far gone to her.

He gave a mocking inclination of his head at her bluntness. 'I drank a couple of cups of black coffee and then took a shower. I can assure you I am now completely sober.'

That he had taken a shower was obvious by his still-damp hair, although even now it was drying back into those riotously dark curls. But the reckless glint had gone from his eyes, the anger from his expression, and in its place had come a weary look, almost of defeat.

'I hope you like what I've chosen for dinner,' she said lightly, some of her tension dissipating now that she was sure she didn't have a drunken host to contend with; she had a feeling this man could be dangerous enough, without that. 'There's a beef casserole, with baked potatoes, and apple pie——'

'I'm sure it will be fine,' he dismissed as a man not much interested in the food he ate, ingesting it only through necessity.

'Yes.' She eyed him frowningly. 'Well, if you would like to wait in the lounge——'

'I wouldn't,' he cut in softly.

Merlyn was filled with a new wariness now as she sensed the speculation in his gaze as it moved slowly over her body, the hair on her nape seeming to stand on end as a ripple of awareness flowed down her spine, her nipples suddenly taut against the softness of her jumper.

'Come here,' Rand suddenly instructed throatily, his stance one of challenge.

Her gaze flew to the hardness of his face. 'What?' she said breathlessly.

His brows rose slightly at her obvious nervousness. 'I said come here,' he repeated slowly, his gaze lowering pointedly to the hard thrust of her nipples beneath the clinging wool.

She felt like a puppet having her strings pulled as she crossed the room to stand in front of him, her eyes a dark stormy green as she stared up at him, her breath caught in her throat as she waited for the master to dictate what her next move should be.

Rand returned her look with narrowed eyes,

the slight rise and fall of his chest indicating the shallowness of his breathing. The bell of the timer on the microwave broke the spell, anger flaring in Rand's eyes—white hot fury turning them from grey to platinum. 'You have flour on your nose,' he declared harshly, turning away.

Her hand rose shakily to wipe away the flour. The gesture was mechanical as she was still watching Rand as he strode forcefully from the room, knowing he had brought her to him for quite a different reason, a reason that he had instantly regretted once he realised what he was doing.

If there had been any women in his life since his wife's death then no one but he—and they—knew about it. Before his marriage to Suzie Forrester he had often been mentioned in the gossip columns, had been a highly eligible bachelor, with numerous women in his life. During his marriage to Suzie, his actions had been just as newsworthy, but since her death he might as well have disappeared, never going to London, and certainly not involved in any of the social whirl he and Suzie had seemed to enjoy so much during their marriage.

But a few seconds ago there had been a physical hunger in his eyes—for Merlyn.

He was drinking brandy again when she brought the casserole up to the dining-room, although he joined her in a glass of wine with their meal, and he didn't go back to the brandy after they had eaten.

'So,' he sat across the room from her, 'you can do magic after all.'

'What?' She blinked up at him, startled by the comment.

'The meal you "conjured" up was very nice,' Rand's voice was mocking.

She moistened her lips, relaxing slightly. 'Thank you, but your cook did most of the work, I just defrosted.'

'You're from London.' It was a statement, not a question.

Merlyn instantly realised it was a mistake to ever relax around this man. 'Yes,' she confirmed warily.

'Decided to get away from the rat-race for a few days, hm?' His scornful tone told her exactly what he thought now of London and the social life there.

'I decided I'd like a change of scenery, yes,' she answered dryly. 'I could have stayed there and had weather better than this.'

'Touché.' His mouth quirked as he glanced out of the window where the rain could still be seen and heard. 'Are you in business in London?' The sharpness in those silver eyes belied his relaxed state as he lounged in the armchair.

This time Merlyn was ready for the directness of his questioning, meeting that narrowed gaze steadily as she answered him. 'No.'

Dark brows rose. 'You're a little cagey, aren't you?' he taunted softly.

'No more so than you, surely?' she challenged with cool confidence.

Rand's mouth tightened. 'I'm not in the habit of relating my life-story to complete strangers!' he rasped.

'Neither am I,' Merlyn returned softly. 'Besides,' she added as she sensed he was about to demand that she tell him exactly what she did in London, 'as you've already guessed, I'm here for a break. And when I get away like this I like to forget all about my work.'

'You're making your profession sound very mysterious.' He sipped at the coffee she had poured him, watching her over the cup's rim.

Merlyn's movements were deliberately controlled. 'I didn't mean to,' she dismissed coolly.

'It isn't the oldest profession for women, is it?' Rand taunted, deliberately provoking her.

She suspected that women had been acting in one way or another since the beginning of time, that they were only now allowed to show they were as capable as men, but she realised that wasn't the 'profession' he referred to. 'Women wouldn't need to provide that service if men didn't want it,' she snapped waspishly. 'It's a question of supply and demand!'

Rand eyed her angry expression with amusement. 'You speak as if from personal experience.'

Her eyes flashed like emeralds. 'I'm twenty-six years old, Mr Carmichael, and I've met my share of——'

'You know my name.' His eyes were narrowed on her suspiciously.

She instantly realised her mistake, although years of training kept her expression bland. 'Anne mentioned that her neighbour had to be her brother-in-law, *Brandon* Carmichael.'

He didn't look convinced. 'You didn't know who I was before you came up here?'

She arched auburn brows. 'Who are you, Mr Carmichael?' she mocked.

Surprise widened his eyes, and then his mouth quirked self-derisively. 'I think I deserved that!'

'I think so, too,' Merlyn nodded, relieved the danger seemed to have passed.

He ran an impatient hand through his hair. 'It's just that since this damned film on Suzie has been announced I've had several reporters trying to find out who I'm sleeping with now!'

Merlyn had received her own share of bad press over the years, although nothing as personal as that. She would have felt as angry as he obviously was, would probably have felt as resentful towards the film and everyone connected with it, too.

'You aren't a reporter, are you?' he grated as she seemed to pale a little.

'No,' she laughed gratefully.

'I hope not,' he scowled. 'Because rain or no rain you would be thrown out in it right now if I even suspected——'

'I'm not a reporter, Rand,' she repeated firmly. 'But I did realise who you were before Anne told me, although looking as you do now I had trouble recognising you.'

'Looking as I do now?' he challenged.

She shrugged. 'The long hair and beard; they went out of fashion years ago.'

'And when they were in fashion I was too damned busy trying to make my fortune to be able to indulge myself in such frivolity!' He stood up. 'But as long as you aren't some damned snooping reporter——'

'I can assure you I'm not,' she said coolly.

'Then I don't give a damn what work you do,' he frowned. 'Or even if you work at all!'

He was being insulting again, and Merlyn couldn't help but smile. 'Are there still such things as "kept" women?' she taunted.

Rand looked at her coldly. 'I'm not impressed by women's so-called independence from men,' he replied heatedly.

Merlyn frowned at his vehemence. 'I don't believe I was trying to impress you,' she snapped. 'Some of us don't have any choice *but* to be independent!'

'And how you all love it,' he jeered.

She shook her head. 'I don't think I know you well enough to discuss this rationally——'

'We aren't likely to get to know each other any better than this,' he bit out.

'Perhaps that's as well.' Merlyn glared at him defiantly.

'Perhaps it is.' Rand's nod was abrupt. 'Now if you'll excuse me,' he added scornfully, 'I have some work to attend to in my study.'

Merlyn felt the tension slowly ease from her body once he had left, aware that confrontation about her profession had only just been avoided, although at what cost. Rand had been married to a woman already well-established in her career long before they met, and yet he seemed to resent women having careers. Had their marriage not been as happy as all the stories about them had indicated? No, she couldn't believe that. A man could resent some aspect of a woman's life and still love her. She was sure Rand had loved Suzie.

Just as she was sure that any 'work' Rand had to attend to in his study would include a bottle of brandy. A man didn't drown his sorrows in alcohol if he hadn't loved the woman he had lost.

Merlyn would have felt a little better about the precariousness of her own position here if she could have talked to Anne again on the telephone at least, but the line was still dead when she lifted the receiver to check. Probably the other woman was as worried about the situation here as Merlyn was!

Having now met Brandon Carmichael, she was surprised that the other woman had had the courage to put her sister's life-story on to paper when Suzie's husband was obviously still so bitter and upset at his loss. She knew it had to be because of Anne's affection for him that the two of them had somehow managed to remain friends, that Rand hadn't cut the other woman from his life for what she had done. Merlyn had a feeling she was going to like Anne Benton very much, knew she had to be a very special lady for Rand to have accepted her book about Suzie.

Anne's book had more or less covered her sister's life from the time she was born, her childhood here, her first love affair, her determination to become an actress against family opposition —something Merlyn could sympathise with— her success in that profession, her marriage to Brandon Carmichael. She had spared Rand nothing in the telling of the latter, had written of his feelings of inadequacy against his wife's obviously wealthy background when his childhood had been spent in an orphanage, his wealth fought for with a ruthlessness that swept many weaker men behind him. That he loved Suzie before everything else in his life had been obvious, as had Suzie's love for him. They had been the golden couple, extremely happy together, Suzie's illness and the battle she had fought to overcome it almost killing Rand too.

It was a battle Merlyn wasn't sure he had yet managed to win.

She envied Suzie Forrester for having known a love like that, had given up any idea of finding such a love herself after the disillusionment of loving unwisely, her dream of having a husband and a houseful of children becoming exactly that. Against her will she was becoming as much of a career-woman as her mother was.

On that depressing thought she took herself up to bed.

It was a strange house, a strange bed, the rain sounding very threatening against the window of her bedroom, and she wasn't sure of her host's frame of mind either, but after the long and tiring day she had had, Merlyn fell asleep almost as soon as her head sank into the downy softness of the pillow.

She woke up just as suddenly!

She had heard a loud crash, instantly fearing that it had something to do with the storm still raging outside. Perhaps one of the towering pine trees that surrounded three sides of the house had come crashing down on top of it; the wind howling against the window sounded gale-force. She had to go and make sure Rand was all right!

His bedroom door still stood open, the room

empty, although the tangle of bedclothes showed that Rand had occupied the bed at least part of the night even if he weren't there now. Maybe he had gone downstairs to investigate the sound of that crashing noise?

She heard another crash, the sound of broken glass accompanying it, and it was coming from downstairs. God, the house was being crushed beneath those monstrous trees! As she rushed down the stairs to find Rand, she became aware of a strange sound coming from the direction of the lounge, like an animal whimpering in pain. She hadn't realised Rand possessed a cat or dog, maybe—

Her hand froze in the action of switching on the light as she realised those mournful groans weren't coming from an animal at all, that it was Rand making those muffled sobbing sounds as he knelt in all his naked glory in front of the fire still burning in the hearth, his face buried in his hands. On the carpet in front of him lay a broken picture frame, only 'Darling, I—' left of the inscription on the half-burned photograph of Suzie Forrester, that and the smile that had to be just for Rand.

Merlyn didn't know whether to go or stay, knew that she was intruding on this man's personal grief. The smashed frame and burnt photograph couldn't have been an accident, not when that same photograph had been standing on Rand's bedside table earlier. He had to have brought it downstairs with him.

Then she saw what had caused the first sound of crashing glass, a brandy bottle lying in several

pieces in the hearth, and from the lack of brandy
with it she guessed the bottle had been empty
before it was thrown. But why had Rand got
himself so drunk that in his rage he had destroyed the photograph of his wife? Whatever his
reason, she knew he would deeply resent her
intrusion, and she was turning to leave when she
realised that the heart-breaking sobbing had
stopped. Her lashes slowly raised as she looked
up to find that silver gaze fixed on her.

A sob caught in her own throat for the ravages
this man's grief had made on his face, his eyes
dull with his private pain, tears still dampening
the soft dark lashes, lines etched into his face, a
face white with emotion.

A shudder racked his body as she looked at
him. 'Rand . . . ?' She half ran to him, and then
stopped, not knowing what he wanted her to do.
She wanted to go to him, put her arms around
him, and comfort him in any way that he would
let her.

As he slowly stood up, the magnificence of his
body bathed in the glow of firelight, she knew
there was only one way she *could* comfort him tonight, that mere words alone wouldn't be enough.

She walked farther into the room, stopping a
short distance from Rand, her hands shaking
slightly as they moved up to slip the straps of her
nightgown from her shoulders, pushing the
material down over her breasts, the nipples
already taut and inviting, the silky garment becoming a splash of black at her feet as it slid down
over her hips to the carpeted floor. She stepped
over it and into Rand's arms.

CHAPTER THREE

IF anything the anguish on Rand's face had deepened by the time Merlyn raised her face from pressing feather-light kisses across his chest, and she pulled away hesitantly.

'No,' he groaned, holding her close. 'I want your magic tonight, Merlyn. I *need* it!'

She could feel the trembling of his body beneath her hands as they rested lightly on his shoulders, could feel the fierce hardness of his desire pressing against her stomach, trembling a little herself as she sensed the force of that desire should it be unleashed.

'You came to me in the midst of a storm, Merlyn.' He swung her up into his arms against his chest with little effort. 'Like a temptress stepping into my darkness.' He placed her gently on the carpeted floor, away from the shattered glass, but close enough for them to feel the fire's flames against their nakedness. 'I want to burn in your fire for just a short while.' He buried his face against the brightness of her hair. 'Warm me, Merlyn. Make me feel you!'

The wanting she had experienced when she first met him hadn't lessened, and yet as she smoothed the tousled hair back from his brow and opened her mouth to his, it was compassion that warmed her. She wanted to ease his pain, even if it meant experiencing pain of her own.

Their mouths moved moistly together, learning, seeking, *possessing*, the fierce thrusts of Rand's tongue giving her a pleasure she had never dreamt of. Rand had forgotten his living nightmare now as he lost himself to the magic of her body, caressing and knowing every inch of her, one of his hands protectively cupping the downy softness that shielded her womanhood. At the same time his head moved down her body until his mouth closed moistly over the turgid peak of one nipple.

Merlyn arched her back pleadingly as his mouth released her to trail moistly down the curve of her breast, gasping her ecstasy as he claimed the other pouting nipple.

Every inch of her trembled with need and, although he had been the one to plead with her, he was now the master, had become the conqueror without receiving the smallest resistance.

But Merlyn needed to touch him too, her hands sliding down the dampness of his back to his buttocks, her nails scraping lightly across his taut skin, feeling the quiver of his flesh beneath her caresses, knowing how to please him instinctively.

She moved determinedly, the aggressor now as Rand lay beneath her, controlling his entry as she moved on top of him, feeling the hard swell of him slowly move inside her, hoping he would put this delay down to an effort on her part to prolong his pleasure. His head was thrown back, his jaw clenched as she lifted herself up before lowering herself for a second time.

'Now, Merlyn,' he gasped his need. 'Don't play any more, take all of me!'

She was trying to. God, she was trying to! But she had never been with a man before tonight!

Rand felt like velvet against her, and she knew her body cried out for him, but the barrier of her virginity had to be overcome first, and it was proving more difficult than she had imagined. The books described it as a sharp pain and then, if your lover was considerate enough, the pleasure began. She didn't remember any of them saying it was like this.

Desperation had replaced passion as she once again lowered herself on to Rand, frustration making her sob as the barrier once again stopped his full entry. She wanted this man, needed him inside her as much as he needed to be there, and yet—She bit into her lip until she tasted her own blood in her mouth as Rand lost patience with what he thought was her game and took matters into his own hands, grasping her hips to guide her down on to him, filling her, engorging her.

After the pain came the most incredible feelings, as if Rand filled every space inside her. She felt overwhelmed, as if she belonged to this man, as if she would always be a part of him now. The tears that ran down her cheeks now were of happiness.

And then the pleasure began, Rand showing her how to move above him to give them both the maximum fulfilment, his eyes gleaming their satisfaction as she gasped weakly at this assault on her aroused senses.

The pressure building within her made her feel like crying and laughing simultaneously, the tumult rising inside her thrilling and frightening her at the same time. What was it going to be like, this physical satisfaction singing along her veins and clamouring for release?

And then she knew. It was like nothing she had ever experienced before.

Warmth, and aching, and fire burst free from the core of their joined bodies, Rand's teeth rough against her breast as he lost control in the river of her convulsions, his hands clenched into her buttocks as he quivered again and again inside her in his own spasmodic release.

They had reached their pleasure in unison, and even in her ignorance Merlyn knew how unique that was in a relationship of familiarity let alone during a first encounter.

Her lips were moistly open, her breathing ragged, as she languorously kissed every inch of his face, from the dampness of his forehead, the tautness of his cheeks, to the pliancy of his mouth. They had shared something so beautiful Merlyn never wanted this moment of closeness to end.

And then she realised that Rand no longer seemed aware of her at all, that he wasn't even looking at her any more but at the fireplace—at the half-burnt photograph of his dead wife. There was a dull, lifeless expression in his eyes that told Merlyn none of his thoughts.

But she didn't need to know them, had known when she offered herself that she had just been fulfilling a need for him. It wasn't his fault that she had broken the rules and felt as if she never wanted to be parted from him again!

He turned back to her with darkened eyes, frowning heavily. 'Did I do that to you?' He gently touched the swollen tenderness of her bottom lip where she had bitten into it at the moment of his possession.

She ran her tongue along the jagged soreness. The bleeding seemed to have stopped now, most of the blood having fallen on Rand's shoulder. 'No, I did,' she dismissed, wondering how on earth she was supposed to untangle their bodies without embarrassing both of them.

Compassion softened the harshness of his face. 'I never meant for that to happen, you know.'

Of course she knew! 'Neither did I,' she said huskily. 'But it's done now.'

'Yes,' he rasped.

She swallowed hard. 'I think I'd better go back to my room.'

'Yes.'

Tears filled her eyes as he made no effort to release her. 'Now,' Merlyn urged desperately.

His gaze held hers as he slowly turned her on her side away from the fire so that she lay beside him, darkness enfolding her as his broad shoulders blocked out most of the glow given off by the flames. 'I'm sorry,' he said suddenly.

She drew in a ragged breath, feeling bereft now that his body was no longer joined to hers. '*I* came to you,' she reminded him.

'Because you pitied me——'

'No!'

He swung away from her to stand up and cross

the room to once again stare broodingly into the fire. 'It's the usual reaction when you find a man crying in front of you like a child!'

'Rand——'

'Go back to your room—please,' he encouraged with a harshness that brooked no argument.

She hadn't been able to help him at all. All she had been able to do was give him a few moments of forgetfulness in her arms and then more pain. He felt as if he had betrayed his wife; he didn't need to tell her that, she just knew.

Merlyn's bedroom looked just as she had left it, the bedside lamp still on, the bedclothes thrown back where she had hurried to see what was happening. But she had changed. Since her disillusionment with Mark she had avoided any real closeness to men. She went out with them, she had a good time, but at the end of the day she always went home alone. God knows she had had her chances for it not to be that way, Christopher Drake only the last in a long line of men who wanted her to share their bed. But she had never found any difficulty in resisting those physical entanglements that in the end brought nothing but heartache.

Until Rand Carmichael. But she had felt no hesitation as she went to him, had felt that it was meant to be, as if she had known that from the moment she first saw him. Could it be that she had been so deeply involved with her research of Suzie Forrester these past months that for a brief time she had thought she *was* her? But that was ridiculous. Wasn't it . . . ?

* * *

Merlyn was already in the lounge when Rand came downstairs the next morning. She had found the broken glass gone from the hearth, the room looking innocent of the stormy lovemaking it had witnessed the evening before.

Merlyn wished she felt as innocent! Her body ached, the slight soreness she was experiencing not alleviated by the lengthy soak in the bath she had indulged in earlier. Her bottom lip was swollen and painful, and she felt altogether irritable. The only good thing about the day seemed to be that the rain had stopped falling some time in the night and with luck the water level on the ford would have gone down enough for her to get out of here. She was going to *walk* to the hotel if she still couldn't drive there; she certainly couldn't stay on here when she and Rand were so embarrassed about last night.

It was after nine when she heard him coming down the stairs, standing up to move nervously in front of one of the tall windows, the bright daylight behind her giving a golden halo to the red flame of her hair, her slender body warmed by fitting black denims and a royal-blue coloured jumper.

She looked warily at Rand as he hesitated just inside the doorway before fully entering the room, completing the task of tucking the black shirt he wore into the waistband of fitted grey trousers as he did so. Now that the confrontation had come, Merlyn didn't know what to say to him. What does a woman say to the complete stranger she made love with the night before!

Although he hadn't seemed so much of a stranger then.

Rand was eyeing her just as warily. 'Has Mrs Sutton arrived yet?' he asked abruptly.

'No one's arrived.' She shook her head. She had been going to say they were still completely alone, but in the circumstances that didn't sound right at all.

He frowned. 'I wonder——'

Both of them were startled when the telephone began to ring, Rand striding across the room to answer it. Merlyn watched him beneath lowered lashes, still finding it incredible that she knew his body more intimately than she knew her own. Any magic that had taken place last night had to have been instigated by Rand!

'Yes,' he was speaking to the caller now. 'Okay, we'll see you soon.' He rang off, shrugging slightly as he met Merlyn's questioning gaze. 'Anne,' he provided abruptly. 'She's driving over.'

Oh God, Merlyn thought shakily, how was she supposed to face Suzie's sister after what had happened in this very room the night before! Rand seemed to guess at her dismay.

'About last night——'

'Do we have to talk about it?' she cut in raggedly.

'Not if you don't want to.' He frowned in his effort to read her expression with the daylight reflected behind her. 'But——'

'I don't,' she snapped, her hands moving together nervously. If this was the way a woman felt the morning after going to bed with a man she was glad she had avoided such encounters; she had never felt so uncomfortably out of place in her life!

He ran a hand through his loosely curling black hair. 'I'd been drinking——'

She had known that, had tasted the brandy on his lips and tongue, colour flooding her cheeks as she vividly recalled their insistent probing. 'If that's supposed to make me feel better, it doesn't!' Her eyes flashed deeply green.

'I'm not trying to make you feel better——'

'That's good—because you weren't succeeding!' She was so tense her usual control had gone. 'You see, I hadn't been drinking!'

Rand sighed. 'I'm out of practice with the niceties of these bedroom games, and I'm sorry if all of this is coming out the wrong way.' He didn't notice how pale Merlyn had become as he moved to pour himself a cup of coffee from the pot Merlyn had made earlier. 'Believe it or not, I was faithful to my wife for the eight years of our marriage——'

'Why shouldn't I believe it?' she snapped. 'You loved her.'

'Yes, I did,' he grated bleakly. 'But it isn't fashionable in her world to be faithful to a spouse.'

What was he saying, that Suzie had been unfaithful to *him*? Merlyn had seen too many show business marriages fall apart because of the long separations and the loneliness their work often necessitated. But she wouldn't believe that of Suzie Forrester.

'We were *both* faithful.' Rand seemed to mock

her indignation. 'And since her death——' He
made an impatient movement, as if it still hurt
him to admit she *was* dead. 'I'm just trying to
explain to you why the age-old platitudes of
"how good it was" and "you were wonderful"
don't trip lightly off my tongue——'

'It wasn't that good,' Merlyn cut in hardly,
knowing that as far as she was concerned she
lied; it had been beautiful. 'And I wasn't that
wonderful,' she scorned self-derisively.

Rand's eyes had narrowed. 'You weren't that
bad either. Look, I'm not trying to give you a
rating from one to ten, I just wanted to make you
understand that I don't usually extract that sort of
payment from unexpected guests, that last night
was just—the circumstances were——'

'Unreal,' Merlyn supplied softly. 'They were
completely unreal, as if they happened to two
other people and not us at all.'

He blinked at her. 'Yes,' he confirmed in a
puzzled voice. 'That's exactly the way it seems. I
don't remember the last time I——' He turned
towards the front door as the bell rang, his expression grim. 'That will be Anne.'

Merlyn swallowed hard, dreading her meeting
with the other woman now, feeling as if she had
betrayed Anne's trust in her. 'Please don't let her
realise about last night——'

Rand glared at her. 'Do you think I want that
any more than you do?' he snapped. 'God knows
we've had our disagreements in the past, but
making love to one of her friends would not be
acceptable to Anne at all.'

Merlyn released her breath raggedly as she

waited for him to admit the other woman. She wasn't a friend of Anne Benton's, but she had wanted to be, and she knew that if Anne realised what had happened in this room the night before that she, too, would wonder at Merlyn's motives. She doubted anyone would believe her only 'motive' have been to be with the man she had wanted so desperately from the first. Mistaking this house for the hotel had been bad enough, but making love with Rand had ruined any chance she might have had of convincing him to let her appear in the film, especially as that chance had been slim to start with.

The woman who entered the lounge at Rand's side wasn't at all what Merlyn had been expecting. Anne was a short blonde woman of about thirty who, if one were being generous, could be called cuddly, and if one weren't, would be called plump. Suzie had been tall, ethereally slim, and dark-haired, and her sister came as something of a surprise.

Anne couldn't exactly be called beautiful either, with her even features, but as she smiled Merlyn realised she had something much more than mere surface beauty, that her warm blue eyes glowed with her inner serenity and gave her a charm that couldn't be bought or applied and would never fade.

'Merlyn!' she greeted warmly, crossing the room to hug her, unzipping the anorak she wore over a powder-blue jumper and denims as the heat in the room hit her. 'You're just as beautiful as I thought you would be,' she complimented without envy. 'You really——' The glow left her eyes as she frowned up at Merlyn. 'My God, what happened to your mouth?' she gasped, moving Merlyn out of the light of the window. 'You didn't mention anything yesterday about an accident——'

'I wasn't in an accident,' Merlyn refuted reluctantly, knowing Anne had seen what Rand hadn't; the black and purple bruising about the cut she had made on her bottom lip.

'But you look as if someone punched you in the— My God,' she breathed dazedly, turning slowly to look at Rand. 'You didn't!' She shook her head disbelievingly. 'Brandon, you can't blame Merlyn for any of this, it was my idea that she come up here. You didn't have to do this.' She looked again with horror at the bruising to Merlyn's lip.

'I didn't,' he dismissed abruptly. 'What was your idea? And if Merlyn is a friend of yours how is it that you didn't know how beautiful she is?' His eyes were narrowed with cold suspicion.

Merlyn gave a negative shake of her head as Anne looked at her enquiringly, knowing the other woman had expected her to have told Rand who she was by now. Maybe she should have done, but he was already unfriendly enough without that, and she had had no idea how long she was going to be stranded with him in this way. Cold indifference she could live with, armed warfare was something else! She would have told him the truth before she left, Merlyn knew she owed him that. Although she probably wouldn't have told him in quite this way.

'Because——'

'Because Anne and I have never met before,' Merlyn cut in firmly, giving the other woman a reassuring look before meeting Rand's challenging gaze at her admission. 'I'm an actress, and I——'

'Want to appear in that damned film they intend making about my wife,' he finished thunderously. 'I should have known,' he scorned. 'Arriving here in the storm with some tale about thinking this was Anne's hotel, when all the time——'

'That wasn't a tale,' Merlyn defended herself heatedly. 'Do you really imagine I wanted our first meeting to be made that way?'

'Yes, I think that's exactly what you wanted.' He looked at her in contempt. 'I think you planned yesterday down to the *last detail*!'

All the colour drained from her face at his silent implication that she had intended that they should make love last night all along, that if the opportunity hadn't presented itself the way that it had then she would have made it happen. It was completely unjustified, but she *had* known who he was and she *had* made love with him, and that was all Rand could see at the moment.

'Brandon, please.' Anne shot Merlyn a concerned glance. 'Merlyn only wanted——'

His icy gaze silenced his sister-in-law. 'I know you want this film made, Anne, but I'm sure even you don't realise the lengths your "friend" Merlyn went to to try and persuade me——'

'Anne, would you mind waiting for me outside?' Merlyn cut in shakily before Rand could list those 'lengths'. She was avoiding looking at him.

'I just have a few things to say to your brother-in-law, and then I intend getting as far away from here as I can!'

'But——'

'Perhaps that would be best.' Rand's voice was harsh, his gaze fixed relentlessly on Merlyn. 'Merlyn and I have a few things to say to each other that might shock your sensibilities,' he added with a sneer.

Anne looked at them each in turn, finally settling on Merlyn. 'I'll be waiting in the Range Rover,' she said gently. 'You'll have to leave your car here and collect it another time, I'm afraid; I only just managed to get through with the four-wheel drive.'

Merlyn had no intention of *ever* returning to this house, for any reason. It was a hire-car, she would pay the extra for the hire company to come and pick it up. She certainly couldn't see Rand Carmichael again, for any reason. 'I won't be long,' she assured the other woman.

'An actress!' Rand scorned as soon as they were alone. 'You should be given an award for your performance last night and this morning.' He paced the room, glaring at her. 'A damned actress!' he repeated disgustedly, his contempt obvious.

'I'm not a "damned" anything,' she snapped. 'And actress isn't a dirty word!'

'You're the latest of Christopher Drake's offerings, aren't you?' he accused, ignoring her anger. 'Did you go to bed with him, too, to get even this far?'

In the circumstances it was an accusation

which could have been expected, but that didn't make it any more acceptable. She may have been stupid last night, even more impetuous than she had ever been before in her life, but one thing she was not was promiscuous!

'What a stupid question,' Rand derided himself. 'Of course you've slept with him!'

'You were the one who wanted me last night,' she reminded him chokingly.

'Yes,' he confirmed. 'I wanted you. Do you have any idea why?'

She frowned at the violence of his aggression. 'You seemed upset——'

'Upset!' he repeated with derisive mockery. 'A man kneels before you sobbing like a baby and you think he was just upset!'

Merlyn moistened her lips. 'You didn't seem to want to explain——'

'And you didn't want to ask!' he scorned hardly. 'You just walked naked into my arms!'

She drew in a ragged breath, knowing she deserved his accusations; she hadn't *wanted* to probe into why he had been crying, she had just wanted to be with him. 'You didn't seem in the mood to talk——'

'No—I'm as susceptible to the beauty of a woman's naked body as the next man!' He looked at her with dislike. 'And when a wanton throws herself at you like that you don't stop to ask questions, you just take!'

'It wasn't like that!' She shook her head protestingly. 'I only wanted——'

'What you wanted you got,' he rasped. 'And you enjoyed every moment of it! But there was something you overlooked in all your greedy little plans—yesterday was the second anniversary of Suzie's death!'

The room swam dizzily before Merlyn's eyes for several seconds. The second anniversary of his wife's death! Anne had started to tell her something on the telephone yesterday just before the line went down, and she knew it had to have been this. If only she had realised. But these last few weeks she had been so intent on researching the living Suzie that the actual date of her death hadn't registered as being yesterday. But if she had known would she really have acted any differently when she found Rand sobbing so brokenly last night?

'Unless of course you did realise,' that silky voice cut in, dangerously soft, 'and decided I would be malleable on a day when Suzie's death was so vivid to me!'

'You know that isn't true,' Merlyn gasped, shaking her head in denial. 'I wouldn't do a thing like that. You——'

'I don't know a damn thing about you—except that you can drive a man wild enough in your arms for him to forget everything else for a short time!' His eyes were narrowed ominously. 'I don't need to know any more than that about you. The answer is no, Merlyn. N.O.—No! Even if I were ever to agree to this travesty being made I wouldn't let a woman like you defile Suzie's memory!'

Merlyn would take his other insults, but not that one. Suzie Forrester had been a beautiful and lovely woman, but Merlyn wouldn't accept being told she wasn't fit to portray her! All she had done wrong was to want this man, and she wasn't even sure that had been so wrong. She had gone to him when he needed someone, and at the time he hadn't seemed to mind.

'You know all these things you're saying about me aren't true,' she challenged him angrily.

'I told you, I know nothing about you—and I don't want to know!'

'You know something about me you aren't willing to admit to yourself,' she bit out. 'Why is that, Rand?' she cried bitterly. 'Does it make it difficult to put the blame for last night on me?'

His eyes were cold, angry slits between lush lashes. 'I don't know what you're talking about.'

'You may have been a faithful husband, Rand, but you had plenty of years before you met Suzie to experience every type of lovemaking there is. And although you haven't admitted it, you have to know that last night was my first time with a man!'

CHAPTER FOUR

'I know it had been a while for you——'

'The first time,' she insisted.

It had troubled her last night that Rand hadn't been aware of her innocence, and then she had been so lost to the ecstasy they were sharing that she had put it from her mind. But she knew he *had* to have been aware of that barrier he had breached, of the reason for her tears.

She continued to watch him challengingly.

'You're an actress——'

'I couldn't *fake* something like that!' she protested.

'Of course you could, it's done all the time in the marriage bed,' he taunted.

Merlyn shook her head disbelievingly. 'Do you really think that?'

'*Yes!*'

'Then I pity you——'

'I told you last night, I don't want your damned pity——'

'After you had already taken it,' Merlyn shot back. 'If Suzie could only see you now!'

He became deathly still, his body taut with tension. 'What do you mean?'

She sighed, accepting that he would never believe he had been her first lover—or he just didn't *want* to believe it. 'I feel as if I've come to know her rather well since reading Anne's book——'

'It was incomplete,' he rasped.

'It was written from your wife's notebooks; you gave them to Anne yourself.'

'Notes only tell a person's random thoughts, not what the person was really like.'

'Anne knew her sister well enough to know what she was "really like", and I've come to know her as well as I could without actually meeting her. And I know she would be disappointed in you——'

'Because I refuse to acknowledge the dubious virginity of a woman who gave herself to me for gain?' he scorned viciously.

'You didn't just bury your wife two years ago,' Merlyn told him shakily. 'You put your ability to care for other people in beside her!'

His mouth twisted. 'This isn't a scene from some B-movie with some hackneyed happy-ever-after ending where the hero throws himself into the heroine's arms as he realises he's fallen in love with her! And I've heard all the lectures I need to from Anne.'

She flinched at his scorn; she hadn't expected her criticism to suddenly transform him into a man who could love again, she wasn't that naïve, but she had hoped that his cynicism wasn't so deep-rooted that he wouldn't even listen when someone was concerned about him.

'Because *she* cares for you——'

'And what's your angle, Merlyn?' he jeered softly. 'Or do I really need to ask!'

It was useless trying to reason with this man,

she didn't even know why she felt the compunc-
tion to try. And yet she felt as if she had let down
Suzie's memory in some way by not being able to
reach Rand through the barrier of his bitterness.

'Anne's waiting,' she said abruptly. 'I hope you
don't mind if I leave my car here until I can
arrange to have it picked up. I—I hope you realise
Anne knew nothing about—about the things
you're accusing me of?' She looked at him
anxiously, having done enough damage without
ruining his relationship with his sister-in-law
too.

Grey eyes looked at her coldly. 'Anne could
never be involved in anything that sordid, I'm
well aware that it was all your own idea.'

He was meaning to be insulting, and he was
succeeding more effectively than he could guess.
The last thing she would ever be involved in
would be sleeping with anyone to get herself a
role on screen or stage. And if Rand had known
anything about her at all he would have realised
that.

But he didn't know anything about her, as she
really knew nothing of the man he was now. Two
years ago he had been the loving husband of
Suzie Forrester, had been her constant support as
she struggled with the illness that wanted to take
her away from him; God was the only one that
knew what he had become in the interim. Merlyn
and Rand were just two strangers who had made
love, primitively, mindlessly. She had broken all
of her own rules with a man who cared nothing
for her, a man she had wanted in a way that was
totally alien to her cautious nature, and she

would just have to learn to accept that and get on with her life.

Nevertheless, she had to try one more time to explain her actions to this man. 'I didn't plan what happened last night——'

'Would you just get out of here?' he cut in disgustedly. 'And tell your friend Drake not to send any more of the hitherto unknown actresses up here who have shared his bed to get their chance at the big-time; the next time my physical reaction might be a violent one! If it makes *you* feel any better,' he added contemptuously, 'you could probably have played Suzie; you certainly felt like her when I was inside you!'

Merlyn blanched at his cruelty as he revealed what she had feared, that he had imagined she was Suzie as he made love to her!

She turned blindly and stumbled out of the room, out of the house, her eyes swimming with unshed tears as she climbed up beside Anne in the Range Rover.

'I put your case—Merlyn?' Anne frowned at her worriedly. 'My God, Brandon *didn't* hit you, did he?'

Not anywhere that it showed. Inside, where it mattered, she was battered and bruised, her last shreds of self-respect stripped from her with Rand's last deliberately cruel taunt.

She blinked back the tears. 'Could we just get away from here? I—I really don't feel like talking about it right now.'

'Of course.' Anne still looked concerned, putting the Range Rover in gear, driving the large vehicle with a confidence born of familiarity.

'Merlyn?' she prompted gently once they had been driving in silence for several tension-filled moments. 'I know Brandon can be impossible at times——'

'He's a cold, calculating bastard,' she stated flatly, feeling as if he had stripped the very soul from her body.

Anne gave a ragged sigh. 'He's that, too,' she acknowledged heavily. 'But he hasn't always been this way.'

'I'm sure even he was a pleasant baby,' Merlyn allowed, feeling numb from the heart up.

The other woman gave a rueful smile. 'I meant a little more recently than that.'

She knew exactly what Anne meant, knew that Rand Carmichael had changed on the death of his wife. But he wasn't the only person ever to lose the one he loved in that tragic way, and it didn't give him the right to hurt her as he had, intentionally, coldly.

'I understand all that, Anne,' she said flatly, her eyes revealing her inner pain. 'But it doesn't help me at the moment, maybe later . . .'

Anne frowned. 'What did he do to you?'

Last night was going to be buried as far back in her memory as she could push it, never to be thought or talked about again. 'Nothing,' she bit out. 'Let's just say this trip was a mistake, that I failed in what I set out to do, and leave it at that.'

'If that's what you want,' Anne agreed slowly. 'But once Brandon's anger has calmed down——'

'I'm the one who's angry, Anne,' she cut in forcefully. 'And I certainly won't change my mind!' Nothing was worth the humiliation she had suffered at Rand Carmichael's hands.

'I'm sorry,' the other woman said with genuine regret. 'Still, that doesn't have to stop your staying on at the hotel with us for a few days; I'd like to get to know you after we spoke so much on the telephone.'

And Merlyn just wanted to get away from here and never think of Rand Carmichael again! But Anne had been friendly and kind to her from their first telephone conversation, and maybe if she just stayed on overnight and left in the morning it would placate the other woman.

'Maybe I will.' She didn't commit herself to the few days Anne had mentioned, turning to stare out of the window, making a determined effort to admire the spectacular countryside about her that hadn't been visible yesterday through the fog and the rain. High mountains dipped down into lush green valleys as far as the eye could see, and in those valleys Merlyn knew the lakes would be nestled, trees growing along their edge in abundance.

'Here we are,' Anne said with satisfaction as she turned the Range Rover into a narrow driveway much like the ones Merlyn had taken by accident the day before, the scent of pine from the towering trees surrounding them coming in through the partly-opened window next to Anne.

A long sprawling building much like a very large log cabin stood gracefully beside a large lake, its mellowed pine structure giving an air of warmth and beauty even before one entered.

'It's lovely!' Merlyn told her incredulously, seeing by the pleased expression on the other woman's face that her impulsive praise was appreciated.

'James designed and organised the building of it all himself.' Anne's pride in her husband's undoubted accomplishment was obvious. 'Come inside and see the rest of it,' she invited.

The inside was all pine too, warm and mellow, the main building housing all the entertainment, from the two restaurants, the club house, pool and sauna, to the health and beauty salon. And then at the back, not visible from the entrance, were two additional buildings, exact replicas of the main building, attached to it by two totally glass and pine constructed corridors that gave unhindered views of the surrounding mountains. These two outer buildings were the living accommodation, and Anne showed Merlyn to her room herself. The furnishing was more expensively comfortable than anything Merlyn had ever seen, from the thick brown carpets to the soft beige leather suite.

'James says that if you're going to do something you should always do it with style!' Anne laughed her enjoyment at Merlyn's awe-struck expression.

'This is style with a capital S!' She sank down on to the quilt-covered bed in the adjoining room to her lounge. 'I can't wait to meet the man who master-minded all this.'

Anne's eyes glowed merrily. 'Give me a few minutes to change out of these clothes and get back into my "hotel proprietor" garb and then join James and me at the pool for coffee; we usually get together there this time of day. And I know he's looking forward to meeting you, too.'

Thoughts of Rand were kept firmly at bay as Merlyn unpacked her suitcase, changing into tailored red trousers with their pleated waistline, tapering at the ankle, and a black silk blouse which tucked in at the belted waistline. She looked coolly elegant, and more confident of herself than she had felt since she left home yesterday morning with such high hopes of this visit to the Lake District.

Yesterday morning? It seemed much longer ago than that, she realised with a suppressed shudder.

She had no trouble finding her way back to the main building, the whole place geared for simplicity, including finding your way about. She was glad she had chosen to wear a blouse, instead of the jumper the weather called for, as the heat from the pool enveloped her. She seemed to have arrived before Anne, and——

'Looking for someone?' an amused male voice cut in on her reverie.

She turned to face the man, feeling as if she could drown in the liquid warmth of his deep brown eyes. Dark hair brushed away from the face of one of the most handsome men Merlyn had ever seen, the white shorts and open T-shirt he wore moulded to the lean fitness of his body. The tennis-racket he carried was indicative of at least one of the ways he maintained that fitness. At any other time she might have felt interested enough to pursue the acquaintance, but not when she was still raw from her encounter with Rand.

Her smile was coolly dismissive. 'As a matter of fact, I am,' she nodded, her attention returning to the pool where several adults and children were cavorting in the heated water oblivious to the dismal weather outside.

'Could I offer you a cup of coffee while you wait?' the man suggested, indicating the coffee pot and cups that stood on the table beside them for anyone to help themselves to after their swim. Several tables were placed about the pool's side, the padded chairs around them covered in a restful green material that exactly complimented the abundance of foliage about the room.

Her smile was frosty this time. 'No, thank you,' she bit out with emphasis.

'Then perhaps I could——'

'No!'

'You must be new here today, I haven't seen you about before,' he smiled pleasantly.

And she was sure he made a point of meeting all the women young enough to find his looks and charm appealing. He had chosen the wrong woman this time! 'Please,' she sighed her impatience, 'I'm waiting for——'

'Ah good.' Anne hurried out to her, the design of the royal-blue dress suiting her ample curves perfectly, the high heels on her sandals giving her extra height. 'The two of you have already introduced yourselves.' She beamed her pleasure.

'No, we——' The man Merlyn was rapidly suspecting of being James Benton returned her gaze with the same dawning realisation. 'Merlyn!' He grinned at her discomfort, holding out his hand.

She limply returned his firm handshake, deciding that the next stranger she met she would presume was the last person she had suspected; she certainly hadn't even guessed that this was Anne's husband James.

She grimaced—cringed, actually. 'I'm sorry if I seemed rude to you just now——'

'You didn't.' He gave her an understanding smile, those brown eyes twinkling merrily.

'What did you do?' Anne frowned her confusion as they all sat down.

'What did *I* do,' her husband corrected ruefully. 'I thought I was playing the concerned hotel manager, and Merlyn thought I was trying to pick her up!'

Merlyn blushed as he put into words what she had already realised, all of his friendliness a few moments ago made in an effort to make her feel at home. 'It wasn't quite like that. We——'

Anne grinned at her discomfort too now, sharing a look of intimacy with her husband. 'That makes a change, it's usually the female guests who try to pick James up!'

Merlyn was well aware of the fact that not by a word or deed had James given the impression he was trying to be more than helpful, that she had just *assumed*— If Elizabeth Taylor walked in here right now and told her she was Beth Jones she would take her word for it! Her judgment was sadly off beam lately.

'I really am sorry if I seemed rude to you,' she grimaced at James.

'Hey, after a run in with Brandon you're entitled to feel a bit jumpy,' he sympathised. 'And

I'm not exactly dressed for the part of debonair hotel manager,' he agreed wryly.

This man would look someone of authority no matter what he did or didn't wear, possessing an animal grace that bespoke confidence in himself and his abilities.

Merlyn complimented him on the design of the hotel, avoiding the subject of Rand Carmichael and the night she had spent at his house as his unwelcome guest.

If the truth were known she didn't feel all that well. Her throat was sore, her nose felt ticklish and irritated, and her head ached. But after the mess she had already made of her visit, she felt the least she owed the Bentons was to be sociable now that she had arrived, joining them for dinner in their private lodge a short distance away from the hotel through the trees.

Just being with the other couple was enough to show Merlyn how wrong her first impression of James as a flirt really was; the married couple were obviously very much in love, constantly touching with a warmth that bespoke intimacy, their expressions rapt as they gazed into each other's eyes. After the cool respect her parents showed for each other, the Bentons' relationship was quite an eye-opener for her.

But she felt even more ill by the time James walked her back to her suite, her eyes stinging too now, and she knew it wasn't just from the cold she could feel coming on. Anne and James had the closest, most special relationship she had ever seen, and the nearest Merlyn had ever come to feeling that sort of love herself had been when she looked at Rand Carmichael for the first time and knew she wanted him. And that wasn't the same thing at all.

'What happened between you and Brandon last night, Merlyn?' James spoke in the darkness.

Her face drained of all colour, and the pounding in her head became stronger. She swallowed hard. 'He made it clear he doesn't want anyone, least of all me, portraying his wife,' she explained huskily.

'That was this morning, I'm talking about last night.'

Merlyn kept her face averted, knowing those deep brown eyes could become hypnotic if she let them, and that beneath the gentleness of his love for Anne he could be as ruthless as the next man. She shrugged. 'What makes you think anything happened?'

His mouth quirked at her evasion. 'It may have escaped your notice, but the rest of us call him Brandon.'

'So?' she challenged, having noticed that discrepancy herself, but putting it down to the fact that last night he had wanted to forget who he really was as he made love to her.

'So you tell me,' James prompted softly.

'He let me sleep in his spare bedroom because he had no choice,' she dismissed hardly.

'Is that all?'

'What else were you expecting?' She forced lightness to her expression as she turned to face him on their entrance to the hotel reception.

He made a rueful expression. 'Well, I haven't seen too much of Brandon lately; his choice not

mine,' James added hardly. 'But he always used
to be able to appreciate a beautiful woman.'

'Appreciate, James?' she mocked with raised
brows.

'Enjoy,' he drawled.

Her eyes flashed. 'The most enjoyment Rand
found with me was this morning when he told me
to get out of his life and stay out,' she related
bitterly, knowing she spoke the truth. He hadn't
found physical release with Merlyn Summers last
night, he had made love to Suzie, his wife.

'I'm sorry.' James took her hand in his. 'He
wasn't always like this.' His head shook regretfully. 'The four of us used to have a lot of fun
when we were together.'

'You and Anne, and Rand and Suzie,' Merlyn
said abruptly.

'Yes,' he sighed, seeming lost in thought. 'It
feels like another lifetime.'

Merlyn had no wish to hear about the cosy
foursome they had made. 'You had better get
back to Anne, she'll be wondering where you
are,' prompted Merlyn lightly. 'And I want to get
a good night's rest before going back to London
tomorrow.'

'You're sure we can't persuade you to stay on a
few more days?' said James regretfully.

They had been trying all evening, ever since
she had told them she would be leaving in the
morning. 'No one could do that!' she told James
vehemently.

As it happened it wasn't a *someone* that prevented her leaving but a *something*; she woke up
in the morning with a raging temperature, a

rasping sore throat, and legs that refused to support her to the bathroom let alone all the way back to London!

The chill she had picked up during her constant dousings when she arrived raged for three days and nights, the fever finally breaking on the third night. She woke up to find Anne sitting beside her bed, the other woman instantly putting down the book she had been reading to bend over her concernedly.

'How are you feeling?' she probed gently.

'I hurt,' Merlyn managed to croak. 'All over!'

'That's to be expected,' Anne nodded, talking softly, seeming to know without being told that any loud noise would hurt Merlyn's throbbing head. 'Can I get you anything?' she prompted.

Merlyn sipped the cool water Anne helped her sit up to drink, her face deathly pale even from that small effort as she lay back against the pillows.

'Don't try and talk any more,' Anne encouraged. 'Just go back to sleep. You'll rest properly now that the fever has broken. And you'll want to look your best when Christopher arrives . . .'

Merlyn fought the waves of sleep that washed over her, trying desperately to take in what Anne was saying about Christopher. The sleep defeated her.

She was out of bed and sitting in a chair in the lounge when Christopher arrived the next day, having been admiring the view of the lake out of the long glass doors that opened out on to her small off-the-ground balcony.

Not knowing who to contact when Merlyn became ill, Anne had finally telephoned Christopher and he had promised to let her parents know she was all right, at the same time informing Anne that he would be down himself once he had finished filming. Merlyn had smiled ruefully when Anne related the last a little indignantly; that sounded like the Christopher she knew and liked, work had to come first.

Not that they were close enough for her to expect him to come rushing up here to her side anyway. Although Anne seemed to have formed a different opinion, acting as if she were sure Christopher were the love of Merlyn's life, insisting on helping her wash and dry her hair and adding a little make-up to her pale face, and getting out a silky black nightgown for her to put on beneath her robe. The nightgown wiped all the amusement at her new friend's antics from Merlyn's face; it was the one she had worn the night she went to Rand.

Christopher did little to allay the impression of intimacy between them when he arrived just after lunch, presenting her with roses and chocolates before kissing her lingeringly on the lips. Merlyn didn't need the dusting of blusher Anne had insisted on as colour flooded her cheeks.

'Nice to see you again, Mrs Benton,' he greeted the other woman warmly, his arm still about Merlyn's shoulders as he sat on the side of her chair.

Anne returned his smile. 'I'll leave the two of you alone. Please join James and me for afternoon tea once Merlyn has settled down for her nap,' she invited Christopher.

'She has the makings of a drill-sergeant,' Merlyn said dryly once the other woman had left. 'Do you know that she had me drinking hot milk this morning?' she added disgustedly as Christopher chuckled. 'To build up my strength, she said. It's all I can usually do to take the stuff in tea and coffee!'

Christopher grinned at her discomfort. 'Did you drink it?'

'Anne may give the impression of being a cuddly blonde,' Merlyn muttered, 'but underneath that warm exterior beats a heart of pure ice!'

'You drank it,' laughed Christopher softly.

Merlyn gave him a disgruntled look. 'She stood over me until I did! But she wouldn't have succeeded if she hadn't caught me at a time when I'm feeling too weak to fight her,' she defended irritably. 'And what about you just now?' She frowned at him. 'You don't usually kiss me hello like that.'

'I didn't like to disillusion the cute but domineering Mrs Benton,' he said ruefully. 'When she telephoned and told me you were ill and I said I'd come up as soon as I could get away she assumed we were lovers, and I didn't like to disappoint her.'

'You mean she bullied you into acting out of character too,' Merlyn said with satisfaction.

'Well . . .'

'And you were too frightened of her to tell her your only interest in seeing me was to find out if I had managed to talk to her brother-in-law and

persuade him into letting me star in your film!'
she accused.

Christopher arched dark blond brows. 'You
know damn well that isn't my only interest in
you,' he drawled. 'You just won't let me pursue
my other one!'

During their brief acquaintance, his efforts to
persuade her into his bed had been made with an
arrogant lack of subtlety that told her he usually
found little resistance to his physical interest in a
woman. And yet it was all done with such good
humour, Christopher not at all offended when
she refused him, that she realised plenty of
women would probably find that very indifference a challenge worth pursuing. Unfortunately
—for Christopher!—she wasn't one of those
women. But she couldn't help liking him, and
she thought that liking was returned. Even if
Christopher was surprised to find himself just a
friend rather than a lover.

'So how did you get on with Carmichael?' He
stood looking down at her, his hands thrust into
the pockets of his fitted trousers, his careless
treatment of them straining the expensive
material.

Christopher was everything Merlyn usually
found attractive in a man, good-looking, unde-
manding, with that intrinsic streak of ambition
that made him such a power to be reckoned with.
Why couldn't he have been the man she had
wanted so mindlessly? At least with him his
emotions were all up-front, and he would never
have hurt her so deliberately the way Rand
had.

'I'm sure Anne must have told you about my blunder,' she began.

'About thinking his house was the hotel.' Christopher nodded. 'I thought it was a good idea.'

Her eyes blazed wide with anger. 'I did not do it deliberately,' she bit out forcefully. 'It was raining, I was lost, and I didn't——'

'Oh, come on, Merlyn,' Christopher scoffed. 'Carmichael may have believed that, but we both know——'

'Rand Carmichael didn't believe anything of the sort.' Merlyn stood up shakily. 'And *we* don't know anything of the sort either,' she snapped, glaring up at him. 'Can't you see that by making that mistake I ruined any chance I may have had of talking to him rationally and calmly?'

Christopher looked at her consideringly. 'That depends,' he said slowly.

'On what? You—Christopher?' she questioned sharply. 'You don't seriously think I went through with your preposterous suggestion that I go to bed with him to get his approval?'

'I never once made that suggestion——'

'You implied it,' she flared.

'If I implied it you didn't say no to the idea either!' he accused heatedly.

Merlyn's hands were clenched at her sides. 'It was too contemptuous an idea to even merit an answer! You got off lightly at the time, Christopher,' she told him scathingly. 'The last man to suggest that to me ended up with an eye so discoloured it ruined his pretty looks for several weeks!'

His expression sharpened with interest. 'You mean you hit him?'

'Yes!'

'Do tell,' he invited softly.

Merlyn gave him a disparaging look. 'I make it a rule never to think about snakes and rats and other nasty things that go bump in the night.'

Christopher whistled through his teeth at her vehemence. 'Whew, am I glad we only got as far as managing to be friends.'

Her mouth twisted. 'You came dangerously close today to ending even that,' she warned.

He sighed. 'I'm only trying to establish what happened between you and Carmichael. You're the one who's being evasive.'

'Because nothing happened,' she snapped. 'Nothing at all.'

'And the film?'

'Now what was it he said to me about that?' She pretended to try and recall the words that had been burned into her heart. 'His last words to me were "Get out. And tell Drake not to send any more of his mistresses up here for my consideration or I might not be responsible for my actions!" That might not be word perfect, but it conveys what he wanted to say!' She didn't add that he had also said he had pretended she was Suzie while he made love to her.

'Arrogant bastard,' Christopher cursed with a scowl of anger.

Yes, Rand was arrogant, even more so than the man who stood before her, but if the two of them weren't adversaries in this matter they were so much alike they would probably have become friends.

'Now you know,' she shrugged.

'And what am I supposed to do about the film now?' Christopher frowned heavily. 'We're supposed to start work on it in three weeks, damn it!'

'Without a leading lady, unfortunately,' she drawled.

His eyes flashed with anger. 'I can't do that; "Suzie" is in nearly every damn scene!'

She knew that only too well, also knew that despite her personal dislike of Brandon Carmichael she would still have liked to have played the part of his wife in the film.

'Maybe if I went and talked to Carmichael——'

'I wouldn't if I were you,' Merlyn advised. 'He gave me the impression he would enjoy beating you to a pulp for even daring to suggest making the film in the first place!'

'This is ridiculous! You——'

'Merlyn, you shouldn't be walking about,' a scandalised Anne scolded her as she barged unannounced into the room. 'You only got out of bed this morning,' she fussed as she manoeuvred Merlyn into the bedroom. 'She's been very ill, Mr Drake.' She turned to include Christopher in her censure.

'It was my fault, Anne,' Merlyn tried to explain as she was firmly pushed down on the bed, her slippers removed and the covers pulled up to her chin before she could protest. 'Christopher and I were just——'

'It's time for your rest,' Anne cut in dismissively, her tone brooking no argument.

Merlyn grimaced at Christopher over the top of the bedclothes. 'I told you, I'm sure she was in the army in another life!'

Anne blushed prettily at the rebuke. 'The doctor said you weren't to overdo things to start with,' she reminded Merlyn of the instructions the kindly man had given her this morning when he called as he had every other morning since she had become ill.

'I don't think he meant you to take him quite this literally.' Merlyn struggled to sit up as the other woman tucked the bedclothes in so tightly she could barely move.

'I think I'll go and join your husband for that afternoon tea,' Christopher put in hastily at Anne's mutinous expression, making good his escape before her wrath fell on him.

'Coward!' Merlyn glared at the door as he closed it behind him.

'He's very handsome, isn't he?' Anne remarked casually as she stood watch over Merlyn as she drank down the fresh lemonade she had brought in for her.

'Says the woman married to the handsomest man for three counties!' Merlyn smiled.

Anne blushed again. 'James *is* gorgeous . . .'

'Even if he does have a sergeant-major for a wife!' She eyed the other woman mockingly.

Anne giggled. 'I'm getting into practice for when the children come along!'

'Are they imminent?' Merlyn asked with interest.

'Not too imminent,' answered Anne mischievously. 'To tell you the truth, we're having too much fun!'

Merlyn chuckled too. 'Still at the rehearsal stage, hm?' she teased.

'Oh no,' Anne denied, a satisfied curve to her full lips. 'We prefer to think of it as practising; we already have the act perfected!'

Merlyn watched the other woman as she pulled the curtains closed in preparation for her taking a nap, envying Anne her wonderful husband and happy marriage. She had only shared the sensual closeness she could see in Anne's glowing eyes once in her life, and the man hadn't shared that closeness with *her*.

For all that she had protested at being put to bed in that peremptory way, she sank back weakly against the pillows once Anne had left the darkened room, the effort of getting up to greet Christopher having tired her more than she had expected or realised. Her eyes fluttered closed within seconds of her relaxing.

She was having the most wonderful dream, that warm ache once more making her limbs feel like jelly, just wanting to stay like that as she felt the moistness of that mouth moving over her body.

'Rand . . . ?' she groaned, unable to wake from the deep sleep to see if this were dream or reality.

'I'm here, Merlyn,' a soft voice soothed. 'Give to me!'

Even now those knowledgeable lips were tugging on the aching hardness of her nipple, its twin being caressed in the same way with the gentle flick of a thumb-pad.

Her breathing became ragged as those lips moved down the flat contours of her stomach, teeth nibbling at the inside of her thighs before closing with erotic intent on the seductive core of her womanhood.

Tension filled her body as she felt the first flick of that tongue, the movement becoming a rhythm that made her writhe and gasp while remaining a prisoner to the onslaught.

She moaned her protest as that mouth left her, her moan turning to a ragged gasp as a knowing hand took over that rhythm at the same time as that mouth tormented her nipple.

The double attack on her senses made her strain into that hand, wanting more, wanting— Her gossamer moistness closed readily about the maleness that entered her, her back arching to match the fierceness of the thrusts.

She could feel the excitement building within her, could feel her release was imminent, felt herself filled with liquid warmth as the sun, the moon and the stars all exploded together inside her body, the sound of harsh breathing mingling with her own as that mouth finally left its caressing of her breast.

Her body felt cold at the removal of those lips, shivering as her thighs knew the same chill before the warm blankets once again became her cover. She reached out for the heat that was being denied her, only to feel it elude her before it slipped completely away . . .

*   *   *

Merlyn trembled as she awoke, never having known the eroticism of such a dream before, knew that her body had become a slave to that fulfilment even while she slept.

Colour warmed her cheeks, her breathing shallow as she acknowledged that. Even if the dreams had been a result of a return of the fever they had still been so very real. How Rand would laugh if he knew the hunger he had awakened in her! And how he would mock her if he knew it had been Rand himself she had imagined making love to her.

If she had imagined it. It had seemed so real . . .

Anne had left the door to Merlyn's room unlocked since she had become ill, so that she didn't need to disturb her every time she came in, she had said. Suppose someone, some unknown someone had come into her room while she slept and made love to her until she responded? Which had taken all of two seconds!

But who could it have been? Christopher? She didn't think so—he had so many willing women in his life he would have no need to make love to a sleeping woman. Then Rand? That idea was even more unlikely!

But it had *felt* like Rand. She had responded to *Rand*. She had *called* him Rand.

No, it couldn't have been. The man who made love to her had been a gentle lover, intent only on arousing her until she attained release. Rand certainly hadn't given the impression of those gentle feelings towards her the last time they spoke together. But if it hadn't been a dream

—although she was fervently beginning to hope it *had* been—and there really had been a man, then he had made love to her; no one in their right mind could ever call it rape.

Her eyes widened apprehensively as the door opened and Christopher came in, a jubilant expression on his face, seeming not to notice as she dived back beneath the bedclothes to hide her nakedness. Merlyn paled as she saw the nightgown she had worn to go to bed in earlier lying on the floor beside her.

'Ah, you're awake at last,' Christopher exclaimed excitedly. 'You——'

'What do you mean, "at last"?' she questioned warily, swallowing hard, her nakedness now when she had gone to bed in a nightgown putting a completely different light on her 'dream'. It had happened!

'I looked in on you earlier,' he dismissed. 'You were——'

'You did?' she pounced sharply. Oh my God, it *had* been Christopher!

He nodded impatiently. 'You were sleeping like a baby——'

'I was?' Her voice was doubtful.

'You were,' he confirmed with an angry frown. 'Would you mind letting me complete a sentence every now and again, I have something important to say!'

Oh no! Merlyn closed her eyes as giddiness washed over her.

'It's fantastic! Wonderful——'

'It is?' She opened her eyes to look at him uncertainly, wondering how she could tell him she had been responding to another man and not him at all. 'Christopher——'

'Merlyn!' He glared her into silence. 'And you told me you hadn't used your feminine charms on him,' he chastised.

Her expression sharpened suspiciously. 'Christopher, what are you talking about?'

'Well, if you would let me finish, I'd tell you.' He gave an irritated sigh. 'While I was having dinner with the Bentons—incidentally, that was why I came over to see you; Anne took to heart your sergeant-major comments and decided a change of scenery might do you good, and——'

'Christopher, please!' Her nerves were completely on edge, and she just wanted a straightforward explanation of what he was talking about.

'Carmichael arrived just as we were sitting down to dinner,' he announced triumphantly.

Merlyn swallowed hard, sure her face was devoid of all colour. 'He did?' she said faintly. Rand had been at the hotel this evening; had he also been in her room?

Christopher frowned his impatience with her. 'You could show a little more enthusiasm.'

Her eyes flashed angrily. 'Do I have anything to feel enthusiastic about?'

'We all do; he's agreed to let *you* star in the film,' Christopher told her excitedly. 'Now tell me again that you didn't go to bed with him!' He looked at her challengingly.

Three days ago Merlyn had been in no doubt about the fact that she and Rand had made love. It was this evening she wasn't too sure about . . .

CHAPTER FIVE

She still wasn't sure about that two weeks later when the whole of the film crew descended on The Forest hotel with the intention of using the actual location for any of the outside shots, a convincing replica of the inside of the house Suzie and Rand had shared being built in the studio.

Neither was she any nearer finding out why Rand had changed his mind and agreed to let her be in the film.

As soon as she had been well enough to venture out of the hotel after she had the flu, she had borrowed the Range Rover and driven over to the house to see Rand. The housekeeper, a tall woman with iron-grey hair and an indomitable disposition, had very politely, but firmly, informed her Mr Carmichael had gone away on business. Anne had confirmed it when Merlyn had explained where she had been, and Rand hadn't returned by the time she left two days later.

Why *had* he changed his mind about the film being made and with her starring in it? She didn't believe for one moment that it had anything to do with their making love. Although Christopher didn't agree with her. He had remained convinced that she had seduced Rand, and nothing she said could persuade him to think otherwise.

And she had tried. The two of them had continued to see each other occasionally once she returned to London shortly after he had, although their main topic of conversation had obviously been the film they were going to work on together. And Christopher had refused to believe she had just spent the night at Rand's house and then left. Maybe she hadn't been too convincing in her repeated denials of intimacy between them; after all, they weren't true.

She had thought a lot about that totally real dream, although it hadn't returned, and she had decided that she could, in her fever, have thrown off her own nightgown. That would certainly explain its presence on the floor. She was clutching at straws, she knew, but there was no other way she could live with the memories that haunted her.

She felt anticipation mixed in with her apprehension at returning to the Lake District.

She drove the whole way up in her own car this time, wanting the use of it for the weeks she would be there. Thankfully it wasn't raining this time, although the sky was overcast.

Anne was her usual warm self when she came to see Merlyn in her room shortly after she had arrived. 'Do they really need all those people and equipment?' she grimaced after hugging Merlyn. 'I know our busiest part of the season is over, but I feel like we've been invaded the last few days!'

Merlyn chuckled. 'We really need all those people and equipment.'

'James is in his element,' Anne groaned.

'Although I'm not too sure about his interest in the actress who's supposed to be playing me!'

Merlyn could see the other woman wasn't really concerned and, considering the closeness she and her husband had, that wasn't surprising. 'It must be a little weird meeting your double,' she nodded.

'Not at all,' Anne grinned. 'Oh, she has my colouring, but she's a lot slimmer than me, and one thing James does like about me is that I'm cuddly. Or so he tells me,' she added dryly.

'I'm sure he means it, too,' Merlyn laughed.

'So am I,' Anne nodded, completely confident. 'I grew up thinking all men wanted a woman that looked like a beanpole and, within a few minutes of meeting James and deciding I didn't stand a chance with him, he turned around and told me he likes to know he's holding a woman in his arms, not a matchstick with bumps!' She laughed huskily. 'I became a woman that very night—and it's been that way ever since.'

'I can see that,' Merlyn smiled.

'Talking of good-looking men——'

'Which we were,' she acknowledged teasingly.

'Which we definitely were,' Anne rejoined. 'The man who's going to play Brandon is absolutely gorgeous!' She rolled her eyes expressively.

'Gary Parker is handsome——'

'Gary Parker had to back out at the last minute,' Anne frowned. 'Didn't Christopher tell you?'

'He didn't say anything . . .' Merlyn frowned her own puzzlement. 'Who has he got instead?'

'His name is—Do you know, I can't remember

it?' Anne realised with some embarrassment. 'He isn't a big star, like Gary Parker is, but with his looks he certainly should be!'

'Careful, or James will be the one getting jealous,' Merlyn teased, although the replacement of Gary Parker at this stage unsettled her. The last two weeks had been spent engrossed in her part, and in all the scenes Suzie had with Brandon she had imagined being opposite Gary Parker. She would have to rethink them all.

'Never,' the other woman laughed off the idea. 'Christopher is by the pool, he said for you to join him as soon as you arrived.'

'He's working hard already, I see,' she derided, searching through her case for her bikini.

Anne took her remark seriously. 'Actually, he's working on the screen-play, something about it seems to be bothering him.'

'I was only joking,' Merlyn told her. 'Everyone in the business knows he's a workaholic.'

'Oh, I see.' Anne gave a self-conscious laugh. 'You'll have to excuse my ignorance; my sister may have been a star but my contact with the business has been very limited. Suzie always kept this part of her life completely separate from her career.'

Merlyn nodded, familiar with the habit of maintaining some privacy in her life. 'I'm surprised you dared to write the book.'

'Because of Brandon,' Anne nodded. 'He was all for my telling people how strong and determined Suzie had been, until he realised there was going to be a film too!'

'He's publicity shy, isn't he?' Merlyn acknowledged ruefully.

'Only about those last years with Suzie,' the other woman excused. 'He doesn't give a damn about any other aspects of his life appearing in newspapers.'

'Why is that, do you suppose?' asked Merlyn softly.

'You would have to ask him that,' Anne dismissed briskly. 'But I would say he just considers that part of his life too private to become public knowledge.'

Merlyn would say she was right, and to give Anne credit, although she had written quite extensively about Suzie and Rand's early married life together, she hadn't given any intimate details of their life together after Suzie became ill, had concentrated the rest of the book on Suzie's fight for life. Although that hadn't stopped a few intimate scenes being included in the screenplay, purely fabrication and guess-work on the part of the person who had written it with the help of Anne's book, but Merlyn was going to have to play those scenes anyway.

'Is Rand back from his business trip yet?' She feigned casualness.

The other woman nodded. 'You know, I've never been able to get over the way you call him Rand,' she frowned. 'He—Oh damn,' she muttered as the bleeper attached to her dress-belt interrupted her. 'I have to go,' she apologised. 'I'll see you later.'

Rand was back. She might even get to see him in the near future. But dare she ask him the questions that had been plaguing her the last weeks? She doubted she would have the nerve for that, and there was no guarantee he would put in an appearance; he had given them permission to film in the grounds, with the strict proviso that none of them was to go near the house.

And she wanted to see him. It had been so long, and she hungered just for the sight of him.

'Can I come in or would you rather be alone?' queried a cheerful voice.

Merlyn gave a guilty start as she turned to face Liza Benedict, the actress, only a year younger than herself, who was to play the part of Anne in the film. Small, and blonde, and a very good actress, she and Merlyn had worked together in the past; she was perfect for the role.

'Isn't this a super place?' Liza added before Merlyn could answer her earlier question. 'I've just got back from filming in Africa; this beats the dust and flies any time!' She made herself comfortable on Merlyn's sofa.

Merlyn liked the other woman, the two of them having kept in touch after they finished working together last time, pleased they were going to work together again. 'You'll have to lose some of that sun-tan before we start filming,' she teased, the other woman's tan very attractive against the blonde of her hair, but too deep a bronze for the English climate.

Liza grimaced. 'I'm sure make-up will take care of that.'

'Yes,' acknowledged Merlyn. 'Well, get your bikini and let's go,' she encouraged lightly.

'Christopher will be doing his realistic impression of a slave-driver soon enough!'

A speculative gleam entered the deep blue eyes. 'Talking of Christopher Drake——'

'Which we weren't,' Merlyn cut in firmly.

'We *were*.' Liza wasn't to be put off. 'I've heard several rumours about the two of you since I got back, and——'

'"We're just good friends",' Merlyn cut in decisively.

'From what I've heard of the dynamic Mr Drake, he doesn't have women friends!'

'I just told you he does,' Merlyn mocked. 'I'm the very first one!'

Liza gave a disappointed grimace and stood up. 'I hope you aren't going to be this close-mouthed about all the gossip circulating; I've been depending on you to tell me who's sleeping with whom!'

Merlyn smiled to herself as Liza went along the corridor to her room to collect her bathing costume. Maybe working on this film wasn't going to be so bad after all—Liza could certainly be a lot of fun to be around.

She didn't look up from slipping on the bottom half of her green bikini as Liza returned. 'Doesn't the fact that Christopher and I have separate rooms at different ends of the building tell you something?' she teased.

'What do you want it to tell me?'

Her fingers crushed the material of her bikini top into her palm as she straightened to look Rand Carmichael in the eye. Her first instinct was to put her hands over her bared breasts, but the idea was lost in a maelstrom of other emotions as she looked at a Rand she had never seen before. His hair was shorter, although still slightly over his ears, and the beard had gone completely, revealing a hard, uncompromising jaw and a mouth that still appeared sensual despite its mocking twist.

He didn't look younger, just different, and as Merlyn continued to look at him, she realised the man in her dream, that realistic dream that still haunted her, hadn't possessed that rasping beard she had known with Rand Carmichael! How long ago had the beard been removed?

His mouth quirked with hard amusement. 'This seems to be becoming a habit,' he drawled.

'What does?' she breathed softly.

'My walking in on you when you're half-undressed,' he mocked, his gaze raking over her contemptuously.

Whatever he was doing here, his opinion of her hadn't changed in the last two weeks. 'Maybe if you tried knocking for a change . . . ?' she challenged, putting the bra to her bikini on with unhurried movements. After all, he had seen it all before.

He shrugged his broad shoulders, the navy-blue shirt taut across their breadth. 'The door was open, I took that as an invitation to walk in.'

She searched his face avidly, wondering if he had just 'walked in' once before; she could read nothing from his expression. 'I was expecting a friend——'

'Male or female?' he taunted. 'Or do I really need to ask?' he scorned. 'After all, you were denying your affair with another man when I arrived!'

Her eyes flashed green sparks at him. 'I wasn't denying anything——'

'I don't see how you could when you got the starring role in this film despite all the odds——'

'Christopher likes to take unknowns and mould them into stars!' she defended hotly.

'You're the wrong height, the wrong colouring, the wrong age——'

'*You* could have stopped it if you wanted to,' she flared.

'I decided you'd earned it.' He moved closer, dangerously so for Merlyn's peace of mind, the heat of his body reaching out to her. 'And any time I want you to you'll earn it again,' he grated harshly.

'What do you mean?' Merlyn frantically searched the cold anger of his face for an explanation to his shattering statement.

'I want you,' he told her calmly, his hands warm on the bareness of her hips. 'And as you aren't averse to giving yourself to me, I intend taking you any time I feel like it. And that includes *now*! Especially now,' he groaned, his dark head bending towards her.

She wasn't just like the moth to the flame, although every time she touched this man she surely got burnt; but she was also like that creature the lemming she had once read about, who ran into the sea at migration and drowned itself. She was burning and drowning at the same time as Rand claimed her mouth with his own.

His jaw was smooth against her as his lips

moved against hers with a mastery that demanded she respond, that she give him what he wanted.

'Rand, please!' She wrenched her mouth from his, pleading with him to release her.

'No.' His eyes were hard as ice. 'I hadn't touched a woman since Suzie until the day a fiery-haired witch with the unlikely name of Merlyn lay down on my carpeted floor and gave herself to me. And now I want her again.'

'Rand. . . .' she gasped weakly at the memories he had just evoked.

'I'm a sensual man, Merlyn. I *enjoy* making love, and your magic is endless,' he grated. 'It's you I want and you I'm going to have. Merlyn's magic,' he mused hardly. 'Weave your spells for me again, Merlyn, I want to be inside you.'

'Me?' she scorned with her last shred of self-respect, the rhythm of his hips grinding against her filling her lower body with a warmth that was already his.

His mouth twisted, his eyes half-closed with the same desire as was in his hardened thighs as they moved against her. 'You,' he bit out harshly, his breathing ragged. 'Now!' he repeated forcefully, stripping her bikini briefs from her body in one deft movement. 'Next time you can undress me—slowly,' he told her huskily as he threw his clothes to the floor. 'Right now,' he drew her bikini top to one side, pushing her backwards on to the bed. 'I don't have the control to wait while you perform that pleasure.'

Merlyn gasped as his rigid shaft entered her, her flesh closing moistly about him as it accepted him, welcomed him. She lay still as she expected him to thrust into her savagely, sate himself, and then leave her.

Rand lay as still as she, although that hard shaft of pleasure throbbed and moved in her softness instinctively, the movements so slight as to be barely perceptible, although the rapid spiralling of their breathing said even that wasn't necessary, the aching need they shared building to a shattering climax for both of them.

It felt so strange, neither of them moving, apart from those inner quivers of flesh that were uncontrollable, and yet Merlyn knew she was about to attain that ultimate fulfilment. Just as she felt herself reach that pinnacle Rand moved savagely within her, this unexpected pleasure at the moment of her release making her groan and arch against him as she felt him spill his seed inside her time and time again.

His face was softened with sensual pleasure as Merlyn gazed down at him as he lay against her breasts like a satiated child that had drunk its fill.

She had expected his lovemaking to be little more than rape, knowing that even though she wouldn't have fought him she couldn't have responded either. Instead, it had been nothing like that, Rand giving not taking.

'Again!' he suddenly groaned, pain in his eyes as he made the admission, his mouth closing hotly over one moist nipple.

If Merlyn had thought he was like a satiated child she soon found that Rand never had his fill, taking and taking until she shuddered her fulfilment beneath him, feeling as if she couldn't give any more as he moved against her in silent demand.

This time her thrusts matched the intensity of his in their feverish clamouring for release, and she knew a pleasure-pain unlike anything before as her body shook and quivered to shuddering satisfaction.

Her arms tightened about him as he tried to move away, his hands firm on her shoulders as he pushed her back down into the bed as he stood up. His body maintained its aura of power even though his passion had momentarily been satisfied.

He gave a hard smile as she watched him dress with eyes full of contentment. 'Don't worry, I'll come back tonight,' he derided the sensuous compliance of her expression. 'This afternoon has shown me that I can't stay away!'

Women were no longer subservient to men, didn't have to accept their physical demands because they were a possession and it was a man's right to take what he wanted when he wanted, as it had been in another era. And yet that was exactly what Rand was asking—commanding! And she wasn't saying no.

'You'll find me a demanding lover, Merlyn,' he told her calmly as he tucked his shirt into the waistband of his trousers. 'So demanding that I expect you to tell whatever man you were waiting for when I arrived that you're no longer available.' His tone was hard. 'I want to be the one who claims your body every night and any other time of the day I want you!'

The thought of being the recipient of this man's

desire made her dizzy. 'And what do I get out of the relationship?' she challenged.

'Me.' His gaze was icy. 'And you do want me, don't you, little witch?'

She swallowed hard. 'No——'

'Oh yes,' he nodded, pulling the sheet from her naked body to kneel on the bed beside her. 'I saw it here the first time you looked at me.' His thumbtips moved lightly over her eyes. 'I taste it here every time I kiss you.' He touched her swollen lips in the same way. 'I see it here every time I caress you.' Those hands moved surely to her breasts. 'And I feel it here every time I enter you.' One hand cupped the moistness of her womanhood. 'You want me, Merlyn, and you're going to have me—because neither of us can say no!'

She did want him—he had already demonstrated how much!—but she also wanted love and affection, things he was incapable of giving. They had touched on the deepest level possible physically, but emotionally they hadn't even said hello.

'Rand, I can't cope with that sort of relationship.' Merlyn shook her head.

'It isn't a relationship, it's an arrangement,' he corrected grimly. 'Be honest with yourself—and me, Merlyn. I didn't force you to do anything just now, you wanted it all.'

Did she love this man? She had a feeling that she soon would if she didn't already—because she *did* want it all. But he was prepared to give so little.

'I can't handle this,' she shook. 'Not now.'

'Because of your work on the film,' he nodded.

'I'm not a monster,' he soothed. 'I understand the demands of your career, and I'll accept it when you're too tired to do more than collapse into bed at night.'

Of course he understood it, he had been the husband of an actress for eight years. But she couldn't be just a body in a bed to him, she wanted more than that. And he couldn't give it.

'No.' Somehow she found the strength to deny him, pushing his hands away to stand up, knowing he watched her as she once again put on her bikini. 'An afternoon—or night—in bed, when you decide you want me, is not something I want,' she told him firmly.

'But you do,' taunted Rand softly. 'You just did,' he reminded her.

Merlyn's mouth tightened at his arrogance. They had been to bed together for a mere hour, had made love twice in that time, and they had spoken little. 'Next you'll be telling me that we're both adults and that there's nothing wrong with taking what we want from each other,' she scorned.

'There isn't,' he rasped.

She gave him a pitying look. 'Find some other woman to satisfy your new-found interest in sex, Rand; I'm not the one for you.'

His mouth thinned, his nostrils flared, and his eyes turned coldly silver. 'I'll be back tonight,' he repeated harshly. 'And I want you to be here.'

'Waiting for you!'

'Yes.'

'I'm sorry,' she replied flatly.

'I won't chase after you like some damned boy!' he warned through gritted teeth.

'Good,' she sighed.

His hands clenched into fists. 'You can't make me burn the way I have for you and then expect to put out the fire by saying no! I won't let you,' he told her fiercely. 'I could live with that emptiness when no woman appealed to me, but I won't live with it when I know you want me as much as I want you!'

Merlyn stood shaking once he had left, not from the threat he had made not to accept her answer, but from the knowledge that he would only have to kiss her for that decision to be meaningless. She didn't understand him, she doubted he really understood himself or the physical demands he had that now tormented and controlled him.

'Wow, visions of Heathcliff, hm?' Liza said in an awestruck voice. 'No wonder you and Christopher are only friends!'

'Liza . . .' greeted Merlyn weakly, knowing her own tousled appearance and that of the bed behind her told their own story. 'I—er—I wondered what had happened to you.' She hadn't given the other woman another thought after Rand's arrival!

Her friend's eyes glowed mischievously as she gave Merlyn a chiding look for her lie. 'Admit it, you forgot my existence after Heathcliff arrived,' she derided. She was wearing a thigh-length robe over her bikini.

They both knew she had, until a few moments ago, a full hour after she was supposed to have gone to the pool with Liza. 'I think he's more of a Rochester than a Heathcliff,' Merlyn remarked lightly.

'Who *is* he?' Liza demanded with great interest.

She could be evasive and say his name was Rand, but as they were all going to be here for several weeks Liza was sure to be introduced to him some time. 'Brandon Carmichael,' she admitted abruptly.

Blue eyes widened with a shock Liza was too surprised to mask. 'Wow,' she finally breathed. 'I mean—well— Er—I didn't realise you knew him,' she said lamely, her gaze moving awkwardly over the rumpled bed. 'What I meant was——'

'Why, Liza, I think you're embarrassed,' she mocked. 'Either that or you have a terrible case of heat-rash. And as it's only about sixty-five degrees outside, I don't think-——'

'Don't tease,' Liza groaned. 'It's just that I thought you were holding out for Mr Right?'

She hadn't been 'holding out' at all, she had just never found anyone she wanted to make love with before. 'What makes you so sure I haven't found it with Brandon Carmichael?'

Liza wrinkled her nose. 'Because everyone knows he's still in love with his wife— Oh dear,' she groaned her consternation. 'I've done it again, haven't I! I'm sorry, Merlyn——'

'Don't be,' she dismissed her friend's apologies with a calm she didn't feel, locking her door behind her as they belatedly made their way over to the pool. 'I'm well aware of Rand's feelings for his wife, and what he wants from me. They bear little resemblance to each other,' she grimaced.

'He's really attractive, though, isn't he?' Liza
mused. 'I wish he had seen me first—I wouldn't
care who he thought he was in love with as long
as it was me he wanted.'

From what Rand had said, it wouldn't have
made any difference whom he had seen first, it
was Merlyn he wanted, Merlyn who had
reawakened his sexual hunger. 'You're welcome
to encourage him if you want to,' she invited
flatly. 'I don't have exclusive rights on him.'

'Maybe we had better stop talking about him
and worry about what Christopher is going to say
to you,' Liza grimaced. 'He didn't seem too
pleased when he asked where you were earlier
and I told him you were lying down for a while.'

Merlyn blushed at the way her friend had
avoided telling a lie, Liza having drawn her own
conclusions about the reason for Rand's visit to
her room—correct ones, as it happened. 'What
did he say?' she frowned.

'I don't know, I beat a hasty retreat back to
my room once I'd told him you would be over
later,' Liza admitted ruefully. 'I decided there
was safety in numbers!'

Christopher was in the oval-shaped pool when
they arrived, indulging in a game of handball
with some of the other crew members. Merlyn
and Liza sat down unobtrusively behind a potted
plant that almost managed to conceal them from
view, ordering a couple of pinacoladas from the
pool waiter.

Liza nibbled at some of the fruit arranged
decorously around the glass rim. 'Maybe he will

have cooled off by the time he gets out,' she said hopefully.

Merlyn's expression was sceptical. 'Maybe Mount St Helens is inactive,' she laughed hollowly.

'Hm,' her friend grimaced. 'I've heard they have similar temperaments!'

Merlyn smiled at her friend's attempt at a joke, although perhaps as that explosive temper of Christopher's was going to be directed at her maybe it wasn't so funny. 'As far as I know it was only a request that I join him by the pool, not an order.'

Liza broke off sipping her chilled drink through the brightly coloured straw. 'With him it's the same thing! I've worked with him before, remember?'

Merlyn vividly recalled the swearing and cursing that had gone on during that three-month period Liza had worked with Christopher just over a year ago; according to her friend, at the time he was a mixture of Attila the Hun and Genghis Khan combined, with a little bit of the Devil thrown in. 'You seem to have come back for more.'

'Because he's brilliant!' Liza scoffed the need to explain her presence here. 'And he's just climbed out of the pool and is coming our way,' she added softly, shooting Merlyn a nervous glance.

She smiled. 'You're welcome to make your escape while you can.'

'Now would I do that to a friend?'

'Yes,' she laughed.

'You're right,' Liza nodded sorrowfully. 'But I

don't have the time,' she managed to mutter before Christopher appeared at the side of their table. Liza, very wisely, buried her nose in her drink, keeping her gaze averted.

'How nice of you to finally join us, Merlyn,' Christopher greeted her with heavy sarcasm.

A face to face encounter with the reputed Drake temper wasn't something Merlyn relished after what had just happened with Rand. She had put on a brave face in front of Liza, was sure her friend hadn't guessed just how devastated she really felt about the time she had spent in Rand's arms; they were both adults, and they lived in a society where physical relationships out of marriage were accepted as the norm rather than the exception.

But inside, where it counted, she was a mass of confusing, conflicting emotions. And Rand seemed to know at least some of that conflict, wanting her in spite of himself, hating himself for the need but driven by an inner hunger. It was a hunger she more than matched.

'Merlyn!' Christopher snapped at her lack of attention to his justified anger.

'Sorry.' She managed to look suitably contrite, aware that they were attracting considerable attention from other members of the crew as they sensed Christopher was going to have one of his famous rages.

'Sorry doesn't excuse your tardiness,' he grated, shooting the cringing Liza a rapier glance. 'If you'll excuse us, Miss Benedict,' he declared harshly. 'I'd like to talk to Merlyn alone.'

Merlyn gave Liza a rueful glance as she responded to what could only be classified as an order—despite sounding like a request. 'See you later,' she told her lightly.

Christopher slid into the chair Liza had vacated, his hair slicked back as he had just got out of the pool, the towel he had used to soak up the excess water from his body and hair draped about his neck, the ends lying against his hair-roughened chest. He had a trim, muscular body; wide-shouldered, narrow-waisted. In fact, the only thing marring his good looks was his furious expression.

'Don't ever pull another stunt like that again,' he leant forward on the table to mutter through clenched teeth. 'You may have gotten the impression the last few weeks that our relationship——'

'Now just a minute,' she cut in protestingly.

'—gives you some sort of special privileges when it comes to discipline on my crew——'

'We haven't started filming yet, Christopher,' she pointed out coldly. 'And we don't have a——'

'—but let me tell you,' once again he continued straight on as if she hadn't interrupted, 'that I expect you to do the same as the rest of the cast—jump when I say jump, don't when I say you don't.'

'I am not a performing dog!' Angry colour blazed in her cheeks.

'You won't be a performing *anything* if I say you aren't,' he returned furiously.

And she had actually been looking forward to working with him, Merlyn thought curiously, as the two of them glared across the table at each other like contestants about to engage in mortal combat.

And then the humour of the situation struck her. On the one hand she had Rand demanding that she have an affair with him to settle both their lusts, and on the other hand she had Christopher warning her not to take advantage of *their* non-existent relationship. She could do without either of them.

'Do you mean that, Christopher?' she asked him softly.

'Yes! No! Hell, I don't know,' he sighed impatiently.

She gave him a rueful smile. 'Make your mind up,' she drawled.

'You knew damn well I wanted to see you——'

'I thought it was socially, not for work,' she told him truthfully.

'I don't have time to be social when I start filming,' he glared. 'I wanted you over here because I intended introducing you to your new co-star. I thought it best if the two of you got to know each other before we actually started filming——'

'But Merlyn and I are already acquainted, Christopher,' cut in a silky-smooth voice. 'It's good to see you again, Merlyn.'

She felt the colour drain from her face, moving slowly to look up at the man who had quietly joined them. He confidently returned her gaze, a man she despised even more than he hated her!

CHAPTER SIX

As she saw him watching her with those grey-blue eyes that could be as cold as ice, she knew he was waiting for her to stand up and make a scene at the idea of working with him. He never had understood her well enough to know how she would react to anything.

'Mark,' she greeted the man she had once contemplated marrying, her voice full of cool condescension. 'It's been so long since I've seen you I thought you must have retired from acting.'

His handsome face flushed at her bitchiness, his short hair so dark it was almost black, his face ruggedly handsome, his stance in the black bathing trunks he wore masculinely aggressive. At twenty-eight he hadn't yet managed to attain the stardom he so avidly sought.

'America beckoned,' he drawled, his anger firmly under control now.

'Really?' She expressed little interest. 'Then what are you doing back here?'

Icy blue eyes narrowed with dislike. 'Starring in a Christopher Drake film,' he bit out challengingly.

Her mouth tightened at the truth of that. And she had to accept that he had the looks to play the part of Rand, a youthful version of the other man. And she knew that he could act brilliantly when he chose to. But it hadn't been accidental that she had avoided seeing him the last six years.

'Strange,' she murmured softly. 'I thought *I* was the star of this film? But I do realise how important success has always been to you, Mark,' she added with saccharine-sweet understanding.

He looked pointedly across at Christopher before his gaze returned to her. 'To us all, surely?' he mocked suggestively.

Heated colour flooded her cheeks at his implication. 'Not that important——'

'You're more beautiful than ever, Merlyn,' he added throatily.

Nausea washed over her at the compliment. 'Luckily I've realised that a person's surface looks, no matter how dazzling, never completely disguise the decay inside!'

Mark returned her challenging look with insolent boredom. 'How interesting,' he taunted. 'I'd love to stay and chat with you a little longer but, unfortunately, I have more important things to do.' He put out a hand to lift a length of Merlyn's hair, maintaining a painful hold as she would have flinched away from his touch. 'Such a pity this flame has to go, it was always your best feature.' With one last painful tug on her hair he walked away.

Merlyn rubbed her pained scalp, blinking back the tears; she had forgotten how physically cruel Mark could be when he wanted to be. 'What did he mean by that?' she frowned at Christopher. 'I thought we had agreed I should wear a wig? I don't——'

'Is there some friction between you and Hillier

that I should know about?' he probed impatiently, ignoring her indignation.

Friction didn't begin to describe the dislike that existed between herself and Mark. She had once thought him the most wonderful man alive, had loved him with the blind devotion only the very young are capable of. And he had shown her how deep his own feelings for her went in a way she could never forget. She had never even tried to forgive what he had done to her!

'We just don't like each other,' she snapped in answer to Christopher's question. 'I'm sure it's nothing we can't both live with.'

Christopher still frowned. 'I've never seen you so antagonistic before, let alone bitchy. You—Oh hell,' he groaned as a sudden thought struck him. 'He isn't the man you grouped together with "snakes and rats and other things that go bump in the night", is he?'

In her estimation Mark Hillier was lower than any of those things, had shown his love for her only weeks before their wedding by asking her to go to bed with the director of the film he wanted to be in after the man had shown his interest in her.

She had been twenty years old, in love for the first—and last!—time, and the man she loved had asked her to prostitute herself for the sake of his career.

Mark hadn't accepted her outraged refusal as final, had tried to beat her into submission when sweet-talk and pleadings failed. By the time he had finished with her *no* man would have found her attractive. He had walked out of her life with the callous advice that she 'grow up'; he had beaten the child out of her!

He had lost the film-part he had wanted so badly to a man who had become internationally sought-after almost overnight, it seemed. Through the years that had been Merlyn's only consolation for what Mark had put her through.

Her glazed eyes focused on Christopher as she realised he was still waiting for an answer. 'No,' she lied, her humiliation at Mark's hands something she was sure Mark wouldn't want to become public knowledge either, confident that the way he had lost his temper with her wasn't even something he would have wanted to boast to his nearest friends about. 'He isn't that man.'

Christopher continued to look at her searchingly for several minutes. 'If you say so.' He gave a slow shrug. 'Just don't let your dislike spill over into my film,' he warned.

To be perfectly truthful, she wasn't sure she could do that. Some of the scenes between Mark and herself were very intimate, a couple of them actually in bed together, and while those sorts of scenes would be awkward enough when performed between two strangers who respected each other, between two people who had once intended marrying and now hated each other, they could just be impossible.

'I'll try not to,' she told Christopher dryly. 'What happened to Gary Parker?'

Christopher shrugged. 'He refused to sign a contract until all the uncertainty had been ironed out, and by the time it had he had agreed to do a series in the States.'

'I wish you had told me,' she scowled, sure she could have handled the meeting with Mark with a little more confidence and less resentment if she had been warned.

Christopher raised his brows arrogantly. 'I make the decisions around here, Merlyn, so don't think——'

'I *think* we've already had this conversation once today,' she sighed wearily. 'And I wouldn't presume on our relationship because we don't have one! We're friends, Christopher. And now I want you to tell me if it's true that you want me to change the colour of my hair?'

He gave an impatient sigh. 'I don't like wigs, they never look realistic, and——'

'And so you want me to dye my hair?' She grimaced at the thought; after all, she had been a redhead for twenty-six years!

'Not exactly. I've spoken to Sheila about it, and she thinks a wash-in colour will work. Of course you'll have to keep washing it in for the duration of the film, but——'

'Obviously,' snapped Merlyn, annoyed that he seemed to have discussed this with everyone but *her*.

Christopher's expression darkened. 'For God's sake, I'm sure this isn't the first time you've been asked to tone down the colour of your hair!' he accused.

She shook her head. 'In the past I've always worn wigs.'

'And I don't——'

'Like them,' she finished heavily. 'You already said.' Merlyn grimaced and sighed. 'I don't suppose I have any choice, do I?'

'No.' He looked at her challengingly.

'Then I'd better go and see Sheila about it, hadn't I?' She stood up.

Christopher smiled. 'There's no rush, you can have your swim first.'

'I'd rather get it over with.'

'You won't be able to swim afterwards,' he warned.

'I'll live with it!'

Christopher obviously found her reluctance very amusing, considered it suitable retribution for her tardiness earlier, no doubt.

But having to sit patiently in front of a mirror while her hair was turned from red to brown was the least of Merlyn's worries, Mark's presence here just making worse an already much-entangled situation. She was going to have Christopher and Mark breathing down her neck during filming, and Rand demanding sexual compliance outside of it.

'All right, love?' Sheila frowned down at her worriedly as she scowled.

'Fine,' she assured the woman wearily, opening her eyes to view the hairdresser's work.

'Well, what do you think?' Sheila turned to the mirror encouragingly.

Merlyn's head span dizzily as she looked at the reflection of the brown-haired woman blinking back at her. Suzie Forrester . . .

Of course, it wasn't Suzie Forrester, it was her, Merlyn Summers. Wasn't it . . . ?

'Amazing, isn't it?' Sheila admired her own handiwork. 'A snip here, and a snip there, and with your hair coloured and styled exactly like hers you even *look* like Suzie Forrester.'

While not exactly the other woman's double, Merlyn could easily have been her understudy. She looked—like a stranger to herself. She felt strange, as if she were two people; Suzie on the outside but Merlyn still on the inside.

Rand! Oh my God, what would Rand say when he saw this change in her?

'Merlyn?' Sheila once again frowned her concern at the younger woman's lack of response.

Of course she was Merlyn. And Rand had to have realised a certain amount would be done to make her as much like his wife as possible. He would have to accept the changes in her.

But could she? She studiously avoided looking at her reflection while verbally praising Sheila on the success of the colouring and styling, needing time to adjust to seeing a stranger in the mirror.

'Maybe I was wrong about your hair after all.'

She had thought she had made it to the sanctuary of her room without being seen by anyone she knew, the key to her door already in her hand as she stopped in the corridor to turn and face Mark. 'I take it that was meant as a compliment?' she scorned.

He sauntered over to join her, fully dressed now in denims and a loose-knit shirt, while Merlyn still wore her bikini beneath her robe. 'What else?' His gaze moved lazily over the resentment on her face. 'You're so provocative when you're angry,' he murmured with appreciation.

She pushed his hands away as he would have

put them on her shoulders and drawn her close to him. 'And your line in seduction is as hackneyed as it was six years ago!'

His mouth quirked with lazy amusement. 'You didn't find it hackneyed then.'

'I'm sorry, I didn't think I'd ever gone to bed with you?' she scoffed, knowing that she had implied there had been so many men since then that if they had been to bed together his lovemaking hadn't been outstanding enough to have made a lasting impression on her.

His eyes narrowed at the slight. 'That could soon be remedied.'

'I don't think so!' She looked at him with dislike, warding off his hands again as he would have reached for her, wondering what she had ever seen in his overbearing manner all those years ago. But then he had been getting more than the walk-on parts that she had, had seemed experienced and successful, and she had been flattered by his persistence in wanting to take her out. Now she could see him for the callous opportunist that he was.

Mark shrugged ruefully. 'Feeling pretty confident of yourself because you're keeping the director's bed warm, aren't you?' he taunted softly.

Her eyes flashed. 'I didn't do that for you and I've never had to do it for myself!' she spat out. 'Fortunately, some of us can get by on our talent alone!'

'Everyone knows that you and Drake have been sleeping together for weeks——'

'I don't give a damn what everyone *thinks* they

know,' she snapped. 'Christopher and I know it isn't true, and that's all that matters.' Except Rand, she didn't want Rand to hear those rumours and possibly believe them. Not when he already thought it was the truth anyway!

'No, it isn't,' Mark said slowly, threateningly. 'I've never forgotten what you did to me six years ago——'

'What *I* did to *you*?' she repeated disbelievingly. 'Don't you have that the wrong way round?'

'You lost me my big chance,' he grated.

'*You* lost you your big chance,' she scorned heatedly. 'Because you aren't good enough to get by on your acting alone, because——' Her words were cut off as his mouth savagely took hers.

Merlyn fought him with all the strength she possessed, and still it wasn't enough as he crudely pulled her hips into his, her hands trapped against his chest as the movements of his thighs against hers matched the slippery invasion of his tongue to her mouth. She felt herself gag at the penetration of that tongue, anger replaced by blackness as she sensed she was on the verge of collapse. And still that tongue raped her, deeper and deeper——

'What the hell is going on here?' Christopher demanded incredulously.

Merlyn was released so abruptly she swayed unsteadily on her feet, her face completely devoid of colour as she breathed deeply to stop herself from fainting.

'Merlyn!' Christopher realised that it was her now that he could see her face.

'The two of us were just—renewing our acquaintance,' Mark drawled insolently.

'He's lying.' Merlyn looked at him with loathing, turning beseechingly to Christopher. 'He forced himself on me. He sickens me!' she added on a choke.

Christopher shot the other man a searching glance, a nerve pulsing in his tightly clenched jaw before he turned back to Merlyn. 'Are you all right?' he questioned softly.

Her eyes widened. 'Didn't you hear what I just said, he forced himself on me!'

'Get lost, will you, Hillier,' he instructed the other man impatiently, going to Merlyn's side. 'And don't come near her again if you know what's good for you.'

'I didn't realise I would be stepping on anyone's toes,' Mark shrugged, looking at Merlyn challengingly.

'Well now you know,' Christopher replied, his hand in the small of Merlyn's back as he guided her to her room, taking the key from her shaking hand to open the door and follow her inside, watching her with angry eyes as she got herself a glass of water. 'Having an affair with your co-star is not something I like on my films.' His voice was cold.

Her eyes widened indignantly, and she choked on the water she had been swallowing as it got lodged in her throat. 'Christopher, I just told you he forced himself on me,' she gasped when she could get her breath back enough to speak.

He shrugged. 'You didn't look as if you were fighting too much to me.'

'Because he's a foot taller than me and weighs twice as much as I do!' she shouted.

'Calm down,' Christopher said softly. 'There's no need to get excited.'

'I don't want to calm down,' she told him agitatedly. 'Mark Hillier makes my skin crawl——'

'I'm sorry if I misjudged the situation between the two of you.' Christopher held her in his arms until the stiff indignation left her body. 'I don't think you realise how desirable you are.' He lightly kissed her hair and then down her cheek, his body tensing with desire.

Merlyn pulled away from him as he would have claimed her mouth. 'Really, Christopher,' she snapped. 'I've just had to fight off the attentions of one man I don't want!'

For a moment his eyes remained glazed with passion, and then he was smiling. 'Twice in one day would be too much, hm?' he said ruefully.

'Twice too much,' she agreed with a grimace; she had to give him credit, he *did* keep trying.

He nodded. 'I'll try and keep Hillier away from you in future. Maybe Liza will attract his interest——'

'I wouldn't wish him on my worst enemy—and Liza happens to be one of my best friends!'

'Oh well, I'll see if I can find something else to keep him busy. In the meantime, have dinner with me tonight——' He broke off as her telephone began to ring. 'You had better get that.' He turned away to look out of the window at the overcast day, his hands in his trouser pockets.

'Merlyn.' Anne sounded relieved to speak to

her. 'I've been trying to find you all afternoon. I forgot to invite you over for dinner this evening in the excitement of being called away so suddenly.'

Merlyn glanced at Christopher's profile as he stared out of the window, sure that he wasn't seeing the view at all but was lost in some inner thought about the film. 'Actually, I was just about to accept Christopher's invitation for tonight——'

'Bring him along,' Anne said instantly. 'You have to come, Merlyn,' she persuaded as Merlyn hesitated. 'James and I have invited a few close friends over for the evening, and I count you as one of them.'

'Thank you,' she accepted huskily. 'I— Will Rand be there?' The thought suddenly occurred to her.

'I've invited him.' The grimace could be heard in Anne's voice. 'Only he knows whether or not he'll be here. Oh, please come, Merlyn.'

Merlyn laughed softly. 'I'll just ask Christopher.' She put her hand over the mouthpiece as she turned to look at him. 'The Bentons would like us to go over for dinner.'

'Why not?' he shrugged. 'We should try and keep our host and hostess happy.'

She smiled ruefully at his cynicism before answering Anne. 'We should love to come.' She pulled a face at Christopher as he raised his brows at her enthusiasm. 'There is just one thing . . .' There was a pause.

'Yes?' Anne sounded worried.

'Well, you see, I've—I've had to have certain —changes, made to my appearance for the film,' she said in a rush. 'Not very big changes, but—I had my hair coloured brown this afternoon.'

For a moment there was silence, and then Anne gave a tremulous sigh. 'I'm glad you told me. Does Brandon— Has he seen you yet?'

'No.' Merlyn chewed on her inner lip, knowing it was his reaction to her appearance that she feared the most.

'If he does turn up tonight I'll try and fore-warn him,' Anne told her practically. 'You know, I'm beginning to wish I'd never written the book *or* agreed to the film,' she sighed. 'It seems to be causing nothing but trouble. But I was so proud of the way Suzie battled with cancer and won that I wanted the whole world to know about it too.'

'You should be proud,' Merlyn assured her. 'And so should Rand.'

'Proud of what?' Christopher questioned once she had rung off after arranging for the two of them to be at the Bentons' by eight o'clock.

'The way her sister fought against her illness,' she shrugged.

He nodded. 'It's a great story——'

'It isn't just a story, Christopher,' protested Merlyn. 'It happened to a real person!'

'I know that,' he accepted tersely. 'And as far as it goes it will make a good film. But I've been trying to do a little rewriting to the end; it isn't dramatic enough.'

Merlyn stared at him incredulously. 'A woman overcoming an illness that was diagnosed as ter-minal and then dying in a car crash isn't dramatic enough for you?'

CHAPTER SEVEN

MERLYN was still smarting at his insensitivity as she prepared for their dinner engagement that evening. God, *insensitive* didn't even begin to describe his callous attitude. She had known from the moment she met him that Christopher's work and the success of the finished production meant everything to him, but to dismiss the real-life tragedy of Suzie Forrester's death as 'not dramatic enough' seemed inhuman to her. The man was a machine, a total machine, and nothing must interfere with his making the best film that he could.

She had told him all of that earlier and he had shruggingly agreed.

Inhuman was too light a description too, she had ranted at him, and he had only laughed.

Grudgingly she had had to accept that Christopher couldn't help the way he was, that his near-genius prevented him from seeing the Suzie Forrester story as any more than another vehicle for his talent. She didn't like it, but she had to accept it.

She couldn't see Suzie that objectively herself, had lived every moment of Suzie's pain as she read Anne's book, had shared the family's utter despair when the police came to tell them that Suzie's car had gone off the road, killing her instantly as it struck a tree, her beautiful neck broken. How could Christopher say that cruelty of real life wasn't dramatic enough for him!

'Still angry with me?' he grimaced at her stony expression as they walked together to the Bentons' house nestled among the trees.

'No,' she answered shortly.

'You are,' he drawled, his arm moving easily about her shoulders. 'I was only speaking from a director's point of view earlier.'

Her eyes flashed as she glared at him. 'I realise that,' she bit out.

'And you didn't like it,' he acknowledged. 'Let's just forget I said it, okay?'

'And how are we supposed to do that?' The heels of her sandals clicked angrily against the tarmacked road as she walked.

'Well . . . I could tell you how beautiful you look tonight, and you could——'

'Tell you that a redhead's wardrobe is vastly different from that of a brunette's,' she complained. 'And that although black is usually my favourite colour in clothes, it doesn't suit me at all now!' She hadn't realised how attached she was to the red hair that had been the bane of her childhood until it was no longer there. She *liked* being a redhead.

Christopher whistled softly. 'You are in a mood, aren't you,' he taunted.

'Yes!'

It wasn't all Christopher's fault that she was so irritable—although he was responsible for most of it. But she was also nervous about this dinner party tonight, was dreading the fact that Rand might be there too. Just appearing as his wife's look-alike wasn't the way she would have approached this given the choice.

'I see what you mean.' Anne's eyes widened incredulously as she looked Merlyn up and down. 'It's quite remarkable,' she frowned.

'I think the hair in the front is still a little long, but——'

'Christopher!' Merlyn bit out warningly.

'What?' He frowned his puzzlement, his brow suddenly clearing as he realised to whom he had been talking with such professional detachment. 'Not too much of a shock for you, I hope, Anne.' He infused friendly warmth into his voice.

If they hadn't suddenly become the centre of attention as people became aware of their presence Merlyn would have kicked him, brilliant director or not. But the half a dozen other guests in the lounge were openly staring at them now, and she knew it had to be because of her appearance. Her eyes widened apprehensively as the dark haired man stepped from the window alcove into the light. Rand . . .

Everyone seemed to be waiting for his reaction to this phenomenon before showing some of their own, every person's breathing in the room coming to a hushed stop as he moved towards Merlyn. Except Christopher, of course, who viewed the scene with clinical interest.

Rand stood in front of her, darkly handsome in the black evening suit and snowy-white shirt, the glossy blackness of his hair lightly brushing against the collar of the latter.

He continued to look at her wordlessly, and Merlyn felt as if her chest were about to explode from the intake of air that had caught in her throat and stayed there. Why didn't he say something, anything, even if it were only to tell her to get out!

'I think I preferred you as a redhead,' he finally drawled.

The air was expelled from her lungs in a ragged sigh, and she could almost have hugged him for the normality of his comment. Almost. Two things stopped her. They had an audience. And she remembered too well his threat of this afternoon.

'With make-up and the contact lenses Merlyn's had fitted you won't be able to tell the difference,' Christopher was the one to answer him.

Grey eyes chilling over like ice were turned on him. '*I* would know the difference,' Rand told him, dangerously soft.

'Well of course *you* would,' Christopher dismissed. 'But—Ouch!' He glared at Merlyn as she trod on his foot as she moved further into the room.

'Sorry, was that your foot?' she said carelessly over her shoulder.

'You know damn well it——'

'I said I was sorry, Christopher.' She looked at him challengingly.

'Can I get you a drink, Miss Summers?' Rand offered smoothly as it seemed no one was about to win the battle of wills taking place between Merlyn and Christopher.

'Thank you, a small sherry would be nice.' They were acting like polite strangers when this afternoon they had been feverish lovers. But if he could act the part, she certainly could.

'I'll have a whisky, thanks. A large one,' Christopher told the other man without being asked, turning on Merlyn as soon as they were alone. 'You did that on purpose,' he complained as he balanced on one foot to rub the painful bruise she had made on the other one.

'Yes, I did,' she nodded impatiently. 'And I'll do it again if you don't learn some tact.'

'But I only—Oh.' He broke off, grimacing. 'I got a little carried away with the professional satisfaction of knowing we've been able to make you almost Suzie's double,' he acknowledged.

She didn't want to be any woman's double, not even one she respected and admired as much as Suzie Forrester.

She accepted the drink Rand handed her with constrained anger, avoiding his gaze as she sensed he was watching her, her impatience with Christopher increasing as he was lured away with compliments on the films he had directed in the past, soon the centre of attention across the room from them.

Now Merlyn had no choice but to look at Rand. I'm sorry,' she apologised awkwardly.

He shrugged. 'I've met people like Drake before; he didn't bother me.'

'Oh, I didn't mean because of Christopher —although goodness knows he has a skin as thick as a rhinoceros's!' She sighed. 'I meant because of what they've done to my hair.' She looked up at him uncertainly.

'I won't be able to see the colour of it in the dark,' Rand said softly.

Merlyn swallowed convulsively. 'I meant

because it's now like Suzie's,' she croaked, too disturbed to dwell on what *he* meant.

Rand shook his head. 'It's nothing like Suzie's was before she died,' he rasped. 'When she became so ill she had her hair cut as short as a boy's and took to wearing a wig styled in her original way; I think she was frightened of her own hair dropping out from the initial treatment they gave her—before she told them she would find a cure that didn't make her feel more ill than her illness! When she died it was about two inches long all over. It was as soft as a baby's curls,' he added gruffly.

'I didn't know . . .' And Christopher had made her have her own hair coloured so that it looked more natural than a wig!

Rand's mouth twisted. 'Maybe you had better tell Drake so that he can put it in the script!' He looked at her coldly before turning and going back to the array of drinks on a side-table.

'I hope the supplies last,' James murmured at Merlyn's side as he joined her. 'The way he's been knocking the stuff back since he arrived we could run out before dinner is even served,' he explained grimly at Merlyn's questioning look.

'Can't you do anything to stop him?' She watched Rand worriedly as he drank the fiery alcohol as if it were water.

'Can you?' James sighed, obviously not meaning the remark to be taken seriously.

No matter what her feelings were for Rand —confusing as they were, wanting him and yet hating him at the same time—she couldn't stand by and watch him drink himself to death. 'I can try,' she said determinedly.

'Hey, I was only joking——'

'I wasn't,' she told James firmly.

'Then I wish you luck,' he grimaced. 'Anne's planned this dinner party for such a long time, and I don't want her upset,' he frowned. 'Not now.'

Her eyes widened. 'James, is she——?'

'Don't spoil her fun,' he warned. 'She's going to make the announcement during dinner,' he told her conspiratorially.

'Oh, James, that's wonderful!' She realised hugging him was the wrong thing to do about two seconds after she had done it. She had arrived with one man, argued with another, publically hugged her host—and all within about ten minutes of her arrival! These people were going to think that every scandalous thing they had ever heard or read about actresses was true.

'Now that's more like it.' A grinning Anne joined them. 'I didn't marry "the handsomest man for three counties" not to be envied by *every* woman I meet!'

Merlyn laughed self-consciously. '"The handsomest man for three counties" can't be trusted to keep a secret, I'm afraid,' she confided in her friend. 'I was just congratulating him on the prospect of becoming a father.'

Anne punched her husband lightly on the arm. 'By the time I make the announcement it will be unnecessary because everyone will already know!'

James rubbed his arm, his expression one of

wounded indignation. 'Can I help it if I'm the original blabbermouth?'

'No.' His wife glared at him with feigned anger, her eyes as warm and loving as ever.

'I am pleased for you both.' Merlyn hugged the woman who had become such a good friend in such a short time. 'Practice time is over, hm?' she teased.

Anne blushed prettily as she looked at her husband. 'I hope not!'

'Would someone like to let me in on *that* secret?' James looked at the two of them curiously.

Merlyn shrugged dismissively, enjoying sharing the joke with Anne. 'Just women's talk. You know how it is.'

'No—but I'm about to put the thumbscrews on my wife and find out!'

'Ooh, I love it when he becomes a caveman!' Anne giggled.

'I think that's one of the things we have to talk about,' James growled. 'And you,' he turned to Merlyn, 'were about to stop one of my guests drowning himself.'

'What—Oh.' Anne followed her husband's gaze across the room to where Rand stood holding a glass of whisky. 'Oh dear . . .' She looked distressed.

'You shouldn't be upset just now.' Merlyn squeezed her arm reassuringly. 'Don't worry, I'll take care of Rand.' She hoped she sounded more confident than she felt; Rand looked about as malleable as a tiger being held by the tail.

Anne still looked worried. 'I wasn't sure he

would come, and as he started drinking as soon as he got here I didn't even like to warn him about your appearance—although he took that very well. Better than I hoped.' She chewed on her bottom lip, looking up at James. 'Perhaps we shouldn't have——'

'He didn't have to come, darling,' her husband soothed, his arm about her shoulders protectively. 'And we're entitled to live our own lives.'

'Yes, but——'

'It's been two years, Anne, and he'll have to accept, as we have, that life goes on.'

'You're right,' his wife nodded. 'But I can't help wishing that——'

'Will you enjoy your party and stop worrying,' Merlyn instructed lightly. 'I told you, I'll handle Rand, and I will.' Her expression was set determinedly as she crossed the room to his side. His gaze flicked over her disinterestedly before he turned away again. 'Leave some of that for the rest of us, won't you,' she snapped, stung by his dismissal.

His gaze was cold now. 'Help yourself,' he invited in a bored voice.

She drew in a ragged breath. 'Why did you come here tonight, Rand?'

His eyes narrowed at the question. 'Because I was invited,' he shrugged.

Merlyn nodded. 'To share in a happy occasion with Anne and James, not to get drunk!'

'I'm not drunk,' he bit out raspingly.

No, he wasn't. Strangely enough, with each sip of the whisky he seemed to become even more controlled rather than less inhibited as most people did. 'You *are* upsetting our hostess,' she said abruptly.

A slight flush darkened his cheeks as he turned to look at Anne, putting his still half-full glass down on the table beside him with a thud as he saw how pale his sister-in-law was as she made an effort to converse with some of her guests while watching him covertly at the same time.

'You're right,' he agreed as he turned back to Merlyn. 'I should never have come here tonight——'

'I didn't say that.' She shook her head. 'I only wondered *why* you had.'

'Because Anne and James are the nearest thing to a family that I have,' he grated.

'Rand——'

'Why don't we give the gossips something to really think about and get out of here?' His eyes glittered recklessly at the suggestion.

Merlyn wasn't naïve enough to accept the statement at face value as she could have with most other men; Rand wasn't like 'most other men', and he wanted their relationship to continue in a way she couldn't accept.

His mouth twisted as he saw she was about to refuse. 'We could sit in one of the hotel lounges and talk,' he derided.

Talking wasn't something she and Rand had ever done much of, and while the idea appealed to her she couldn't let Anne and James down in that way. Although maybe she would have been doing them a favour by removing Rand from their party.

'Maybe not,' Rand drawled before she could

formulate an answer. 'Talking seems to be the last thing on my mind when I'm alone with you!'

A blush highlighted her cheeks. 'We wouldn't be alone——'

'Forget it,' he cut in harshly. 'I was right the first time, it would give these gossips too much to talk about. And they never could understand why one of the Forresters married one of the *nouveau riche* in the first place!' His voice held contempt for their snobbery.

Merlyn frowned. 'I'm sure you're wrong; James didn't have any wealth of his own when he married Anne, and he's accepted by all her friends.'

'Because he's one of the Bentons, my dear,' Rand mimicked a snobbishly aristocratic accent. 'No money but plenty of class,' he added bitterly.

She shook her head. 'I'm sure you're wrong about the way they regard you.'

'Maybe you're right,' he shrugged. 'Since Suzie's death none of them has spoken to me enough for me to find out!' He gave a harsh laugh.

Merlyn frowned her puzzlement. 'Do you really care what these people think of you?' He gave the impression that he needed no one.

'For myself?' he grated, shaking his head. 'No, I don't care,' he scorned. 'But for Suzie? Hell, yes, I mind!'

'You haven't given them a chance, Rand,' she reasoned. 'James told me he hasn't seen much of you lately, and I gather the two of you used to be good friends.' The latter was a guess, but from the warm way James spoke of the other man she thought it was a correct one.

'The *four* of us used to be good friends,' he corrected harshly.

'Oh, Rand.' She shook her head impatiently at his unyielding attitude.

His expression darkened. 'I really do prefer you with red hair, you know.'

She blinked at the sudden change of subject, guessing by the way his gaze was fixed on her hair that her movement had drawn attention to it. 'So do I,' she sighed. 'But Christopher insisted.'

Rand's narrow-eyed gaze turned to the other man as he continued to be the centre of attention across the room. 'Suzie told me when she worked with him that he's a brilliant director,' he bit out abruptly.

'He is,' Merlyn nodded.

Icy grey eyes turned back to her. 'Have the two of you been lovers long?' he rasped.

She caught her breath. 'I told you——'

'And Anne told me a different story,' he scorned. 'All about his concern for you when you became ill last time you were here.'

Merlyn became suddenly still, looking at him warily. 'You know I had the flu when I was here before?' She watched him closely, still uncertain if that man who had made love to her had been part of her fever or if he had really existed.

Rand met her gaze steadily. 'Anne told me all about it.'

'When?'

'When?' he repeated softly, his brows raised in silent mockery.

'Yes.' The colour had returned to brighten her cheeks. 'Before or after I left?'

He shrugged. 'Is it important?'

'Yes! No! Probably not,' she decided heavily; it was unlikely she would ever know the truth about that night.

Rand watched her with narrowed eyes. 'You don't sound very sure.'

'Yes, I——' She broke off gratefully as Anne announced dinner was ready, suppressing the shiver of awareness that shot down her spine to hang suspended between her thighs in a warm acknowledgement of Rand as he put his hand in the middle of her back to escort her in to dinner.

She was deluding herself if she thought she would ever be able to deny this man, tonight or any other night he wanted her.

'If I had known before you left,' he remarked softly as he stood behind her to pull back her chair for her to sit down, 'I would have come over here to see for myself how you were. Wouldn't I?' he murmured throatily against her ear before straightening and moving farther up the table to take his seat several places up from her.

Merlyn stared at him with wide eyes, and he returned that gaze blandly before turning to converse with the woman sitting at his side, seeming engrossed in the breathless conversation of the beautiful woman.

'You seem to be much better at PR than I am.' Christopher drew her attention back to him as he sat next to her, his expression mocking as she turned to him with sudden awareness.

'And what is that supposed to mean?' she answered resentfully.

He raised darkly blond brows. 'What do you think it meant?' he derided.

'You tell me.' Her eyes flashed a warning of her anger should he imply one more time that she was involved with Rand.

He shrugged, holding up his hands defensively. 'Hey, I'm just glad you managed to avert a scene just now. I'm sure the Bentons are too.'

Her mouth tightened. 'Rand isn't drunk,' she denied coldly.

'No?' Christopher scorned. 'Almost a bottle of whisky in one evening is normal consumption for him, is it?'

Merlyn looked at him with narrowed eyes. 'You know, you aren't a very nice person.'

He grinned unabashedly. 'None of us bastards in life is. And I mean none of us, Merlyn,' he added in gentle warning.

Her head went back in challenge. 'Meaning?' Her question was abrupt.

He shrugged. 'Meaning it takes one to know one. Carmichael will hurt you, Merlyn,' he warned again.

'Rand and I don't even like each other,' she returned scornfully.

'With the sexual tension that exudes from the two of you I don't think it's necessary you actually *like* each other,' Christopher replied just as scornfully. 'It's just lucky no one took out a match when you walked into the room; we would all have gone up in flames!'

'Oh, eat your soup!' advised Merlyn crossly, trying to concentrate on her own steaming bowl of onion soup.

'Does one eat or drink soup, I've never been able to decide,' Christopher drawled, having scooped up a spoonful and now surveyed it with a jaundiced eye.

'One gets it into the mouth any way one can without spilling it down one's chin!' Merlyn valiantly began to eat—or drink—hers.

She studiously avoided looking towards the end of the table where Rand sat, although as there were only ten people seated at the meal, none of them was sitting too far apart around the oval.

The lovely blonde woman who had first engaged Rand in conversation seemed to have been invited as his dinner companion, whether by Anne to even the numbers up at her table or as Rand's personal guest, Merlyn didn't know. Whatever the arrangement, the woman stuck doggedly to his side as they all moved back into the lounge after the meal.

Merlyn felt a little lightheaded with the sherry she had drunk before dinner, the wine they had consumed with the meal, and then a glass of champagne that James had insisted everyone had to prematurely 'wet the baby's head'. But she wasn't too fuddle-headed not to notice when Rand and the beautiful blonde made an unobtrusive exit together.

She had told him to find some other woman to make love to, but she hadn't expected him to do it this quickly after her refusal.

'A fast worker, our Mr Carmichael,' Christopher drawled as he lounged on the sofa at Merlyn's side.

'"The pot calling the kettle . . ."?' she snapped, wishing she didn't mind so much that Rand had gone off with the other woman. But she did. She *did*!

He shrugged. 'Maybe she's an old family "friend",' he mocked.

'Rand hasn't touched a woman since——' She broke off, breathing heavily in her agitation.

'Yes?' Christopher queried interestedly.

Merlyn put a hand up to her temple. 'Could we leave now? It's been a long day, I have the start of a headache, and I also have this demon of a director who expects me to be in make-up at five a.m.'

'The way the weather has been against us lately we'll be lucky if we can start filming before five *p.m.*!' her 'demon of a director' complained grimly.

'They forecast rain again for tomorrow; do you really think it's the best day for the lake shot?'

As was normal when filming, the scenes weren't being shot in any sort of sequence, and Merlyn had been a little dismayed when she had looked at the schedule for tomorrow to see that they intended shooting the scene where Suzie had just learnt she was terminally ill. She had rowed out to the middle of the lake she had spent so much time on as a child to try and come to terms with the diagnosis. It had been a relatively clear day today, but there had been a chill wind howling through the trees, and the thought of possibly having to spend hours out in the middle of the lake in that weather was not at all appealing.

'With the long-term weather forecast I've had in there aren't likely to be any "best days",' Christopher told her morosely. 'Besides, a nice overcast day will help set the mood!'

'If you're going to start being insensitive again I'm definitely leaving!' Merlyn stood up decisively. 'Just try and remember that the Bentons are your hosts here.'

The fresh air hit her like a slap in the face, but she instantly felt better, the effects of the alcohol wearing off almost instantly after a wave of dizziness. It was dark and cold, but the lake was illuminated by several strategically placed lights, and she walked over to its edge to stare out over the grey water where a beautiful woman of thirty-five had tried to come to terms with dying—and failed.

Suzie had decided as she sat out in the middle of this expanse of water that she wasn't going to die without a fight—and she hadn't.

Merlyn let out a small scream of surprise as she felt an arm go about her waist. 'Christopher, I told you——' she broke off, her vision accustomed to the darkness now, and the man standing at her side wasn't Christopher. 'Rand . . . ?' she breathed huskily.

'Yes.' His eyes glowed cat-like in the dark.

'I thought you had gone home with what's-her-name.' She blinked up at him.

'I drove Deborah home when we discovered her car wouldn't start—and I left her there.'

'I don't think that was the idea,' Merlyn mocked breathlessly.

Rand gave a rueful shrug of his powerful shoulders. 'It wasn't a very subtle approach,' he conceded. 'But if she had tried it a month ago it might have worked. Even yesterday it might have worked,' he added huskily. 'But not since I've made love to you again and found that it was just as good as I imagined it was.'

'Rand, this is impossible——'

'I know,' he groaned achingly. 'I behaved like a madman this afternoon, coming to your room the way that I did.' He shook his head dazedly. 'I didn't intend for that to happen. I didn't *want* it to happen. But after it had—! I wanted you again and again, and the only way seemed to be to go on with what's between us,' he said grimly.

'And now?' Merlyn's expression was uncertain as she looked up at him in the darkness.

'I watched you tonight.' His words were husky. 'You're a very beautiful woman.'

'Thank you,' she accepted in a puzzled voice.

'Anne likes you.'

'I like her too,' she nodded, even more puzzled by the conversation.

'I realise that,' he replied tersely. 'The two of you are friends.'

'And you disapprove of that friendship.'

'It's nothing to do with me,' Rand continued. 'What I'm trying to say is that this afternoon my need for you outweighed my common sense.' He moved away from her abruptly. 'I will not go sneaking around Anne's hotel to sleep with a green-eyed witch called Merlyn!'

She swallowed hard, had been expecting him to say that he had realised he liked her too, although in retrospect perhaps that was expecting a little too much! Rand despised her and the need she made him feel, and she knew he hated her for that as much as anything else.

'Perhaps we should say good night now while this conversation is still within the realms of being polite?' she bit out. 'Because as I told you this afternoon, I don't want you either!'

He glanced towards the hotel. 'Drake waiting for you, is he?' he scorned.

'As far as I'm aware, Christopher is still at the party,' she dismissed contemptuously.

Rand's eyes narrowed. 'Why?'

'Because he wasn't ready to leave!' Merlyn told him with barely contained impatience. 'He's far from being the only attractive man in the crew!' she added tauntingly before walking off without so much as a backward glance.

She half expected Rand to come after her, only half relieved when he didn't, the other half disappointed. Tonight she wanted him as never before!

She had nothing to fear from him in going back to her room now, staring at her reflection in the mirror for a long time before turning away disgustedly. Inside she was still Merlyn Summers, outside she had no idea who she was.

She couldn't sleep, despite knowing of the early call she would have in the morning, shifting restlessly about in the bed, not wanting to think of Rand but unable to stop herself. Was he as haunted by sleeplessness as she was or had he gone back to see if Deborah's offer was still open?

She gave a choked sob, turning to bury her face in the pillow. She couldn't bear to even think of Rand with another woman.

Finally the tears stopped, and she lay back in the twilight between sleep and wakefulness, exhausted by her emotions.

The noise outside her window brought her completely awake again.

'Rand?' she called instinctively, getting out of bed to pull back the curtains.

A dark figure stood outside the window, moving quickly away as Merlyn threw the curtains back completely.

She silently began to scream.

CHAPTER EIGHT

WHEN she realised there was no sound coming from her throat she turned and ran, unlocking her door to speed into the corridor—straight into the solid hardness of a human body.

This time she began to scream in earnest.

'Merlyn!' Rand grasped her arms to gently shake her. 'Merlyn, what's wrong?' he demanded.

'Rand!' She clung to him thankfully. 'Oh, thank God it's you!' She fell weakly against his chest, her fingers curled into the thick wool of the navy blue jumper he wore.

'It's all right,' he soothed gently, stroking her hair as he held her against him. 'It's all right,' he reassured her as she continued to shake with fright.

She turned fearfully to look back into her bedroom. Moonlight shone in the window unhindered by any dark spectres outside her room. 'It's gone,' she shuddered with relief.

Rand frowned down at her. 'What has?'

She swallowed hard, dry sobs still catching in her throat. 'There was someone or—or *something*, outside my bedroom window,' she told him shakily, chewing on the knuckles of the hand that didn't still cling to him.

Rand's expression darkened ominously, and he set her firmly aside before moving stealthily into her room and over to the window, pushing back the nets before opening the window to look outside.

'Rand, no!' Merlyn moved towards him instinctively. 'He could still be out there!'

He was shaking his head as he reclosed the window. 'There's nothing out there now except maybe an owl or two.' He pulled the curtains back over the window before moving to switch on the small bedside lamp. 'Are you sure you didn't imagine it?' he prompted softly. 'You aren't used to the noises of the country, and——'

'The noise I heard was someone trying to open my window,' she cut in forcefully. 'And the dark shape I saw outside wasn't a giant bat either!' She knew he was only trying to comfort her, but she was too agitated to respond. Someone *had* been outside her room! Breaking in—or looking in?

'That safely rules out Dracula, then,' Rand muttered.

'Rand!' she gasped her hurt at his derision.

'Sorry.' He ran a hand through the thickness of his hair. 'It shook me up a little having you come flying out of your room screaming like a banshee! And you did say it could have been a *something*,' he reminded her.

She made an uncomfortable movement. 'I was upset when I said that,' she snapped.

'And you aren't upset now?' He raised dark brows.

'No.' And strangely she wasn't, the argument with Rand having calmed her more quickly than anything else could have done. 'Although I'm a little puzzled as to what you were doing outside my room at . . .' she glanced at the red-illuminated clock on her bedside table, 'one-thirty in the morning?'

'I changed my mind,' he told her harshly.

'About what?' Merlyn frowned, noticing for the first time that he had changed from the dinner suit into denims and the navy blue jumper.

He gave a ragged sigh, his eyes narrowed. 'Sleeping with a green-eyed witch called Merlyn.'

Her breath caught in her throat. She only had his word for it that that was his reason for being here. *He* could have been the person outside her room; there was a door to the outside beside the next room. And yet what reason would he have for not admitting to being outside? She couldn't think straight any more, felt emotionally drained, and the warmth of his arms beckoned.

'Just for tonight?' she asked warily.

'I don't know,' he admitted truthfully. 'But I have to have you tonight. I can't sleep until I do.' His voice shook with the admission.

It was mindless, completely inexplicable—to either of them—this primitive force that compelled them to want each other against all the odds the way that they did. Maybe she was a witch after all and had fallen victim to one of her own spells. Rand certainly seemed to think it was beyond his power to resist her and all that she offered.

'I need you tonight too.' She held out her arms to him. 'I couldn't sleep either.'

He trembled slightly as he held her, his heated gaze moving down the length of her body. 'Where did you think you were going just now dressed like this?' He slipped the thin strap of her pale green nightgown from her shoulder, his lips moving moistly across the creamy flesh he exposed.

'I was looking for help.' She groaned low in her throat as he pulled the material down over one breast and drew her aching nipple into his mouth for the briefest of caresses.

'And instead you found me,' he rasped, cupping her bared breast while his lips closed moistly on the other nipple through the silky material of her nightgown.

Her head fell back as she shuddered her pleasure, not answering him as she became lost in the delight of his caresses.

Her bed had grown cold since she had left it, but as Rand stripped off his clothes and quickly joined her there they were both set alight in the flames of their passion, their caresses fevered, those caresses mixing pain with pleasure as they surrendered to their emotions.

Merlyn's nails raked from the muscle of his shoulders to the tautness of his buttocks as he thrust smoothly inside her, bringing them both to a tumultuous climax that left them a tangle of perspiration-damp bodies and raggedly uneven breathing.

'Rand?' Merlyn finally prompted when he made no effort to speak.

He moved slowly, raising himself up on one elbow to look down at her with dark eyes. 'Did I hurt you?' he groaned. 'I lose all control when I touch you! You must think I don't know how to make love with consideration and gentleness.'

She shook her head. 'Was that what either of us wanted just now?'

'I don't know what I want any more,' he replied in self-disgust.

Merlyn sighed. 'Maybe if you stopped self-analysing everything——'

'But I don't understand what's happening between us,' he groaned. 'I don't *want* any of it!'

He didn't need to tell her that, she knew that every time he came to her he did it in spite of himself. 'Can you live without it?' she prompted huskily.

'For the moment, no,' he answered, his eyes pained. 'I came over here in the middle of the damned night because I needed to be inside you!'

'And now that you are?'

'Can't you feel it?' he said shakily. 'Even the satisfaction doesn't last; I instantly want you again. It's never been like this for me before. I——' He broke off as he realised exactly what he had said—and its import. 'It isn't the same thing,' he rasped. 'I *loved* Suzie.'

She closed her eyes to shut out the pain. 'Please, Rand, if you're going to leave, go now!'

'I can't!' The admission was dragged from him as he pushed her hands down beside her head and held them there as his mouth claimed hers and his thighs began to move against her.

She had no idea what time it was when they both fell asleep through exhaustion, but it seemed only a matter of seconds before Merlyn's early morning call came. She picked up the telephone, answering the automatic call before she realised it was one, putting the receiver down with a groan as she rolled over—to look straight into silver-grey eyes.

'Rand . . . !' She had half expected him to be gone when she woke up, sure that actually 'sleeping' with her, an act of intimacy in itself, hadn't been part of his plans when he came to her last night.

His hand was gentle as it smoothed the tangle of hair from her face. 'I know, you have to go to work,' he acknowledged indulgently.

'Yes.'

'I should be leaving too.' He sounded regretful. 'You look so young without make-up.' He looked at her searchingly. 'No more than a child.'

His mood had softened this morning, and she moved closer to him. 'Do I feel younger too?'

'No,' he groaned huskily as the tautness of her breasts nestled amongst the curling black hair on his chest. 'May I see you again tonight?' His hands caressed her from breast to thigh.

'You said you didn't intend sneaking about the hotel to sleep with me,' she reminded him.

'So I won't sneak,' he shrugged, although his expression was serious.

Merlyn looked at him searchingly, his hard face softened by sleep—and something else, something he wasn't even sure of himself. He was so close, so endearingly close, that she could see the silver in the grey of his eyes; flecks of light among the darkness, the swarthiness of his skin, the dark stubble on his chin and over his top lip. Her gaze stopped there, an indulgent smile curving her lips as she gently touched the hardness of that jaw. 'Why did you do it?' Her voice was husky in the quiet stillness of the early morning.

'I didn't.' Rand's voice was gruff. 'Last night I just walked in. It was late——'

'No,' she laughed huskily. 'I meant why did you shave off the beard and moustache?'

'Oh that.' He nodded. 'The lady in my life told me it was old-fashioned,' he told her blandly.

Her eyes glowed at his first attempt to tease with her. 'Actually, I quite liked it. It felt quite —sexy.'

'Is there any pleasing you?' Rand mocked disgustedly.

'Oh yes.' Her voice was deliberately provocative.

'I thought you had to go to work?' Even as he reminded her of that he was pulling her within the close confines of his body. He laughed huskily at the wistful longing in her eyes that warred with the reluctant way she slipped out of his arms, falling back on the pillows to watch her as she got out her clothes for the day.

Suddenly that smile faded, his eyes darkening with pain.

'Rand?' Merlyn moved to his side, instantly sensitive to his mood. 'What is it?'

He captured her hand in his, pressing it to his lips, kissing the inside of her wrist. 'Memories,' he rasped.

'Memories?' she prompted softly.

He rested his face against her arm. 'Of other mornings like this,' he told her gruffly.

Her breath caught in her throat. How stupid she was; he must have shared hundreds of mornings just like this with Suzie. 'Rand——'

'It's all right.' He looked up to meet her gaze, forcing the memories to the back of his mind, although there lingered a shimmer of emotion in his eyes. 'Go and get yourself dressed and then off to work; you can't be late your first day.'

'But——'

'I said I'm all right, Merlyn.' His voice was suspiciously husky. 'Now go, please!'

She swallowed hard, wanting him to talk to her about those memories, sure that talking would help. Maybe tonight . . .

She squeezed his arm before going into the adjoining bathroom to shower and dress, dreading going back out to the bedroom to find him gone. Like a thief in the night. Only he hadn't stolen anything, she had given freely. And she would go on giving, as long as he would let her.

He was dressed and sitting in the lounge when she came out of the bathroom.

The relief at finding him still there must have shown in the blinding smile she gave, but she didn't care.

Rand stood up, his hands thrust into his pockets, his gaze not quite meeting hers. 'I'll mention the possibility that the hotel has a prowler to Anne,' he said abruptly.

Merlyn frowned as she remembered her fear of last night. 'Do you think that's what it was?'

'Either that or someone just trying to get a look at the film star,' he smiled as he put his arms about her.

'I'm not a star——'

'Yet,' Rand drawled. 'But you will be.'

'If all they wanted to do was get a look at me

they could do that in the daylight,' she said dryly.

'But it wouldn't be as much fun!'

Merlyn sobered. 'Do you think it was a prowler?' She knew his teasing had just been a diversion to the nervousness she still felt about last night.

'It couldn't have been a dream?'

'No!' She trembled at the memory of just how *real* that person outside her room had been. As real as that last 'dream' she had had?

'It's all right.' Rand's arms tightened about her. 'Don't think about it any more. I'll be with you tonight and every other night.'

Every other night. It sounded so permanent, and yet Merlyn knew that what he hadn't added was every other night 'she stayed here'. After that she would be returning to London to complete the filming there and Rand would remain here. They would have a few weeks together at most. It wasn't long with the man she believed she was falling in love with. That wasn't true, she *knew* she was already in love with him. Maybe she had loved him from that very first moment she looked at him and wanted him; she knew she had to already have been in love with him before she came back yesterday, or she would never have *come* back.

'I do have to go now.' She could hear the reluctance in her own voice.

He nodded. 'Or your director-genius will be down on you.'

'Will you join me for dinner tonight?' She didn't want to let him go; he seemed so much gentler this morning, and she had no guarantee that mood would continue throughout the day.

'Give me a call when you get through for the day.' He put her firmly away from him.

She didn't exactly feel ecstatic with happiness as she joined the rest of the crew for their early morning breakfast in the restaurant that had been especially set by for this early meal, but she did feel more light-hearted than she had for a long time, for over a month to be exact . . .

'My God.' Christopher paused next to the table she shared with Liza and a couple of technicians on his way out of the room. 'Get back to make-up as soon as you've drunk your coffee; you're supposed to looked ravaged by grief, not already ill!'

If looks could kill her 'director-genius' would have dropped to the floor at that moment! 'I haven't been to make-up yet,' she muttered as they became the cynosure of curious eyes.

Christopher squinted down at her. 'You mean you always look this awful in the mornings?'

Her teeth grated together as the rudeness of his statement brought several titters of amusement from adjoining tables. Her head went back in challenge. 'I didn't sleep very well last night,' she snapped.

'I don't wish to know about your sleeping arrangements,' he said disgustedly. 'God, I hope you have the stamina for this!'

Christopher might be the most brilliant director in England today, might even command respect from the glittering world of Hollywood, but as far as Merlyn was concerned he drew a zero for tact and good manners, their conversation being listened to avidly by every person in the room now, including those who were trying to pretend otherwise.

'I have the stamina to cope with everything you throw at me,' she bit out furiously.

He looked at her scathingly. 'I wish I had your confidence,' came his parting shot.

'You——'

'Calm down, Merlyn,' Liza's hand on her arm stopped her from following Christopher as he smiled and talked pleasantly to several of the minor actors on his way out. 'You have to give him credit,' she said ruefully as Merlyn slowly subsided into her seat. 'Even when you know it's coming it's impossible not to retaliate.' She shook her head.

'Know what's coming?' Merlyn returned distractedly, heated colour still burning her cheeks at Christopher's public humiliation of her.

'You mean you didn't know?' Her friend looked astounded.

She gave an irritated frown, that small bubble of euphoria that had accompanied her after leaving Rand's arms completely burst. 'Know what?' she prompted with impatience.

Liza chuckled softly. 'The thing to remember here, Merlyn, is "know thy director",' she misquoted. 'It's like this,' she patiently explained as Merlyn still looked blank—and disgruntled. 'Christopher Drake is the sort of director who believes that the emotions of love or hate between him and his leading lady enhance both of their performances, his from behind the cameras, hers in front of them, and you've assured me he isn't the reason you look as if you haven't slept all night——'

'He isn't!' Colour once again darkened her cheeks, and not because of anger this time.

'—then it was obvious he was going to pick an argument with you this morning,' Liza continued lightly. 'Any argument——'

'Not to me!' Merlyn glared after him resentfully.

'I can see that now,' Liza sympathised. 'I wish I'd known earlier, I could have warned you.'

'Warned me that he's a sadistic, bad-tempered——'

'Brilliant director,' Liza finished wryly. 'You'll see, you'll go out there today and act your socks off just to "show him"! There's a method in his madness.' Her friend laughed softly. 'I've seen him in action before.'

'He'll see *me* in action if he tries to humiliate me that way again,' Merlyn muttered, her embarrassment still paramount even though the two technicians had now left their table and the conversation seemed to be flowing smoothly in the room again.

'Hey, it's nothing personal,' Liza dismissed lightly. 'Shelley Graham threatened to scratch his eyes out when we were all filming together.'

'I'm surprised she didn't walk out if he treated her that way.' Merlyn knew the well-known actress's temperament as well as anyone else who had ever heard of her; fiery was a mild description!

Liza gave her a sideways glance. 'She solved the problem another way.'

'I don't see how—That's intimidation!' she gasped as she realised exactly what that 'other way' had been.

'Shelley didn't look as if she minded too much,' her friend laughed at her outraged expression. 'In fact, I think that bad beginning added spice to their relationship.'

'Well, it isn't going to work on me,' Merlyn told her firmly. 'I do not want Christopher Drake as my lover.'

'Because of Heathcliff?' Liza asked with interest.

'Rochester,' she corrected dryly.

'Whatever,' her friend teased. 'In that case I should watch yourself around Christopher, away from the cameras he may be a pussycat——'

'I've never found him in the least like a pussycat,' Merlyn scorned the description.

Liza grinned. 'I didn't say he didn't have a few claws even then——'

'A few!' she scoffed, pushing away her empty coffee-cup.

Her friend laughed. 'You haven't seen anything until you've seen him in action behind the cameras.' She shook her head. 'He's earnt every foul name he's ever had thrown at him!'

Merlyn soon learnt that—to her cost. Christopher was like a Jekyll and Hyde character, and Hyde took over behind the camera!

He was a perfectionist to the point of faultlessness, their first four attempts at filming her anguished acceptance that she was actually ill declared by him to 'look like a cow in labour', 'like she had just lost her favourite puppy', 'like someone had stolen her ice-cream', and the final humiliation, 'like she had just been told her lover was a married man'!

Merlyn stood up in outrage. 'Now just a damned minute——'

'That's it!' Christopher cried excitedly from a neighbouring boat where he was supervising the scene. 'If you stood up just like that and gazed up at the sky, as if challenging the elements themselves. Brilliant, Merlyn.' His eyes glowed his pleasure. 'Absolutely brilliant!'

Maybe other actresses in the past had been grateful to accept these crumbs of praise after the most callous of insults from him, but Merlyn had been ridiculed and sitting out in the middle of this lake with the wind ripping into her for over two hours now, and she wasn't about to *thank* the man for putting her through that! She was cold, and miserable, and she *hated* Christopher Drake, she decided.

'Christopher, I think——'

'I know, and it's fantastic,' he cut in enthusiastically, looking up at the cloud-filled sky. 'Now if we can just wait for that black cloud there,' he pointed it out to the cameraman, 'to get behind her as she stands up, it will be perfect.'

Merlyn's protestations at his insulting behaviour were lost as he excitedly issued new instructions to the rest of the people involved.

She was furious with him, intended telling him so as soon as she got off this lake; she might lose all control and actually attempt to drown him if she tried to tell him now.

Twenty minutes later she was still sitting in the

small row-boat waiting for the black cloud to be in the exact position Christopher wanted. Now she knew why she had stuck to theatre work the last few years; there you didn't have to wait for the position of a cloud as your cue.

It was late afternoon when Christopher declared himself satisfied with a take that would probably only use up thirty seconds of the actual film, the light too bad by then for any more filming today.

Merlyn was grateful for the blanket that was wrapped about her shoulders once she got to shore, cupping her frozen hands about the coffee-cup that was thrust into them.

'You were wonderful, Merlyn.' Christopher put his arm about her shoulders.

She turned to glare up at him. 'And you were a bastard!'

He chuckled. 'All the best directors are,' he mocked without rancour.

'Yes.' She ruefully acknowledged that he had finally wrung a performance out of her that she was sure would require every member of the audience to reach for their handkerchieves.

'You go take a shower and warm up and then we can meet for dinner later,' he suggested lightly.

Dinner. She was having dinner with Rand this evening. Christopher had demanded such intensity of feeling from her today that she hadn't even had time to think about the man she loved.

She couldn't quite meet Christopher's gaze. 'I can't,' she excused. 'I—I have other plans.'

'Hillier?' he challenged. 'I told you I don't

approve of relationships between my leading man and lady.'

'Only between *you* and your leading lady, hm?' she scorned.

'Someone's been talking,' he drawled.

'Not soon enough,' she bit out. 'I like you, Christopher, and I think you're the best director there is in the country today, but I won't put up with your insults again the way I've had to today.'

'You won't?' His eyes were icy.

'No,' she declared, not in the least cowed by his cold arrogance. 'It may work with other actresses but not with me. I don't want an affair with you but neither do I want to feel the lash of your tongue every day. You didn't get where you are today by stereotyping the people you work with.'

He frowned at the rebuke, the chill fading from his eyes. 'And you react better to gentler handling,' he guessed. 'Okay, I'm sorry about today, it was force of habit. I'll try not to be so hard on you tomorrow.'

She wasn't so sure he could keep to that promise, but she felt better for making her feelings about his behaviour today known. 'Here.' She thrust what was left of her coffee into his hands. 'And I'm not seeing Mark Hillier later.' She grimaced at the idea. 'Give me credit for better taste than that!'

Christopher laughed softly. 'I've never been able to work out what it is that turns us all into neurotics once filming starts. Individually we're all capable and talented people—I wouldn't have anything less on my film crew!' he added with his usual arrogance. 'And yet once we start to work and the adrenalin begins to flow the most unlikely relationships occur!'

'*Nothing* is more unlikely than Mark and me,' she assured him with distaste. 'Now, why don't you go and find one of those "talented" women and get them to tell you how wonderful *you* are. With one word of advice,' she added dryly. 'I wouldn't bother with Liza; she was the one who told me what a swine you are!'

'Really?' He turned to seek out Liza as she talked animatedly with one of the cameramen as he packed away for the day, his eyes gleaming with sudden interest. 'She's quite beautiful, isn't she,' he mused slowly.

'Christopher——'

'I never can resist a challenge,' he cut smoothly across Merlyn's warning, slapping the empty coffee-cup back into her hands. 'See you later.'

Merlyn watched in dismay as Christopher tersely dismissed the man Liza was talking to, speaking softly to the other woman before she shruggingly accompanied him back to the hotel. Merlyn smiled as she too turned to leave; she knew Liza better than Christopher did, and her friend wasn't easily impressed.

'Didn't he believe you last night?'

She stiffened at the sound of that mocking voice, resignedly turning to look at Mark. His hair had been styled to look more like Rand's had three years ago, shorter than Mark usually wore it, the three-piece suit and snowy-white shirt donned for the role he played too, as the scene with Suzie out in the lake ended with her pained gaze focusing on her husband as he stood watching her from the shore. Despite the changes in his appearance, Mark was unmistakably Mark, and Merlyn knew it had been the identity of the man playing Rand that had resulted in her unusually stilted acting today.

She gave a weary sigh as she looked at him. 'It's been a long day, Mark, and I'm not in the mood for your innuendoes,' she stated flatly.

His handsome mouth twisted derisively. 'Drake appears to have lost interest in you— already.'

She drew in a deep breath. 'Christopher was never "interested" in me,' she scorned. 'So if you thought that little scene you created last night would cause trouble for me you were mistaken.'

'I think you underestimate your own attraction,' he drawled, his gaze moving over her insolently.

'And I think you *overestimate* yours!'

'If you get lonely in your big bed, just give me a call,' he sneered. 'I might be able to find you the odd free night.'

'You can—' She broke off, looking at him questioningly. 'How do you know I have a big bed in my room?' she asked sharply.

Mark looked taken aback at the question. 'All the rooms have double beds——'

'No, they don't.' She shook her head, unable to stop the trembling that suddenly racked her body.

'Well mine does,' he dismissed tersely. 'And I just assumed yours did too. Good God, Merlyn, it was only a casual remark, there's no need to make a scene about it.' He glanced about them awkwardly, although most of the crew had gone back to the hotel by now, glad to get in out of the cold.

'Someone was creeping about outside my room last night, and——'

'Well, it wasn't me,' Mark cried in disgust. 'I have better things to do with my time than try to get a glimpse of your unimpressive body through your bedroom window——'

'How did you know they were outside my window?' she pounced, her eyes wide. 'I only said they were outside my room!'

Mark gave her a pitying glance. 'Well, whoever it was could hardly expect to see you through a closed door,' he mocked. 'Lighten up, Merlyn. You probably imagined the whole thing.'

'No—no, I didn't.' She shuddered at the memory of how frightened she had been.

'Well, it wasn't me,' he said again more firmly. 'I happen to have been in a certain young lady's bedroom all night——'

'Which young lady?' Merlyn demanded to know.

He frowned. 'I'm not going to tell you that,' he dismissed irritably. 'It's none of your damned business who I go to bed with.'

'Then you can't prove where you were last night,' Merlyn challenged triumphantly, sure she had solved the mystery of who had been outside her room last night. Mark had said he had never forgiven her for the fact that she had lost him that film role six years ago, and he was vindictive enough to enjoy half frightening her to death.

'I don't have to.' He slowly shook his head, looking at her frowningly. 'Merlyn, I know we had our differences in the past, but— Are you sure you haven't been imagining things?'

She flushed at his almost condescending tone; he made her sound as if she were some hysterical female on the verge of a nervous breakdown. 'No, I'm not imagining things,' she snapped. 'There was someone outside my room last night.'

Mark shrugged. 'Then I suggest you look elsewhere for your peeping Tom,' he mocked. 'My nights are much too busy to be spent hoping for a glimpse of your body.' His gaze raked over her insolently again. 'It just isn't that unique,' he drawled before striding off.

God, was he right, was she becoming paranoid?

Maybe if it had been the first time something like that had happened to her she could have taken it in her stride, but it was the memory of that vivid dream she wasn't sure was a dream the last time she stayed here that haunted her. What if the man had been real then too, and last night he had come back to sneak into her bed again?

She had to be with Rand, he was the only one who made her feel safe.

CHAPTER NINE

By the time she had showered and changed, her feelings of fear down by the lake seemed fanciful even in her emotional state. Of course she wasn't only safe when she was with Rand, no one was trying to hurt her, just frighten her a little. And despite what he said she still hadn't discounted Mark as the culprit; she knew only too well that he was capable of anything.

But she wasn't going to dwell on that any more, had her evening with Rand to look forward to. Besides, she was too tired after the long day she had just spent to think about it any more.

'Goodness, you look worn.' Anne frowned her concern when Merlyn opened the door to her knock.

'The same can't be said of you; you're glowing!' She invited the other woman in by stepping back and opening the door wider.

Anne grinned. 'No morning sickness either; I'm expecting to come down with a bang pretty soon!'

'I don't see why you should, my mother said the only thing that made her pregnancy bearable when she was carrying me was that she wasn't sick at all,' she smiled.

'Suzie was really sick with hers, although we all thought—' Anne broke off, stricken by what she had unthinkingly revealed. 'I don't suppose you can forget I said that?' she groaned.

Merlyn moistened her lips, swallowing hard. 'But Suzie never had a baby . . .' she croaked, stunned by what Anne had just said.

'No,' Suzie's sister acknowledged heavily. 'I told you there were some things in the last few years of Brandon's marriage to Suzie that I omitted from the book; that was one of them. I only wanted my book to encourage other people who were diagnosed as terminally ill not to give up, not make Brandon suffer. He's already suffered enough.'

'Suzie lost the baby?' Merlyn's breathing was shallow.

'Yes,' Anne nodded abruptly.

'Oh God.' She groaned at the cruelty that had taken that other life from Rand. A child could have been the one thing to help him after Suzie's death, and *she* had blithely told him how her own parents had blamed each other for her existence before sending her father off to be sterilised so that the mistake shouldn't happen again! No wonder he had needed another drink after she had told him that; he had lost *his* chance to become a father.

'Merlyn?' Anne frowned worriedly at how pale she had become.

'Sorry.' She attempted to shake off the shock she had just received. 'It was—a surprise.'

'Yes,' Anne acknowledged levelly. 'Now you know why I was so worried about Brandon's behaviour last night,' she sighed.

With good reason. At the beginning of the

evening Rand had been like the man she first met; full of bitterness. As he had been yesterday afternoon when he came to her room and demanded to take her so savagely . . .

'Anne,' she spoke shakily. 'When did you tell Rand about your baby?' She swallowed hard.

The other woman sighed again. 'Well, just announcing it at the party last night seemed too callous a thing to do so I invited him over for lunch yesterday. He—took it quite calmly at the time.'

Too calmly! He had come to her room after Anne told him about her baby with the intention of hurting someone as badly as he was hurting. And she could never tell him that she understood the pain that had driven him that day because she could never tell him she knew about the baby he had lost, his and Suzie's baby . . .

'I'll never tell anyone what you've just told me.' She squeezed Anne's arm reassuringly. 'As you said, some things belong only to them.'

Anne nodded. 'You're very fond of Brandon, aren't you?' she probed gently.

Delicate colour brightened Merlyn's cheeks. 'I—barely know him,' she answered truthfully, realising how little she really did know him—or the demons that drove him.

'He told me there was someone outside your room last night,' Anne said slowly. '*Late* last night.'

The colour deepened in Merlyn's cheeks. 'He —he walked me back to my room——'

'Merlyn,' the other woman cut in chidingly. 'Brandon is a very attractive man, only thirty-nine, and he deserves to make a new life for himself if he can. Besides,' she added with a smile, 'James and I like you so much.'

She sighed. 'It would be pointless to deny that I'm seeing Rand, but I really don't think you should make too much of it. We're just two consenting adults who are attracted to each other.'

God, she sounded like one of those bed-hopping women that she despised who explained away their behaviour with words like 'consenting adult' and 'mutual attraction'. She wasn't a prude, and she realised soon after her break-up with Mark that if she had really loved him she would have let him make love to her, would have wanted to make love to him too, that if there had been any other man since then that she had really cared about she wouldn't have hesitated to go to bed with him. She just couldn't stand it when people explained away their sexual promiscuity as experimentation for that 'one perfect relationship'. Half of them didn't recognise it when it did come along because they were too busy 'experimenting'!

'Brandon likes you very much.' Anne touched Merlyn's arm reassuringly. 'You're the first woman he's shown an interest in since—well, since——'

'Since Suzie,' finished Merlyn softly. 'I know that. It's a big responsibility.'

Anne nodded understandingly. 'But he's already changed a little since you came here, taking an interest in his businesses again, shaving off that dreadful beard.'

'I quite liked it,' she said lightly, glad that Anne

had taken her relationship with Rand so well. It could have been very awkward for all of them if she hadn't.

Anne gave her a sceptical look. 'It was awful!' she grimaced. 'Anyway, I didn't come over here to probe into your relationship with Brandon——'

'Or to tell me things I didn't hear.' Merlyn once again assured her of her confidence being kept strictly between the two of them.

'No, I actually came to tell you that the police have been informed about the prowler last night——'

'Do you really think that's necessary?' She frowned her surprise.

'Brandon does,' Anne told her as if that said everything—and perhaps it did; he could be a very forceful man. 'About this other business —I'm not usually so careless. I think it's just that you've become such a friend these last few weeks that I forgot you didn't know.'

'It didn't become public at the time?' she asked slowly.

'Oh no.' The other woman shook her head. 'Suzie was only a few weeks pregnant when they—when they discovered her illness. I think it was finding out about that that brought on the miscarriage.'

Poor Rand, being dealt two such tragic blows in one go. No wonder he was so bitter. And no wonder he was determined never to love again, to take only the physical gratification of the moment that Merlyn could give him. She couldn't expect any more from a man who had lost so much.

'Just care for him, Merlyn.' Anne seemed to sense her despair. 'He has so much love to give.'

Learning of the child Suzie had been going to give him changed their relationship yet again, Merlyn realised after Anne had left. She understood what had brought him to her room the afternoon before, knew that it had been completely different from when he came to her last night. Last night he really had needed *her*, and not just to block out the unhappy memories Anne's pregnancy had given him.

It was something to build their relationship upon. She hoped.

'Coming over to dinner?' Liza invited when Merlyn answered the door to her.

'I thought you would be with our "pussycat" of a director,' she taunted.

Liza grinned as she strolled into the room, the bright orange dress she wore suiting her sunny personality. 'He really was a bastard to you today, wasn't he,' she dismissed.

'I think you're being over-generous, Liza,' she mocked. 'Am I to take it his mood will be improved tomorrow?' Merlyn raised questioning brows.

'Not because of anything I've done,' her friend shrugged, dropping down into an armchair.

'In that case, he'll probably be worse than today.' Merlyn's eyes rolled expressively.

'Never mind, he'll have someone else to vent his anger on then. He's concentrating on that scene with Mark in the gazebo, remember?' she prompted.

Merlyn remembered. The 'scene' with Mark

was one of those purely fictional ones that had been put in to provide the 'romance' in the film, 'Suzie and Brandon' making love in the glass and pine gazebo beside the lake after Suzie stepped out of the boat.

Anne had actually written that Rand had been at the doctor's office with Suzie when she got the results of her tests, so it was ludicrous to assume the couple had made violent love in the gazebo after Suzie had told him of her illness herself. But film directors, and certainly film companies, didn't particularly care for the accuracy of those minor facts as long as the story was fast-paced and moving. They also seemed to think that a little sex thrown in for good measure never did anyone any harm.

Merlyn had known the scene was scheduled for tomorrow, and was dreading having to do it with Mark, of all people.

'Did I say the wrong thing?' Liza grimaced as she saw her expression.

'Yes,' Merlyn sighed. 'What do you think about Mark Hillier?'

Liza grimaced. 'I haven't seen him act yet.'

'I didn't mean from a professional point of view,' she replied dryly.

'He seems okay,' her friend shrugged. 'How do you feel about seeing your ex-fiancé again?'

Merlyn's eyes widened as she stared open-mouthed at Liza. 'How did you know that?'

'When we first met you were still very bitter about what he tried to do to you,' Liza reminded her. 'I'd never forget the name of a louse like that!'

Merlyn couldn't help laughing. 'You certainly see things in black and white!'

'A rat of the first degree,' Liza nodded. 'I certainly don't envy you out there in that draughty gazebo with him tomorrow,' she shivered.

She grimaced. 'It has to be warmer than the rowing-boat today.'

'Not without your clothes on!' Liza said expressively.

Merlyn's breath seemed forced from her body before she became completely still. 'What did you say?' she finally managed to croak.

'You can hardly make love with your clothes on, Merlyn,' her friend scorned.

'It's supposed to "fade off into the sunset" when they start to make love,' she bit out tautly.

'Well I don't know,' Liza shrugged dismissively. 'Why ask me? I just know that Christopher was talking of restricting the crew to the minimum to save you and Mark any embarrassment.'

'He *has* to be joking,' Merlyn said through gritted teeth.

'I somehow don't think Christopher ever jokes about his work,' Liza grimaced.

Neither did she, but if he thought she was going to be agreeable to any nude scenes—especially in an exposed gazebo with Mark Hillier—he was in for a disappointment!

Liza uncurled herself from the chair as she stood up. 'I've seen that look on your face before, and I don't want to be anywhere within range when the sparks start to fly!'

'Where is Christopher now?'

'Don't ask me, I dumped him after his first

improper suggestion.' Liza's look spoke volumes. 'You could try his room. He was probably as cold as the rest of us earlier; as far as I know he's human!'

He was going to know he was very human by the time she finished telling him what she thought of his idea that she and Mark strip off in the gazebo!

He conveniently wasn't in his room when she rang, and he didn't answer the page she had the hotel receptionist put out for him either. Coward, she muttered to herself. He had to know Liza would tell her about his bright idea for tomorrow, just as he had to know how she would feel about it.

She felt completely depressed when she rang The Forresters and the housekeeper told her Rand wasn't home yet.

'As soon as he comes in could you tell him I called?' she requested heavily.

'I'm just on my way home now; you only just caught me as I was going out the door.' The woman managed to convey her disapproval of that fact even down the telephone line. 'But I can leave your message on the pad here for him to read. With the others.'

What others, Merlyn wanted to demand, but knew she wouldn't get an answer. Being the last on a list of other messages, some of them perhaps from other women, one of them maybe even from the lovely Deborah, didn't please her one bit. But there wasn't much she could do about it.

An hour later Rand still hadn't arrived or returned her call, and so she tried the house once again. This time not even the disapproving housekeeper answered her call.

Where was he? Anne said he had taken up the reins of his businesses once again; did that mean he had gone to London? Tired of the confines of her room she headed towards the lake. The gazebo stood across from the hotel like a mockery to her anger.

It was a beautiful structure, pine like the hotel, with windows taking up the top half of the walls of the rounded construction. Inside it was like a one-room cottage, with a pine floor partly covered by a couple of scatter rugs, and a sofa and chair to sit on as you gazed out at the pine-covered mountains beyond the hotel.

Merlyn deliberately avoided the building, walking along the jetty to the small landing area that the family used to moor their boats.

It was so still and peaceful after the day's hectic activity, and she took a moment to drink in the tranquillity.

A board cracked beneath her foot with a suddenness that sent her tumbling through the air, the coldness of the water closing over her. She felt as if she took half the lake into her lungs as she went deeper and deeper under the water, blackness and an ominous rushing sound surrounding her.

She was drowning!

She began to thrash her legs to and fro in an effort to get back to the surface, felt one of her shoes leave her foot as she did so, the narrow-skirted dress she wore impeding her movements and clinging to her body like a restrictive skin.

Weeds tangled against her thrashing limbs, and she cried out soundlessly at their slimy tentacles, immediately taking in more water, choking, desperately needing to take air into her lungs.

If only she could reach the surface, if only she could *breathe*! God, she was going to drown out here and no one would even know about it until they found her body in the morning. No one even knew where she had gone. Why hadn't she——?

Suddenly she felt something close about her waist as she was forced through the water to the surface, drawing air into her starved lungs even as she choked up the water she had taken in, her arms going around Rand's neck as she clung to him, tears streaming down her face as she sobbed with the relief of being alive.

'Are you all right?' he rasped.

'Yes,' she sobbed.

'What the hell happened?' demanded Rand, his arms about her as he kept them both afloat.

'I don't know,' Merlyn choked. 'I—Oh I'm just so glad you found me!' She couldn't seem to stop clinging to him, frightened to let go in case the black water closed over her again. 'Don't let go of me, Rand. Please, don't let go!' She trembled uncontrollably.

He drew in a ragged breath, his eyes silver in the moonlight. 'You're safe now, Merlyn,' he assured her gruffly. 'You're safe!'

For all his confidence, she still clung to him when he had managed to push her out of the water up on to the bank, pulling himself out beside her to lay back panting on the grass.

'Well my life had become a little dull before you exploded into it,' he smiled, his chest heaving up and down from the effort it had taken to subdue her panic enough to get her over to the bank and out of the water. 'Thunderstorms, prowlers, and now this!'

She gave a shaky laugh, her head resting on his chest, relieved just to be alive.

'What happened?' Rand probed again softly.

'I—You're shivering,' she realised, sitting up to look down at him. His shirt clung to him wetly, as did his trousers, but at least he had had the good sense to throw off his shoes before jumping into the water, she realised as she ruefully looked down at her own feet where only one sandal remained. Her stockings were laddered in several places, her green dress as covered in mud as was the rest of her. They both looked a mess.

'Let's go inside.' He pulled her to her feet and over to the warmth the gazebo offered, picking up his jacket and shoes as they passed them. 'No electricity,' he told her as she looked around inside for a light-switch, finding a box of matches in a cupboard with a familiarity that told of his use of the gazebo in the past, striking one to light the oil lamp that stood on a small table. 'And there should be some blankets in here.' He lifted up the lid to an ottoman that also seemed to serve as the coffee-table as it stood in front of the sofa, taking out one of the blankets to wrap it around Merlyn and another one to drape about his own shoulders. '*Now* I could do with the brandy I've been drinking like water lately,' he said as Merlyn huddled down into the blanket as she sat on the sofa.

Her teeth chattered uncontrollably. 'Have I thanked you yet for saving me?'

'I'm just glad I saw you when I did.' His expression was grim as he paced the small room, at least they were out of the biting wind in here. 'I almost didn't,' he scowled. 'With that green dress and dark hair you were camouflaged pretty well against the trees. Then just as I was locking the car something made me glance over here. Just in time to see you fall in!'

'I didn't fall in.' She huddled beneath the blanket, tucking her feet up underneath it. 'The planking gave way.'

He looked at her and frowned. 'It did?'

'Mm,' Merlyn nodded, starting to feel a little warmer now. 'It must have been rotten. With all this rain that isn't surprising,' she added wryly.

'No,' Rand acknowledged.

'If one more weatherman tells me it's the wettest summer for years . . . !'

'Yes,' he grimaced his agreement.

This was ridiculous. They were lovers, Rand had probably just saved her life, and here they were discussing the weather like polite strangers sitting in a dentist's waiting-room.

'You received the message that I'd called, then?' She certainly didn't have the experience to know what the next move was in an affair!

'Did you think I wouldn't?' Rand frowned.

She shrugged. 'Your housekeeper gave me the impression she didn't approve of my calling you. Or maybe she just isn't used to women telephoning you?' she added hopefully; that 'with the others' still rankled.

He gave a grimace, peering out of the window where the rain had once again started to fall. 'It isn't you she doesn't approve of, she just knows you stayed at the house that night. It's a village community, Merlyn,' he answered her dismayed expression. 'Little goes on here that someone doesn't know about.'

No wonder she had received such a frosty response the one time she had actually met Mrs Sutton and then again on the telephone this evening; the other woman hadn't given the impression that the twentieth century had caught up with her yet, let alone the 'permissive society'.

'Do you mind?' She looked closely at Rand, his face unyielding in profile.

He turned slowly to look at her. 'Do you?' His voice was husky.

She shrugged. 'Why should I mind anyone knowing about a relationship that even I don't understand?'

Rand's eyes narrowed as he stepped away from the window. 'What is there to understand?'

'You!'

His mouth twisted. 'That would be a case of "the blind leading the blind". I don't understand me either,' he rasped. 'And besides the fact that your very existence is a medical miracle, I know little or nothing about you either. What you like, what you dislike.' He shook his head.

She was cold and wet, would probably have been hysterical if it weren't for his comforting presence, and yet the mention of her own birth reminded her of the child he and Suzie had lost, and she deliberately made her reply lightly enquiring. 'Disregarding all the injustices of the world, like famine, and drought, and——'

'Yes, disregarding all those,' he drawled.

'Just my own personal likes and dislikes?'

'Yes,' he nodded.

'We're both soaked through and you want to discuss my likes and dislikes?' she laughed.

Rand returned the smile. 'We don't have anything else to do.' He looked pointedly at the rain.

They both knew that wasn't true, her desire for him reflected in his eyes, and yet with the condition they were both in anything else but talking was impossible. 'Which would you like first?' she said lightly. 'I have three real loves in life, and only one real hate.'

His brows rose. 'Then we'll save that one until last,' he drawled, sitting opposite her in the chair, the lamp giving a golden cast to his features as it stood on the table beside him.

'Well,' her eyes glowed, 'I love cats. I don't just like them, you understand, I love them. All colours, shapes and sizes. Of course I haven't had one of my own since I left home, it wouldn't be practical when I now live in a flat and go away so much. But one day, when I can afford it, I'm going to buy a big old house somewhere in the country and fill it with cats!' Colour heated her cheeks as she realised she had probably just described his house to perfection. 'When I can afford it,' she added defensively.

'Then people will *know* you're a witch,' Rand

teased softly, completely relaxed. 'What's your second like?'

'Rain. Walking in it. Usually.' She gave a pointed grimace to the weather outside. 'Even I've had my fill of it this year!'

He gave a throaty laugh. 'And your third love?'

'Burnt biscuits,' she announced with relish.

'*Burnt* biscuits?' he repeated slowly, as if he must have misheard. Or hoped he had!

Her mouth quirked. 'Actually, I love burnt toast too, but I think burnt biscuits comes first.'

'Of course,' he agreed as one humouring a slightly deranged person.

Merlyn chuckled. 'You did ask!'

'Hm.' He seemed to question his own sense in doing so. 'Why *burnt* biscuits?'

'Because they taste the best,' she shrugged carelessly.

'So if I ever want to bring you a gift I forget about roses and chocolates and bring along burnt biscuits instead?' he drawled dryly. 'Mrs Sutton would have a fit if I asked her to deliberately burn her delicious cooking!'

Remembering the lovely meals the housekeeper had left him prepared in the freezer, Merlyn thought the other woman would probably resign on the spot if he made such a request. But the thought that Rand might like to bring her a gift at some stage in their relationship filled her with a warm glow. 'I don't eat chocolates,' she told him huskily. 'But I do like roses. White ones.'

'And now for this intriguing one dislike you have,' he said abruptly.

'It isn't that interesting,' she declared, realising by his suddenly withdrawn manner than she had over-stepped some imaginary line by telling him her preference in flowers.

'Tell me anyway,' he invited softly.

She pursed her lips. 'I hate being called "Ms"! I told you it wasn't very interesting,' she shrugged uncomfortably.

'But it is,' he mused. 'Very interesting. You're an independent lady, have a successful career, should be just the sort of woman who would revel in the featureless Ms!'

'Featureless,' she repeated with feeling. 'That exactly describes it. If women are so liberated they can obviously do without men why do they need to hide their marital status behind Ms!'

'You really don't like it, do you,' Rand chuckled incredulously.

'I don't see the need for it, women that are so liberated they really believe they don't need any-one else, not even emotionally, usually refuse to change their name or wear a ring when they marry anyway. I certainly can't see any insult or slight being implied by being called Miss when it's so obvious a man isn't needed for a complete and fulfilling life any more!'

Rand stood up, determinedly crossing the room to sit down beside her on the sofa, unfold-ing the blanket from about her with deft move-ments. 'There's still one thing you need us for,' he murmured as his head bent towards hers.

Her last observation definitely hadn't been a personal one. 'Oh but——'

'*You* need me for his,' he groaned before his mouth claimed hers.

Thunder crashed and lightning flashed overhead as that kiss went on and on, Merlyn flushed and breathless when Rand at last raised his head. 'That remark wasn't meant on a personal level,' she gasped before he could demonstrate a second time how much she needed him. 'I'm not ashamed to admit that I need you.' She caressed the lean hardness of his cheek.

His eyes were dark. 'I need you too. But not here, and especially with the two of us like this!'

She fully understood what he meant by the latter. Where they were drying off the odour from the lake water and weeds was becoming quite pungent; they both needed a shower.

'You haven't told me any of your likes or dislikes yet,' she teased. 'Besides smelly lakes!'

'Right now that is paramount on my list of dislikes.' He stood up to turn off the oil lamp, leaving the moon as their only illumination. 'But one of my likes—loves—supersedes even that.' He flung open the door to the gazebo, the wind and rain instantly blowing inside. 'I *love* making love to you.' He held out his hand in silent invitation.

Merlyn looked from the heavy rain falling outside to Rand, drowning in those beautiful silver eyes. She stood up to take off the one shoe she still wore, putting her hand in his as they ran out into the storm together.

They were laughing with the sheer joy of just being together by the time they reached her room, undressing quickly to step under the shower, their gazes locked as they slowly washed each other beneath the soothing spray, Rand's body forging with hers in a tempest of emotions much stronger than the storm thundering outside.

'We never did have dinner,' Rand murmured some time after eleven, the two of them lying naked together in Merlyn's bed.

'Still hungry?' She mocked the feast he had made of her body the last two hours.

His eyes gleamed with mischief. 'Anne's chef does a lovely Club sandwich!'

'At this time of night?' Merlyn groaned.

'*Especially* this time of night,' Rand assured her, already picking up the telephone to place an order for two of the sandwiches and a bottle of wine.

'I suppose you do realise that you've just ruined my reputation.' She quirked mocking brows as he replaced the receiver after making the order. 'This room is supposed to be let to a single lady.'

'Want me to call them back?' he teased. 'Tell them we've changed our minds?'

As it always did, their awkwardness together fled when they were in bed. 'Very funny.' She gave him a playful punch on the arm. 'But I——' She broke off as the telephone began to ring. 'Who on earth——!'

'Yes, this is room 202,' Rand confirmed down the receiver. 'Of course you can speak to Miss Summers.' He held out the receiver to her, seeming to be having difficulty in keeping a straight face.

Merlyn understood why as the room-service waiter identified himself and asked if an order had just been placed from her room, colour flowering in her cheeks as Rand got out of bed to move out of earshot of the telephone before he burst out laughing.

Merlyn was so fascinated by that throaty laugh that she answered the waiter in a vague voice. God, Rand was *beautiful* when he forgot his bitterness and gave in to genuine humour.

'Ask him not to forget the coleslaw,' he prompted dryly.

She made the request before she realised what she was doing, quickly ending the call to glare at Rand. 'It will be all over the hotel by tomorrow,' she groaned.

'No, it won't,' he assured her lightly. 'The staff here can be very discreet. Why do you think he telephoned back to make sure he had the right room?'

'So that someone didn't end up with a free meal after I refused to pay for it because I didn't order it!'

'You watch too many films,' he derided mockingly. 'The man was merely checking that he didn't go to the wrong room and interrupt the wrong couple!'

'And I thought Anne ran a respectable hotel!' Merlyn feigned dismay, enjoying the exchange immensely.

'She does; it's the disreputable film-crew she has in residence that are dragging down the tone of the place,' Rand told her, tongue-in-cheek.

'Not nice,' she reproved with mock indignation. 'Just because I can't stay out of your arms is no reason to suppose the rest of the cast are behaving as disgracefully.'

'No? When we came in earlier I saw two couples who certainly weren't married to *each other* go into rooms down the corridor.'

Merlyn frowned. 'Anyone I know?'

'I would say you knew all of them,' replied Rand. 'But Drake wasn't one of the men, if that's what you're wondering.'

'I wasn't,' she denied. 'At least, not for the reason you're implying.' How could she explain to him that if Christopher had found a woman to divert his attention he might be more amenable to her tomorrow when she told him she wouldn't do a nude scene with Mark. 'I only——' She broke off as a knock sounded on the door. 'That was quick,' she muttered as she stood up to pull on her robe, belting it tightly about her waist as she moved to answer the knock.

'Want me to hide in the bathroom?' Rand taunted softly.

She gave him a scathing glance. 'Wouldn't that be a little pointless in the circumstances?'

'I think so, yes.' He gave an abrupt inclination of his head. 'But it's up to you.'

'You could try putting something on to save the poor man's blushes,' she snapped. 'But that is up to *you*.'

He mockingly pulled on his trousers, dry now, but very badly stained from the lake water.

Merlyn waited only long enough to be sure he had zipped up the trousers before opening the door, her polite words of invitation to the room-service waiter dying in her throat as she saw it was Christopher who stood there.

What on earth could he want at her room at this time of night!

She quickly turned to look at Rand, knowing from his expression as he regarded the two of them with narrowed eyes that he was wondering the same thing—and drawing his own conclusions.

CHAPTER TEN

CHRISTOPHER was obviously looking at their half-naked state and drawing his own conclusions too—only his were the right ones.

'I didn't realise I would be interrupting anything,' he drawled softly, his blue gaze speculative. 'I received a message that you wanted to see me as soon as I got back, Merlyn.'

She still had her doubts about his having *been* anywhere, but she certainly wasn't going to start discussing her aversion to a nude scene in the gazebo with Mark in front of Rand. 'It can wait until tomorrow,' she answered tautly.

'If you say so,' he shrugged. 'I wouldn't have bothered you this late at night but the receptionist seemed to think it was urgent.'

'It wasn't,' she muttered through clenched teeth. 'At least, nothing that can't wait until the morning.'

'If you're sure . . . ?' He still lingered in the open doorway.

Her eyes flashed. 'I'm sure, Christopher,' she told him with controlled anger.

'Okay.' He didn't argue. 'Good night, Merlyn. 'Night, Carmichael,' he added mockingly.

Merlyn let out a ragged sigh of relief as she leant back against the closed door, looking apprehensively at Rand as he stood across the room from her, his hands thrust into his trouser pockets. Despite his bared chest and tousled hair he didn't even look approachable, let alone like her lover.

'Why did you need to see him?' Rand spoke suddenly in the awkward silence that had followed Christopher's departure.

She put a hand up to her temple as she moved away from the door, feeling the tension there. 'I—There's a scene I'm not too happy about.' She knew she sounded evasive, but how could she tell Rand that it was intended that she should be naked tomorrow when she played the part of *his* dead wife!

'Surely you ironed all that out weeks ago?' Rand's eyes were narrowed.

'Christopher likes to—improvise, as he goes along,' she admitted.

'And you aren't happy about the improvisation he has lined up for tomorrow?'

Merlyn swallowed hard, moistening her lips, praying he wouldn't ask what those changes had been—and knowing she couldn't be that lucky. 'No.'

'What is it?'

'I——' Saved by the knock on the door; it had to be the food this time!

She rushed to open the door, gratefully pulling the slightly dazed waiter inside, giving him a dazzling smile as she signed the bill.

'You're right,' she told Rand once the waiter had left, clutching his more-than-generous tip. 'The sandwiches do look delicious. And I will have just one glass of wine.' She sat cross-legged on the bed with the tray in front of her, looking up at him expectantly as he made no effort to join her. 'Rand?' she prompted with a quick smile, hardly daring to breathe as she waited to see if he would join her or continue to probe into tomorrow's filming. She felt some of the tension leave her body as he slipped off the uncomfortably stained trousers before joining her on the bed.

Merlyn hadn't had a late-night feast like this since she was at boarding-school and one of the other girls had received a food hamper, not protesting as Rand repeatedly topped up her wine glass, feeling quite heady by the time they removed the tray and empty wine bottle from the bed.

They made love slowly, lingering over every new delight, Merlyn responding with a lack of inhibition she had no control over, snuggling down against his chest as they lay replete in each other's arms.

'Never feel you have to deliberately keep something from me, Merlyn.' He smoothed her hair as he softly spoke. 'You don't owe me any explanations, about anything.'

She wanted to explain to him, to try to make him understand why she was so upset, she just didn't want to hurt him by revealing what Christopher intended doing with the gazebo scene. But it had been a long day, a tiring one, and she was exhausted by their avid need of each other that didn't seem to lessen but intensify.

Instead of explaining she fell asleep.

*   *   *

'A whole morning,' Christopher ranted as he paced the room. 'I've lost a whole morning's filming!'

'Well, I'm sorry,' Merlyn said impatiently. 'If I'd known that I would have waited until tomorrow before falling through the deck!' She glared at him.

'Very funny,' he argued back. 'You could have let someone know of the damage you had done.'

'Again, I'm sorry, but at the time I was more concerned with saving my life——'

'You saw me late last night— When you were obviously concerned with Brandon Carmichael,' he realised disgustedly. 'And just how long has that been going on?' he accused.

Her face was flushed. 'None of your——'

'If you had only told me about the deck then I could have got it repaired.' He ignored her indignation as he returned to what was really bothering him. 'And——'

'In the middle of the night?' She gave him a sceptical look.

'—then we wouldn't have wasted the whole morning,' he finished exasperatedly, glaring at her.

'I repeat,' she said through gritted teeth. 'In the middle of the night?'

'Of course,' Christopher dismissed. 'And then we wouldn't have wasted the whole——'

'Morning,' Merlyn finished wearily. 'Speak for yourself,' she muttered. 'I've enjoyed my morning.' She had woken up with a headache and an unwillingness to do any work today. Her day had brightened considerably when she found she

didn't have to. 'Would you care for a game?' She
lent on her cue as she stood next to the snooker-
table in the hotel games-room.

'No,' he replied in irritation.

'Perhaps not,' she grimaced, deftly pocketing a
red ball, quickly followed by the black.

Christopher's eyes widened. 'Where did you
learn to do that?'

She gave him a vague smile while replacing the
black ball on its spot before pocketing another
red. 'One of the advantages of having such an
older brother. One of the few,' she added with
feeling. 'As we were both at boarding-school he
never had a partner for snooker during the
school holidays!'

'You could be a professional,' Christopher said
dazedly as she pocketed one ball after another
with complete accuracy.

'No, I couldn't,' she taunted. 'I'm an actress,
remember.'

His scowl returned. 'I couldn't believe it when
we went to set up this morning and found that
gaping great hole where you were supposed to
step up off the boat!'

'A gaping great hole big enough for a body to
fall through—mine!'

'All right, all right,' he sighed. 'You weren't
hurt, were you?' he asked grudgingly.

'At last,' she said with feeling. 'No, I wasn't
hurt. But if it hadn't been for Rand——'

'Carmichael was out there with you?' Christopher queried with a frown. 'What were you
doing, practising the gazebo scene?' he taunted
knowingly.

'Oh yes, the gazebo scene,' repeated Merlyn, dangerously soft. 'I'm glad you brought that up.'

Christopher raised his brows in innocent enquiry. 'I gather there's something about it that isn't to your liking?' he said mildly.

'*Something* about it?' she echoed with suppressed anger. 'Liza told me that you intend for us to play that scene nude now!'

'Knowing what a little gossip she is, I thought she might,' he drawled with satisfaction.

'I realise that,' she declared in anger. 'And you have to know that I won't do it.'

'Won't, Merlyn?' he repeated, as if he had never heard the word before.

And maybe he hadn't. *He* was the star around here, for all that he remained behind the camera. 'It isn't supposed to be played like that, Christopher,' she tried reasoning with him. 'They're supposed to sink on to the sofa together, kissing passionately, while the scene fades away to leave the rest to the audience's imagination. That was the way we discussed it——'

'Don't tell me how to direct my film, Merlyn,' he responded icily. 'I know how we discussed it, I just happen to have decided it should be more explicit. The audience doesn't like having things left to their imagination any more. This isn't some damned love-story,' he added scornfully.

'But it is,' protested Merlyn. 'It was because Suzie loved life, because she loved Rand, that she fought her illness and won.'

'It was because she didn't want to die,' he jeered. 'It had nothing to do with love, for Carmichael or anything else. The human body has a wonderful resilience to survive, against all odds.'

Merlyn shook her head. 'Faced with the same prospect, I don't know if I'd have had the same strength.'

'Why not?' Christopher drawled. 'You love life. And Brandon Carmichael,' he added softly.

Her breath caught in her throat as a blush flamed in her cheeks. 'Christopher——'

'Hey, I'm not criticising,' he chided. 'I'm for anything that keeps him happy—and out of my way.'

Her eyes darkened. 'That isn't the reason——'

'Look, Merlyn, your reasons are your own,' he assured her briskly. 'I just hope you're sure of his.'

Merlyn became suddenly still. 'What do you mean?'

He shrugged his broad shoulders. 'I just hope, for your sake, that he isn't looking at you and seeing his wife.'

He didn't, of course he didn't! And yet Christopher was only putting into words what she feared herself. She was playing the part of Suzie, had been made to look like her; Rand couldn't be blamed if it was Suzie he saw.

'Forget I said that,' Christopher said self-disgustedly as he saw her stricken expression. 'It's probably just sour grapes on my part; I did want you myself, remember,' he confessed.

She gave him a rueful smile, the warmth not reaching the bleakness of her eyes. 'Only because you knew I wasn't interested.'

'Well, if there was no challenge in the conquest

it wouldn't be worth bothering about, would it?'

Did all men think that way about attracting women? Did Rand? Because if he did she was very much afraid she had been no challenge to him whatsoever, had been his from the beginning.

'Not there, Merlyn,' Liza complained as she squirmed. 'Lower!'

She massaged her friend's aching back lower than the point between her shoulder blades which was the exact spot Liza had been complaining about seconds earlier. 'What on earth have you been doing?' she mocked as the girl groaned as the ache was eased farther down.

Liza sat forward in the chair while Merlyn stood behind her, her head back as she flexed her aching muscles. 'We didn't all spend the day thrashing all comers to the snooker-table,' she moaned. 'Christopher decided the weather had cleared enough this afternoon to do my scene on horse-back. I haven't ridden a horse since I was ten years old and didn't know any better! I was so tense today my back became locked.'

'Poor you,' Merlyn consoled.

'The horse wasn't too happy about it, either,' her friend said with feeling. 'I'm too much of a lady to tell you where else I hurt, but it *is* painful!'

Merlyn chuckled softly as Liza's awkward way of sitting told her exactly 'where else' she hurt. 'Never mind,' she encouraged. 'It's done now.'

'No, it isn't,' Liza groaned. 'Christopher said I looked like a puppet whose strings had got all tangled up; he's going to reshoot it tomorrow before the gazebo scene. Talking of the gazebo scene,' she half turned to Merlyn, the stiffness in her back preventing her from turning all the way around, 'you must have taken quite a fall last night.'

'I thought I was going to drown,' confirmed Merlyn with a shudder of remembrance.

'I saw Mr Carmichael over there this morning before the men started work,' Liza nodded. 'He looked grim. Hey, do you think I could call him Rand like you do, it seems a little strange calling one of my best friend's lovers Mr!'

'Call him what you want,' Merlyn said absently. 'Rand was at the gazebo this morning?'

'Mm.' Her friend nodded again, once more enjoying her massage. 'He was probably imagining what could have happened if he hadn't been there to save you.'

Rand had left her this morning shortly after six o'clock with the intention of going home to change before flying down to London for the day; so what had he been doing at the gazebo?

'Ouch!' Liza complained indignantly as Merlyn's nails dug into her back. 'I don't have to call him Rand if you would rather I didn't,' she teased. 'You don't have to get violent about it!'

Merlyn stepped away from her friend, her smile weak. 'It was an accident,' she excused. 'I think you should have a nice soak in a hot bath now. It might help ease your other point of pain,' she added dryly.

Liza stood up with difficulty. 'I'll never be able to get back on that horse tomorrow.' She moved stiffly. 'Maybe I shouldn't have lied when

Christopher asked if I'd ridden a horse lately!'

Merlyn chuckled. 'Our director is certainly demanding.'

'No luck with him about the gazebo scene?' her friend asked directly.

'No,' said Merlyn with feeling. 'Christopher is adamant he wants it played that way.'

'Mark seems to be looking forward to it,' Liza told her sympathetically.

Merlyn hadn't spoken to Mark all day, but she hadn't needed to, his knowing looks enough; he really was looking forward to tomorrow afternoon. And Merlyn didn't need anyone tell her why. The two of them had been engaged to be married six years ago but their most intimate caresses had been when Mark touched her breasts; tomorrow afternoon he was going to take great pleasure in touching more than that!

'He has nothing to worry about,' she said crossly. 'He'll be wearing as much as if he were going for a swim.'

'Are you seeing Rand tonight?' Liza wisely changed the subject.

Merlyn wasn't sure. He had said he would call her when he got home, and he hadn't called yet. In view of his housekeeper's reaction yesterday when she telephoned him, she was loath to call him again.

'I don't know yet,' she revealed truthfully. 'He'll call me if he gets back in time to come over.'

'If he hasn't called within the next hour come and rescue me from the bath and we'll go and have dinner together. We haven't had time to catch up on all that gossip yet.'

'See how you feel once you've been soaking for a while,' Merlyn advised with humour.

With her usual exuberance, Liza bounced back to full mobility after her bath and, as Rand still hadn't called, Merlyn joined the other woman for dinner in one of the hotel restaurants.

'Good evening, ladies.' James came to stand by their table. 'Is everything satisfactory?'

Merlyn returned his smile. 'Well, the steak was a little more delicious than I'm used to, but I think I could learn to live with that. Why don't you join us?' she invited as the waiter brought their coffee.

'Miss Benedict?' He looked questioningly at Liza before making any move to sit down.

'Please,' she smiled. 'I never refuse the company of a handsome man.'

'Unless they're married, of course,' Merlyn put in dryly as the couple continued to smile at each other as James sat down.

Liza gave James a rueful smile. 'It's terrible when you have your conscience sitting next to you!'

His eyes glowed darkly brown. 'But *we're* married. In a way,' he drawled.

'So we are.' Liza's expression brightened. 'In that case—— Don't look so worried, Merlyn,' she laughed her enjoyment of the exchange. 'James and I are only having fun.'

Merlyn was well aware of that. 'But if I don't play the Jiminy Cricket, who will?' she teased.

'I will,' Anne announced lightly. 'You're wanted on the telephone, Merlyn,' she told her softly once she had her attention. 'Over by the desk,' Anne explained. 'It's Brandon.'

She breathlessly thanked the other woman before hurrying over to take the call, hardly aware of excusing herself before she did so. She hadn't consciously allowed herself to think of Rand all evening, and yet she knew that at the back of her mind she was thinking of nothing else, just waiting to hear from him.

'Merlyn?'

His voice sounded different on the telephone, more brusque, not at all like the man who had whispered eroticisms in her ear this morning as they made love. 'Yes,' she confirmed huskily. 'Rand?'

'I'm still in London,' he announced flatly.

She bit back her gasp of disappointment. 'When do you expect to be back?' She deliberately made her voice light, casually enquiring, vividly remembering what Christopher had said earlier about 'no challenge in the conquest making it not worth bothering about'.

'I'm not sure,' Rand answered abruptly. 'Some time tomorrow, perhaps.'

'I'll miss you.' The admission was an involuntary one, and she bit her lip painfully after she had made it.

'Will you?' He sounded sceptical.

'Yes,' she confirmed almost resentfully as she sensed that scepticism.

'How did that scene go today that you weren't too happy about?' His voice was brisk again.

'We didn't do it,' Merlyn sighed.

'Why not?' he demanded sharply.

'I—er—The conditions weren't right,' she evaded. It was ridiculous to keep the nudity scene from him, she knew, when he was sure to see the completed film. And yet she didn't want him to know about it just yet.

'I see,' Rand said slowly. 'I'll possibly see you tomorrow, then.'

'Yes. But—Rand!' she cried before he could ring off, giving a self-conscious smile at the maitre d' as he stood a short distance away, having turned to look at her curiously as she raised her voice. 'I will miss you,' she repeated inadequately to Rand, her voice softer now, the maitre d's attention returning back to the diners.

'I told you I'll see you tomorrow,' he said tersely. 'I don't want to keep you from your meal any longer.'

'Oh, I've finished my meal, we were just sitting around talking.'

'Really?' he said disinterestedly. 'Then I won't keep you from that.'

'We were only gossiping— Rand, what's wrong?' She frowned her confusion with his coldness towards her. Had he tired of her already and this was his way of ending things?

'Wrong?' he echoed icily. 'What could possibly be wrong? I've been delayed in London on business,' he told her, his voice edged with impatience. 'One of those dislikes of mine that we didn't get around to discussing last night is that I can't stand possessively jealous women!'

Merlyn felt the colour drain from her face. Jealous? Did she have anything—*anyone*—to be jealous of? God, he was right, she *was* jealous! Since Mark she hadn't allowed herself to care for any man, least of all to become possessive about one, and it was that Summers pride and emotional independence that helped her now through this awkwardness with Rand.

'I think you're talking about the wrong woman, Rand,' she said with cool dismissal. 'Now, if you'll excuse me, I *do* think my coffee is getting cold.'

'*Only* the coffee?' he scorned.

Merlyn frowned. 'I'm not even going to pretend to understand you, Rand,' she sighed. 'I have a feeling you were right last night, you *don't* understand yourself either. You certainly don't seem to know what you want, especially from me. I have to go,' she said impatiently. 'I have another early call tomorrow.'

She took a few minutes to compose herself before rejoining the others at the table, finding James had gone now, Anne and Liza chatting companionably together.

'Sorted out yet which one of you belongs to James?' prompted Merlyn lightly as she sat down.

'I do—by default,' Anne drawled, her eyes glowing with humour. 'Liza dropped out when she heard that James likes to eat biscuits in bed.'

'I can't stand crumbs on the sheets,' Liza acknowledged wryly.

'I take it poor James left in disgust?' Merlyn quirked her brows.

'Come to think of it he did leave soon after that,' Anne nodded. 'How's Brandon?' Merlyn sobered.

'Busy in London,' she supplied abruptly, not quite able to meet the other woman's gaze.

His sister-in-law nodded. 'It's good to see him

so interested in his work again.' She stood up. 'Ah well, back to the grindstone,' she said without rancour, obviously enjoying her thriving hotel.

'It may be good for Brandon,' Liza said slowly, watching Merlyn intently once they were alone again. 'But is it good for you?'

Merlyn looked at her with feigned surprise. 'What does it have to do with me?'

'You look as if you've lost five pounds and found a penny!' her friend observed.

Merlyn sighed. 'I don't understand Rand, and I'm not even going to pretend to. My only consolation is that he doesn't understand himself either! Come on.' She stood up decisively. 'Let's get out of here,' and she strode from the room without waiting to see if Liza was following her.

'Slow down,' Liza puffed from behind. 'My back has stiffened up again.'

Merlyn relented, matching her strides to Liza's painfully slow ones. She felt charged with energy, needed to be doing something, and at almost eleven o'clock at night there wasn't too much to do.

'I know, let's go dancing!' Merlyn suddenly realised the discothèque would still be going.

'In my condition?' Liza groaned, hobbling along at best.

'Hm.' Her friend's enthusiasm wavered. 'I just don't feel like going to bed yet.'

'Then how about a quiet game of cards in one of the lounges?' Liza suggested hopefully. 'It's about all I'm fit for tonight.'

'I'm being selfish,' Merlyn realised heavily.

'And stupid. We both have to be up early tomorrow.'

'Don't remind me!' Liza grimaced.

Merlyn gave a tender smile. 'The best thing for you is a good night's sleep.'

'I'm not even sure that will do any good; they'll probably have to tie me on to the horse's back.'

While she didn't exactly look equestrian class Liza did very well the next day, Christopher declaring himself satisfied with what he had after only the third take.

Merlyn was pleased for Liza, but it meant they were now ready to film the scene she had so been dreading. The mere mention of the word gazebo had become a nightmare in her mind, and once she left here she never wanted to see one again.

The planking seemed as good as new when she tried her footing on it, and the first part of the scene went perfectly the first time. It was only as Mark took her in his arms that she froze up, conscious of exactly who he was.

'For God's sake,' Christopher burst out impatiently. 'Merlyn, this is the man you love. Mark,' he added hardly, 'you aren't about to throw her to the floor and rape her. This is the woman you love and you need to be as close to her as you possibly can.'

Merlyn thought Christopher's first description of Mark's acting more apt as they went through the scene time and time again. Mark just didn't have it in him to even *act* gentle with her.

'Like this!' Christopher finally lost his temper completely, taking over Mark's part, standing so close to Merlyn that their bodies almost touched, but not quite, his big gentle hands cupping either side of her face as his eyes gazed into hers with a love that revered and adored. 'I love you, Suzie. God, how I love you . . .' He groaned the words Mark should have said in the role of Brandon before his mouth lowered to hers.

Merlyn's arms slowly crept about his neck as she became lost to that kiss, knowing they were both acting parts even though it felt so *real*.

Christopher raised his head at the sound of the spontaneous applause from the technicians he had deemed necessary for the scene, turning to scowl at all of them until they were silent again, his baleful glare settling on Mark. '*That's* how you make love to a woman,' he told him scathingly as he put Merlyn briskly away from him.

Mark shrugged, strolling forward to take over from Christopher. 'Maybe you've had more practice at it with Merlyn than I have,' he said carelessly.

Blue eyes narrowed, the air suddenly still, even the wind that had been whipping about them all afternoon ceasing for those few seconds. 'What's that supposed to mean?' The very quietness of Christopher's voice was menacing.

'I meant more *recent* practice, of course.' Mark wasn't in the least daunted by the other man's anger.

'Explain,' Christopher demanded.

'Can't we just get on with the scene?' Merlyn put in awkwardly, the stunned surprise she had felt at Christopher's intensity of passion quickly replaced by apprehension at Mark's challenging attitude. 'We——'

'Explain,' Christopher barked at Mark a second time, his eyes as cold as ice.

Mark shrugged again. 'I told you the other day that Merlyn and I were becoming *reacquainted*.'

'Yes, but—Merlyn, in your dressing-room,' Christopher snapped, suddenly becoming aware that they still had an avid audience. 'Now,' he ordered through gritted teeth.

Her 'dressing-room' was one of several caravans they had parked where they were convenient to their location, but not too intrusive on the other guests.

Merlyn turned fatalistically to face Christopher as he closed the door forcefully behind him.

'When I asked you about Hillier——'

'I told you we didn't like each other but we could live with it,' she cut in tautly.

His eyes flashed. 'What's going on out there is "living with it"?'

Her face became flushed. 'Don't blame me for that, Christopher, I'm doing my part——'

'You act as if he's about to abuse you, not make love to you!'

'Maybe because that's the way he makes me feel——' She broke off abruptly, breathing heavily as she realised what she had said, a speculative gleam in Christopher's eyes now. 'Mark Hillier just doesn't appeal to me—even when he is pretending to be someone else. Now can we just leave it at that?' It was a futile hope at best; Christopher never 'just left' anything!

'He is that man from your past,' he realised impatiently. 'And you told me he tried to use you to——'

'Christopher, please!' said Merlyn tensely, her hands twisting together in front of her.

He gave an angry sigh, moving about in the small confines with his customary restlessness. 'Great! This is just *great*,' he ground out forcefully. 'I wish to God I'd known that before I took him on.'

'So do I,' Merlyn's reply was weary. 'But it's done now,' she added shakily.

'Do you want me to try and break his contract——'

'God, no!' she refused with a gasp. Mark would *never* forgive her if he lost another starring role because of her.

'Okay, but if he lays one finger on you——'

'He already has, Christopher, you saw him do it,' Merlyn sighed. 'I think today is probably a repercussion of that.'

He gave a groan. 'As if I don't already have enough problems on this film with the author of the book constantly breathing down my neck, and you having an affair with Suzie Forrester's husband——'

'I thought you said that was helping you,' she reminded him tightly.

'It's a double-edged sword,' Christopher scowled. 'If you don't *keep* him happy it could just make him all the more difficult to deal with afterwards. Oh, what the hell.' He threw up his hands in disgust. 'I'll send Irene in to retouch your make-up while we all take a break. But in ten minutes I want you back out there and acting like Mark Hillier is the man you love and don't ever want to leave!' he warned.

She didn't need to ask him to make that clear to Mark too, could tell by the light of battle in his eyes as he left her that he intended making his feelings even more clearly known to the man, that he was as angry about the actor's open defiance earlier as he was about the taut situation between Mark and Merlyn. She could almost pity Mark during the next few minutes. Almost . . .

Whatever Christopher had said to him—and by the very fact that Christopher had never been all that particular about making his displeasure known in public she knew someone was bound to relate the chastisement word for word to her some time before the end of the day—Mark, as Brandon Carmichael, couldn't have been more in love with her.

He was so gentle as he lay her back against the sofa, so reverent as he slipped the clothes from her body, his mouth so erotically sensual against her own, that he quickly overcame Merlyn's awkwardness with the situation, and as she closed her eyes she could even believe it *was* Rand making love to her.

The tension left her body completely as her fingers laced in the vibrant dark hair at his nape, his skin smooth and muscled beneath her searching lips. She forgot everything, the cameras, the technicians, Christopher, as she became lost to the wonder of Rand making love to her.

She was on fire as that dark head moved down her body, gasping as his mouth caressed the peak of her breast, her eyes closed as she drowned in Rand's touch.

'Love me,' she groaned. 'Oh God, love me,' she encouraged achingly.

'Merlyn . . . ?'

She blinked open dazed blue eyes, staring up into Mark's puzzled face, not Rand's . . .

'Damn it, Hillier,' Christopher exploded. 'What the hell do you think you're doing?'

Mark raised his head to glare across the room at the other man before easily levering himself to his feet. 'That wasn't in the script,' he complained. 'What was I supposed to say to that? She——'

'You could have improvised, damn it,' Christopher shouted his impatience. 'Couldn't you see she was enjoying it?'

Merlyn gave a pained groan as she bent her knees up into her body in shame, turning away from all the curiously speculative faces. There weren't really that many people present, Christopher had kept them down to a minimum as Liza had said he was going to, but it seemed as if dozens of pairs of eyes were staring at her. *Had* she been enjoying it? She had tried to pretend it was Rand making love to her, but it seemed she had succeeded more than she had dared hope——

'Here.' A harsh voice rasped before something heavy fell about her body.

Merlyn recognised that voice even as she smelt the maleness of Rand on the navy blue jacket he had dropped over her nakedness. She raised startled eyes to look at the man who stared back at her as if she were a stranger to him.

She swallowed hard. 'How long——'

'Long enough,' he bit out with disgust, his eyes coldly silver.

It had been *him* she responded to, *him* she had wanted to love her. But how could she make him understand she had only been able to bear the embarrassment of today by pretending it was him who made love to her!

'Carmichael,' Christopher greeted lightly as he interrupted them. 'I didn't realise you were here.'

'Obviously.' That silver gaze raked over him with open contempt.

'Merlyn is doing really well, isn't she?' Christopher enthused, not at all daunted by the other man's coldness. 'And after the start we had this afternoon it's a relief, I can tell you——'

'*Don't* tell me,' Rand cut in harshly. 'I have no interest whatsoever in hearing about any of your problems. Suzie never did a nude scene in the whole of her career, and I don't intend letting her make one now—even posthumously!'

'But, Carmichael——'

Hooded eyes silenced him. 'You heard me, Drake,' he ordered harshly. 'No nude scene.'

'Rand——'

Fury glittered in his gaze as he looked at Merlyn before turning and walking off.

CHAPTER ELEVEN

'HELL,' Christopher groaned in frustration. 'Okay, everyone, we may as well call it a night.'

Mark was buttoning his shirt as he joined them. 'Can he do that?' he frowned. 'Can he just cut a scene like that?'

'Yes,' Christopher spat out. 'Anything he doesn't like goes.'

Merlyn swallowed hard, still huddled beneath the protective cloak of Rand's jacket. 'You mean I don't have to—have to go through this again?' Her teeth were chattering, but with reaction, not the cold.

The only way she had got through that scene even once was by pretending Mark was Rand, her mortification when she realised how well she had succeeded in doing that such that she wanted to crawl away into a corner and die. But Rand's presence meant she had to face exactly what she had done. He had stood and watched as she made love with another man!

'Hey,' Mark taunted. 'Don't sound so eager to scrap it. As Christopher said, you were enjoying it well enough a few minutes ago!'

'Shut up, Hillier,' Christopher told him caustically as Merlyn gasped her humiliation. 'Can't you tell when a woman is responding to another man and not you?' He sat down on the sofa to take Merlyn soothingly into his arms.

Mark's handsome face flushed angrily at the rebuke. 'I was the one lying there with her——'

'But you weren't the one in her mind,' Christopher declared coldly. 'And women make love with their minds as much as their bodies. It's all right, Merlyn,' he comforted as she still trembled, holding her gently against him. 'It's all over.'

'You mean she was pretending I was Carmichael all the time?' Mark was furious at being told he had been nothing but a stand-in lover.

'Well it certainly wasn't me,' Christopher scorned. 'Now could you get *your* mind out of your trousers long enough to go to my caravan and get Merlyn a glass of brandy; you'll find a bottle in there somewhere.'

'I'm no one's servant——'

'Get the brandy, Hillier,' Christopher told him through clenched teeth. 'And stop being such a stupid bastard.'

Mark looked malevolent before he turned and strode out of the gazebo.

'You've just made yourself a vindictive enemy,' Merlyn murmured faintly, her eyes closed as she lay weakly against Christopher, willing everyone else gone before she had to stand up and put her clothes back on.

'He's been spoiling for a fight ever since he got here,' Christopher dismissed carelessly. 'Now he's got himself an opponent of his own weight! It's you I'm concerned about, Merlyn.' The worry could be heard in his voice. 'I know you said you didn't want to do this scene but I had no idea it was this bad.' He rubbed the chill of her hands in his much larger ones.

'I really won't have to go through it again?' She looked up at him beseechingly.

He shook his head. 'What Carmichael doesn't like is vetoed.' He looked grim. 'I don't like someone else having this much power over my film, but we may as well not bother to make it at all if Carmichael should decide after it's made to speak out against the authenticity of any part of it. The public loved Suzie too much to accept anything less than the truth about her.'

Merlyn shivered in reaction again. 'I wish you had discussed it with him before I—before I had to go through this.'

Christopher grimaced. 'I was hoping he would see it in the context of the whole film; I didn't realise he was going to be creeping around my closed film set!' he added resentfully.

Merlyn wondered what he had been doing there too. Last night he had given the impression that he didn't care if he never saw her again, let alone the way he had seen her today.

'Here.' A very disgruntled Mark pushed the bottle of brandy in front of them.

'Glass?' Christopher queried.

'I brought two.' He thrust the tumblers at them too. 'I thought you might *both* need a drink!'

'What did you ever see in him?' Christopher bit out as he poured the brandy for Merlyn and himself, Mark having left after giving a triumphant smile at the baleful glare he received from the other man.

'At the time, things I didn't have—maturity

and success,' she said dryly.

He raised dark blond brows. 'My, what a bad judge of character you were!'

There was no answering smile for him in her shadowed eyes. 'I don't seem to have got any better with age!' She took a large swallow of the brandy, choking a little, but at last able to feel some warmth returning to her body.

'Carmichael,' Christopher sighed, sipping his own drink. 'Come on,' he decided briskly. 'Let's get you into the warm and then into some clothes.'

'Has everyone gone?' She had deliberately kept her face averted from the doorway.

'No, they haven't,' Christopher told her decisively. 'But you have to work with them all again tomorrow whether you like it or not, so you might as well face them all now.' He put out a hand to pull her to her feet.

Merlyn shook her head, rigid with nervousness. 'I can't——'

'You can,' he insisted. 'And you will. My God, woman,' he groaned in exasperation as she still refused to move. 'Do you think you're the first actress, the first *woman*, to ever pretend it's someone else making love to her just to get through it? Believe me, when your co-star has been eating Indian food the night before, sometimes it's the only way *to* get through it!'

Her mouth curved in the ghost of a smile. 'Are you comparing Mark to a strong curry?'

'I wouldn't compare him to anything,' Christopher said disgustedly. 'The man's an idiot. He had to be to let you go the way he did.'

Merlyn gave him a sharp look. 'He told you we were once going to be married . . . ?'

'Boasted about it, is a more apt description,' Christopher replied. 'Until I pointed out that at least you had come to your senses before you made *that* mistake!'

Her mouth quirked. 'I won't ask how he reacted to that remark!'

'I shouldn't,' he grimaced. 'Even one of the cameramen blushed,' he answered dryly.

She didn't know how she did it but somehow she allowed Christopher to pull her to her feet, wrap the jacket that reached mid-thigh on her more firmly about her, before walking her over to the caravan she was using to change and make-up. The clothes she had been wearing earlier were neatly folded and lying on the chair just inside the door. The colour drained from her face again as she realised someone must have picked them up from the floor and brought them over here.

'This is all my fault.' Christopher frowned as he watched her anxiously.

'No.' She shook her head. 'It's mine,' she said dully.

'Get dressed and we'll have dinner together,' he instructed harshly.

She swallowed hard, shaking her head. 'I couldn't face anyone tonight.'

'Yes, you could,' he told her firmly. 'The only ones with egg on their faces are Mark and me. I'm thick-skinned enough to take it, and Mark's had plenty of years to get used to the feeling!'

She shook her head again. 'I'd rather have a

soak in the bath.' To wash away Mark's touch and the degradation she still felt. 'And then order dinner in my room.' Which she doubted she would be able to eat.

'Hiding?' he enquired.

'Renewing my defences,' she corrected in a subdued voice. 'Did you ever meet Rand when he was married to Suzie?' she asked curiously.

'Once or twice, I think, at parties,' he shrugged with a frown.

'Was he different then?'

'He may have smiled a little more, but I believe he was just as arrogant. Why?' Christopher's eyes were narrowed.

She shrugged. 'I think I would have liked to have known him then.'

'It wouldn't have done you any good; he was married, remember?'

It might even have been worth the pain of knowing he was completely inaccessible to her just to have seen him happy with someone. After today he was just as elusive to her as if he were still married, and he despised her into the bargain.

'Thank you for understanding just now.' She squeezed Christopher's arm gratefully.

'About time, hm?' His tone was self-derisive. 'I really am sorry about what happened earlier.'

'It's over now,' she dismissed.

'And you want to go and hide, forget it ever happened,' he guessed correctly. 'Face it head on, Merlyn, it's the only way.'

'Rand is the one I can't face again.' She shuddered just at the thought of it.

'You think he'll come back?' Christopher raised surprised brows.

Would he? If she had to judge by the contemptuous way he had looked at her earlier as he threw his jacket over her then she would say no. But he had walked away from her before only to come back again because he needed to make love to her. She didn't know what he would do now . . .

She shrugged. 'I doubt it,' she sighed. 'I'm sorry if that makes things awkward for you.'

Christopher scowled. 'Nothing you do could make things here any more difficult for me than they already are. I've been up against flooding in drought areas, and deposed governments replaced by less welcoming ones right in the middle of filming, but this is definitely the worst situation I've ever been in! I'll stick to fiction next time!'

Merlyn wished the whole of the time since she first met Rand hadn't been real. And she especially wished today were just part of a nightmare from which she would eventually wake up.

What must he be thinking of her now, besides the obvious feelings of disgust! It had to be obvious that she hadn't been acting out a response to Mark, that she had been completely dazed when he broke away from her in confusion as she hadn't kept to the script. The whole experience had been mortifying enough without Rand witnessing it!

It felt good to put her clothes on again, although she took Rand's jacket with her when she went to her room, keeping it wrapped about her shoulders, loving the scent of him that it carried. And maybe, just maybe, he would come back, if only to retrieve it.

The water was cold and the bubbles had long disappeared from its scented surface by the time she got out of the bath. There had been no visitors to her room during that time, not even Liza for her customary chat. Maybe her friend had heard all the gossip about her today and was as shocked by her behaviour as Merlyn was herself. Although that didn't really sound like the Liza she knew and loved; her friend's policy had always been 'live and let live'. She never presumed to judge anyone. Besides, Liza, more than anyone else here, knew how she really felt about Mark.

She was picking disinterestedly at the dinner she had ordered when the knock sounded on her door, and as she approached it she wished Anne's hotel, like American ones, had installed peepholes to the doors so that she might now know who was standing on the other side of hers before she opened it.

Rand, in all honesty, was the last person she had expected to see. Even though she had hoped.

She looked up at him with wide green eyes, glad she had chosen to put on black fitted trousers and a bright red blouse tucked in at the waist, knowing she looked coolly elegant. When she had chosen the clothes she had known she would need to feel confident of her appearance if she had *any* visitors this evening. It had to be an improvement on the last time Rand had seen her.

'You have my jacket,' he finally rasped.

Merlyn nodded abruptly. 'I'll get it.' She bit her lip as she turned away.

He reached out to lightly grasp her arm. 'Can I come in?'

She blinked up at him uncertainly. 'I—If you would like to,' she nodded breathlessly.

'I would,' he said huskily, closing the door softly behind him.

Merlyn watched him as she crossed the room to pick up his jacket from the chair she had draped it across earlier. Late this afternoon he had looked furiously angry, now he just looked tired, tired and a little uncertain. Uncertain? It wasn't an emotion she had ever associated with him before.

'Here you are.' She held out the jacket to him.

He made no effort to take it from her slightly trembling hand. 'Do they hurt?'

She eyed him warily at this totally enigmatic question. 'What?'

'The contact lenses,' he explained gruffly. 'I got quite a shock today when I looked into your eyes and saw they were blue instead of green! Drake mentioned something about your wearing contact lenses the other evening, but even so it was—startling.'

Merlyn swallowed hard. 'Christopher believes —he decided that it was Suzie's eyes that made her so hypnotic to watch, the deep deep blue of them. I think he's right, but if you object——'

'He told me about you and Hillier,' Rand cut in harshly.

She gave him a startled look for the interruption. 'Told you what?'

'About the rough time he's been giving you, how you didn't want to do that scene with him today. That the only way you could do it was by pretending he really was me,' he added searchingly.

Colour warmed her cheeks, in fact her whole body suddenly felt warm. 'Rand, I——'

'Did you do that?' he pressured. 'Just answer me yes or no!'

She moistened her lips. 'Yes,' she finally admitted forcefully.

'That's all I needed to know.' The breath left his body in a ragged sigh. 'When I saw his hands all over you today I——'

'On me?' Merlyn looked at him uncertainly. 'But I thought—we *all* thought— We all thought you were angry because I was supposed to be Suzie,' she frowned.

'That was only part of it,' he rasped. 'The rest was all you. I didn't like seeing another man touching you the way I do!'

'Oh Rand!' She moved instinctively towards the shelter of his arms, hesitating before she reached them.

'Merlyn?' He was watching her with narrowed eyes as she faltered.

'Yesterday you said——'

'Yesterday afternoon I telephoned you to let you know I wouldn't be back last night——'

'Last night, you mean,' she corrected tautly. 'I was having dinner when you called, remember?'

'That was the second time I called,' he bit out. 'The first time was late in the afternoon, about four-thirty. When you weren't in your room they thought you might still be out filming——'

She shook her head even as he spoke. 'I told you, we didn't do my scene yesterday, I spent most of the day in the games-room,' she told him frowningly. 'Playing snooker.' She hadn't received that first call!

Dark brows rose at this absently-made addition. 'You play?'

Her mouth twisted. 'If you don't mind losing your money I'll give you a game some time!'

'You play,' he acknowledged dryly. 'Well, obviously the hotel staff didn't know where you were when the call came through, and I was just going to leave a message with them to tell you I had called when one of the actors came in to the reception. They asked him if he had any idea where you were . . .'

'Mark!' she realised with a sinking heart.

'Yes,' Rand grated, his hands thrust into his trouser pockets. 'He said he didn't know where you were either but——'

'That's a lie,' she gasped. 'All the crew knew I was in the games-room!'

Rand sighed. 'He chose not to tell me that, but said instead that you could probably be reached in the dining-room that evening, that you and Christopher Drake spent every moment together that you could.'

'And when you telephoned later that night——'

'You were in the dining-room with a friend!' Rand finished tautly.

'Liza. And she's definitely a female,' she told him softly. 'I didn't even *see* Christopher last night. If I had I would have tried once again to get him to drop the nudity in today's scene. I never wanted to do it in the first place.'

'Drake told me that too,' Rand put in gently.

'Somehow the part of the Good Samaritan doesn't sit well on those cynical shoulders.' Her voice held suspicion.

'He did mention something about "an unhappy actress is a bad actress" . . .' Rand said wryly.

'Now *that* does sound like him!' She gave a husky laugh, her hands twisting together, unsure where they went from here. If they went anywhere.

Rand's eyes narrowed. 'Just how vindictive is Hillier towards you?' he asked abruptly.

She gave a ragged sigh. 'From what you've just told me about yesterday, I would say very.' She had no difficulty at all in believing Mark had set out to cause trouble between Rand and herself, in fact she knew he would take great pleasure in trying to ruin her life for a second time in retribution for what he believed she had done to him six years ago. He had almost succeeded!

'Why?'

She couldn't quite meet Rand's searching gaze. How would he react if she told him she had once almost married Mark? Perhaps that wasn't the question she should be asking herself; how would Rand react if *someone else* should happen to tell him she had once been going to marry the other man!

She moistened her lips with the tip of her tongue, trying to think of a suitable way to tell

Rand about the part Mark had played in her past. Perhaps the blunt truth was the only way.

'Merlyn?' he prompted impatiently at her continued silence.

Her eyes flashed at his compelling tone. 'I was once going to marry him!'

Rand flinched a little, but was soon once again under complete control. 'Why didn't you?'

She looked challengingly into those cold silver eyes. 'He wanted me to go to bed with a director to get him a part in a film!' she revealed almost defiantly.

Rand inhaled sharply, frowning darkly. 'God,' he finally groaned, dropping down into an armchair, his face buried in his hands. 'Oh God!' he groaned again weakly.

Merlyn stood helplessly across the room from him, not knowing what to do. Would he believe her if she said she hadn't done it? He hadn't believed her when she told him he had made love to a virgin.

When he at last looked up at her his eyes were dark with pain. 'Why do you put up with me?'

She frowned at the self-recrimination in his voice. 'I don't understand . . .'

'Neither do I,' he said in disgust. 'I've treated you abominably from the first, insulted you, taken from you, crept into your room like a thief in the night, and yet you don't seem to hate me!' He sounded astounded by the fact.

How could she possibly hate him, for anything he did, when she loved him so much. But she could tell he still wasn't ready to accept the love of another woman, that he perhaps never would be.

'Sexual attraction works two ways, Rand,' she dismissed with a lightness she didn't feel.

Some of the anguish left his expression, and she knew she had said the right thing. 'Yes,' he acknowledged heavily. 'I'm sorry about last night. I'll know to be wary about Hillier in future. If there is a future for us?'

She knew he wasn't referring to a permanent relationship, and she had never expected that from him. 'Why not?' she shrugged with a tight smile. 'I'll order us some dinner—one I'll eat this time.' She gave the cold food that sat on the tray a rueful look. 'And then we can——'

'No,' he cut in harshly. 'There'll be no more eating in your room, we'll go over to the hotel restaurant.'

'Are you sure?' She frowned her concern for the enormity of what he intended doing; if they went to the hotel restaurant no one would be in any further doubt about their relationship.

'Very,' he answered decisively. 'After all, why should Hillier have the satisfaction of even thinking he's succeeded in breaking us up?' he added grimly.

'Right,' she agreed hollowly, wishing he could have said something a little more encouraging, like 'he would be proud to be seen anywhere with her'. But she couldn't ask for too much too soon, and at least he had been honest.

She felt more than a little apprehensive entering the more intimate of the hotel's restaurants with him, felt apprehensive about entering the restaurant at all after this afternoon.

'Just think of them as the audience,' Rand

encouraged softly as she seemed set to panic.
'And you're the "Virgin Queen" looking down
on all her minions.'

Merlyn turned to him with a laugh. '"Virgin
Queen"?' she scorned.

His mouth quirked. 'That's better,' he said with
satisfaction. 'It always worked with Suzie when
she was nervous too.'

He was speaking so naturally of his dead wife
tonight, and Merlyn hoped nothing happened to
spoil that. 'She used to feel moments of nervousness too?' she said disbelievingly; Suzie Forrester
had always seemed so self-confident.

'All the time,' Rand nodded, his hand on her
elbow as he escorted her to their table.

'I wouldn't——'

'Hey, Merlyn, over here,' Liza called out to her
lightly. 'Unless you would rather be alone?' she
asked as an awkward afterthought as she realised
who Merlyn's companion was.

She glanced at the neighbouring table where
Liza sat with one of the cameramen and another
couple, turning back questioningly to Rand.

He headed away from the table for two they
had been directed to and moved over to the larger
table. 'We would,' he drawled, very much in
command as he saw Merlyn seated before sitting
down himself beside her, his knee resting along
the length of her leg. 'But I've been looking
forward to meeting Merlyn's friend Liza,' he
added with a light charm Merlyn had never seen
before.

She watched with awe as he successfully put
Liza at her ease within a couple of seconds of

meeting her, quickly drawing the cameraman and the other couple into the conversation. He may have avoided social functions the last couple of years but he still knew how to be charming when the need arose. Within a few minutes they were all talking together like old friends.

'Gorgeous, gorgeous, *gorgeous*!' Liza said ecstatically when she and Merlyn had excused themselves to go to the powder-room for a few minutes. 'And he's all yours.' She sighed her envy.

Merlyn smiled at her friend's enthusiasm. 'Our relationship goes from one crisis to another, so I wouldn't feel too happy for me!'

'You mean this afternoon?' Liza dismissed, watching Merlyn's reflection in the mirror as she took the time to retouch her lipgloss.

She grimaced. 'You heard!' she said with feigned surprise.

'Greg told me Mark made a complete idiot of himself,' Liza scorned.

'*Mark* did?' she scoffed. 'We both know I wasn't just talking about him. And how long have you been seeing Greg?' she frowned. 'I thought I was your best friend and confidante, no secrets from each other and all that?'

'You are and we haven't. Greg's a friend. Well —maybe a little more than a friend,' she conceded at Merlyn's sceptical expression. 'But it's really too soon to tell if it will become serious. Now just forget all about this afternoon and enjoy yourself,' she instructed as they left the powder-room.

Merlyn followed, and almost came to a full stop

as they walked back to their table; another table for two had been added to theirs and seated at it, his arm about one of the make-up girls, Jennifer, Merlyn thought her name was, was Mark Hillier.

Rand seemed to sense her presence, turning slightly in his chair to meet her horrified gaze, the warmth in his eyes beckoning her to his side. He looked so reassuring, as if he wouldn't let anything hurt her, least of all Mark Hillier. Every step was an effort but she finally made it back to Rand's side, sitting down gratefully as he stood to hold back her chair for her. The hostility crackled from the emerald depths of her eyes as she looked at Mark across the table.

'What stone did you crawl out from under, Mark?' Liza scorned, not having Merlyn's restraint when it came to people she disliked.

Fury glittered in his eyes, making them more grey than blue. 'You——'

'I invited Mr Hillier and his companion to join us,' Rand put in smoothly. 'I wanted to thank him personally for taking my call to Merlyn yesterday afternoon.'

Mark flushed, eyeing the other man warily, instantly on his guard against the silky softness of the threat in Rand's voice. 'I only told you what I could,' he replied defensively.

'Of course.' Hooded eyes held Mark's gaze, but Rand said nothing more, his very silence ominous.

'Wasn't Merlyn marvellous during the filming today?' Mark launched into nervous speech, colour creeping beneath the taut skin in his cheeks as grey eyes glazed over with chilling fury. 'So realistic,' he added with defiance. 'Of course it was nothing new for Merlyn and me, as I'm sure you know?' he challenged.

'Yes.' Once again Rand's voice was silky soft, his hand capturing Merlyn's beneath the table as it moved nervously on her lap, squeezing her fingers with a light reassuring touch.

Mark's eyes flashed his irritation with Rand's complete control. 'You *do* know?' he prompted recklessly.

Dark brows rose. 'That Merlyn once believed herself in love with you?' he returned dismissively. 'Oh yes, she did tell me,' he nodded. 'But as I assured her, we all make a lot of stupid mistakes like that when we're young and impressionable.'

'Now just a minute,' Mark protested in a blusteringly angry voice.

'Some people make those same mistakes when they're older too,' Rand continued in a softly menacing voice that no one could mistake for being in the least pleasant. 'They're the ones who get hurt if they don't realise who the sharks are in life.'

'I think you've just threatened me!'

'Only think?' Rand drawled. 'My, I must be slipping,' he added mockingly.

Mark moistened his lips as he sensed the very real danger emanating from the man seated opposite him. 'Come on, Jenny.' He stood up. 'I think I prefer an intimate dinner for two after all. In your room.'

The tiny brunette blushed at his implication, giving an awkward grimace as she left the dining-room with him, her pretty face animated with anger as she talked to him on the way out.

Merlyn felt some of the tension leave her body. She hadn't known what to think when Rand revealed that he had been the one to invite Mark to join them, still couldn't fathom the man she loved, although in this case he had championed her.

'If I ever acquire an enemy like that one can I call on you for assistance?' As usual it was Liza's mischief that broke the strained silence of the other couple's departure, grinning guilessly at Rand.

He warmly returned that smile. 'You can call on me any time,' he drawled. 'Even without an enemy.'

The conversation became more general after that but Merlyn remained quiet. She knew just how nasty Mark could be, had witnessed it first-hand in a very painful way in the past, and she very much doubted, for all she was grateful for it, that Rand's intimidation of the other man would put an end to his bitterness.

But for all that it was a pleasant evening, Rand easily accepted by everyone as they went through to the bar, showing none of that arrogant reserve Merlyn had always associated with him as he chatted and joked with a couple of other men, Greg included.

'Gorgeous, gorgeous, *gorgeous*,' Liza said in an aside as Rand gave a rich, throaty chuckle.

'You've already said that,' Merlyn reminded her dryly.

'But now I know he's all-through gorgeous. Not all good-looking men are, you know.'

'You don't say!' she replied. Liza's forthright attitude and easy-going manner always had a way of putting things back in perspective. So Mark was still bitter and angry with her about the past, there was nothing he could really do to hurt her, not if she didn't let him.

Liza grimaced. 'From what Rand said about that call, I gather Mark was being his usual nasty self yesterday?'

And he had almost succeeded in breaking her and Rand up. 'Yes,' she answered with feeling.

'Don't worry, Rand will take care of you from now on,' her friend told her confidently. 'Uh oh.' She raised her brows. 'Here comes our tyrant of a director.' She nodded in the direction of the main doorway, Christopher just entering as she did so. 'I haven't forgiven him for making me get back up on that brute of a horse yet,' she said disgustedly.

Merlyn was glad Christopher had put in an appearance this evening; she owed him a debt of gratitude.

'It was myself I was thinking of,' he brusquely dismissed her sincere thanks after she had crossed the room to speak to him privately before he joined the others. 'I thought over what you said and decided things *would* be less awkward here for all of us if you and Carmichael were friends again.'

'Cynic!' She gave a wry shake of her head as he confirmed what she had already guessed; nothing must be allowed to interrupt or disturb his picture.

'It worked, didn't it?' He looked pointedly in Rand's direction.

Rand was watching them in return, his expression bland, although his eyes were questioning.

'I know that look,' Christopher groaned. 'Get back to his side before he thinks *I'm* after you!'

'Coward,' she laughed softly.

'Survivor,' he corrected mockingly. 'From all accounts Carmichael is a possessive bastard.'

Rand hated possessiveness, had reacted violently when he thought she was acting jealously over his time in London. 'I think you have the wrong man, Christopher.' She shook her head.

'You do?' he smiled wryly. 'Then why is he forging a path to your side even as we speak?' He laughed as her eyes widened in surprise on Rand as he purposefully made his way to where they stood talking together, occasionally stopping to talk to someone, but coming over to them none the less. 'A word of warning, Merlyn, the dark brooding ones are always the worst,' Christopher had time to mutter before Rand reached them, his arm moving about Merlyn's waist.

'Drake,' he greeted the man abruptly. 'I think you now have an unhappy actor,' he drawled.

Christopher grimaced. 'What's new?' His reply lacked concern. 'No permanent damage, I hope?' he asked interestedly.

Rand's mouth quirked. 'Only to his ego.'

'That could stand a few beatings,' Christopher scorned. 'As long as you haven't marked his face!'

Rand glanced at Merlyn, her face pale. 'We were just about to leave,' he murmured.

'Don't let me keep you,' Christopher said cheerfully. 'I intend sending this lot off to bed now anyway!'

It had been a strained evening for Merlyn, and she breathed deeply of the fresh air once they were outside and away from the smoky bar.

'I'm sorry,' Rand watched her anxiously. 'Maybe I shouldn't have put you through that, but I felt it was important that Hillier see he had done no lasting damage with his lies.'

'It was,' she agreed abruptly.

Rand still watched her. 'Let's go back to the house for a nightcap.'

She raised startled eyes to meet his. 'You mean *your* house?'

His brows rose. 'Unless you happen to have one around here I know nothing about?'

She hadn't thought she would ever go inside the house again that he had shared with Suzie all those years, had certainly never expected to be an invited guest there. 'Maybe a coffee?' she said uncertainly.

'Fine.' He led her over to the dark grey BMW he drove, unlocking the door for her.

Merlyn was a little apprehensive as they entered the house, following Rand through to the kitchen, automatically moving to the appropriate cupboards to help him prepare the coffee before she realised what she was doing, coming to an abrupt halt.

Rand sighed heavily. 'I was very rough on you the last time you were here, wasn't I?'

'Yes,' she confirmed without hesitation.

He put his arms about her as he leant back

against a kitchen unit, Merlyn's body resting lightly against his thighs. 'That day, the anniversary of Suzie's death, is—well, it's a nightmare.' Rand closed his eyes as he rested his forehead against hers. 'I gave all the servants the day off, intended spending the day with a bottle of brandy, hoping I wouldn't feel any of the pain once I was drunk.'

'And then I arrived,' Merlyn put in huskily.

He gave a ragged sigh. 'And then you arrived,' he nodded. 'And the getting drunk theory went out of the window. I was a bastard to you but it helped me get through the day at least. It was the night I couldn't cope with,' he remembered harshly. 'And then you helped me live through that too!'

'And tonight you helped me,' she told him shakily. 'Like Christopher, you must be wondering what I ever saw in Mark, but he can be very charming when things are going his way.'

'And when they aren't?' Rand watched her with narrowed eyes.

She winced at the memory. 'Then he isn't charming at all!'

'Will you tell me about it?'

Rand's intimidation of Mark earlier had been obvious to everyone present, and she didn't think he was the type of man—no, she *knew* he wasn't the type of man to hold back when he heard of another man using violence against a woman.

'No, I don't think so,' she refused lightly, peering over his shoulder at the newly percolated coffee. 'I will have a cup of coffee, though.'

'Subject of Mark Hillier closed?'

'The coffee smells delicious.'

'Okay, subject closed.' Rand gave a shrug before moving away from her. 'But if he bothers you again . . .' he added pointedly.

'He won't,' she assured him with more confidence than real honesty; Mark had left her alone six years ago because he knew there was nothing else he could do to her, but now she was more vulnerable. And from the sceptical look in Rand's eyes before he carried the coffee-tray through to the lounge, he didn't believe her assurances for one minute anyway.

But as she sat beside Rand on the sofa, a fire newly blazing in the dimly lit room, in a rare moment of tranquillity, she put everything else from her mind except the sheer joy of being with him. Earlier this evening she had believed this closeness between them again would be impossible.

'Are you staying with me tonight?' he spoke huskily against her temple.

'Here?' Her voice was gruff, the invitation so much more than she had expected.

'I'd like to just lie in bed and hold you,' he clarified the invitation. 'No demands, just hold you.'

From the moment they had met they had either been hating each other or making love, and what he offered now sounded wonderful. She didn't know if he realised it, but it was also a tangible step forward in their relationship.

Her eyes glowed as she turned to look at him. 'I'd like that,' she told him throatily, her hand slipping into his much larger one as they stood up to ascend the stairs together.

CHAPTER TWELVE

'So I was wrong about it being Drake you slept with to get this part, it was Carmichael,' Mark scorned with contempt. 'I have to hand it to you, Merlyn, you went right to the top this time.'

Merlyn closed her eyes momentarily as she gave an inward groan. She had successfully managed to avoid Mark the last three days—Christopher, whether by design or necessity, having kept their filming schedules separate. It had been too good to last, she realised that.

They all had the day off today, the rain once again pouring down outside, although many of the crew had still taken advantage of the freedom to go out and see some of the surrounding countryside. Merlyn had preferred to lounge by the pool. Although if she had realised Mark had the same intention she would have revised her plans.

'I suppose it's too much to hope this conversation could actually develop into something pleasant?' she said dryly, looking up from her relaxed position on the lounger beside the pool with jaundiced eyes, feeling better than she had for a long time, even her hair temporarily back to its original colour, her bikini the perfect green of her eyes, intentionally so.

He gave a mocking inclination of his head before sitting down on the lounger next to hers. 'Your boy-friend made a fool out of me the other night, and——'

'You've never needed any help in doing that, Mark,' she snapped.

His body was still wet from where he had swum the length of the pool in leisurely strokes twice before strolling over to join her. Probably someone had once told him how muscular he looked with water glistening on his bronzed skin. The fact that it was true didn't make him any less vain.

His mouth twisted at her mockery. 'You certainly outgrew that childish happy-ever-after theory with a vengeance!'

She looked at him warily. 'What do you mean by that?'

'Carmichael!'

She drew in an angry breath. 'If you have something to say, Mark, then just say it! I'm not in the mood for your innuendoes today.'

'Been spending a lot of time with Suzie Forrester's husband, haven't you?' he taunted.

It was true that she and Rand spent their evenings and nights together, but never again at the house. There he *was* Suzie's husband.

That one night they had stayed there together they had just held each other until they both fell asleep, and it had been enough. It had been better than enough. Until she woke up alone in the darkness to find Rand sitting in the bedroom chair just staring at her as she slept.

'What is it?' she called to him huskily, sitting up in alarm at how still he sat, fully clothed now, his expression unreadable.

He drew in a ragged breath. 'I can't sleep with

another woman in the house I shared with Suzie,' he rasped.

She had closed her eyes on the pain she knew must be reflected in them, fighting for control before she got out of bed to go to him, kneeling at his feet, her elbows resting on his knees as she clasped his hands in hers. 'Then we won't sleep together here again,' she assured him gruffly.

And they hadn't, had spent their nights together in her hotel room. And each morning Rand left her bed to return to his house. Where he became Suzie's husband again.

They had never spoken of that night, and Merlyn had never told him that she knew exactly how he felt about his affair with her. But despite their physical closeness his marriage to Suzie now stood between them like a brick wall. And no matter how she wanted to knock that wall down she knew that she never would.

'She's dead, Mark,' Merlyn said flatly in response to his barb that penetrated more deeply than even he could guess.

'From what I've heard he wasn't much of a husband even before the accident.' His voice was scornful.

Merlyn gave him a sharp look. 'What are you implying now, Mark?' she demanded harshly. 'Another lie you hope will cause me pain?'

'Hey,' he derided mockingly. 'I don't spend my whole life thinking up ways to hurt you!'

'Just half of it!' she returned impatiently.

'Well, I didn't think this up. And I would have thought you would be pleased to hear that the wonderful Rand was reputed to be separated from his wife before she died.'

'That's a lie,' Merlyn gasped, shaking her head, tension in every inch of her body.

Mark's brows rose at her vehemence. 'You aren't pleased?' he drawled.

'Because it isn't true,' she bit out tautly. 'Rand loved his wife very much.'

'Then why did she leave him?' Mark challenged with triumph.

'She didn't——'

'She was in London when the accident happened, he was still up here——'

'Just because they didn't live in each other's pockets doesn't mean——'

'I meant she was staying in London at their apartment, that she had been for some time,' Mark insisted.

That information had been in the newspapers at the time of the accident, and a couple of the more lurid tabloids had even tried to make something out of it. But Rand had denied any estrangement between himself and Suzie, and she believed him. He had loved his wife; he still did!

'She left him, Merlyn,' Mark put in softly.

'How do you know that?' She wouldn't believe him.

He shrugged. 'You know what gossip is like in our business—or perhaps you don't. You're like those three wise monkeys, "see no evil, speak no evil, hear no evil——"'

'Oh I *see* it.' She gave him a pointed look. 'But if you mean I don't care to hear malicious gossip about people who have probably only ever smiled at each other, you're right; I don't like to know about it.'

'Well, this isn't malicious gossip,' he said with satisfaction. 'I heard a rumour about it at the time, and when I spoke to one of the maids here——'

'*Spoke* to her?' Merlyn dismissed scathingly.

He shrugged. 'Can I help it if she's impressed by film stars?'

'Has she *met* any?' Merlyn returned caustically.

Anger flared in Mark's eyes. 'Very funny,' he declared with a noticeable lessening of his amusement at her expense. 'She told me that Suzie Forrester had left the area a week earlier, and no one knew when she was expected back!'

'Rand would have known——'

'Least of all Carmichael,' Mark continued. 'Ask him, Merlyn. You'll see.'

'No!'

'Why?' he taunted. 'Afraid I just might be telling the truth?'

She couldn't believe this, knew how Mark could lie just to hurt her. And yet something Anne had said the other day about 'leaving certain things that happened during the last years of Brandon's marriage to Suzie out of the book' kept coming back to her. And yet surely her sister leaving Rand couldn't have been one of those things? But she knew Anne subscribed to the theory that Rand was the one still alive, the one who could be hurt by certain things about his marriage to Suzie being revealed; *was* Suzie's leaving him only a week before her death one of them?

'I am, you know,' Mark encouraged softly as he sensed her uncertainty.

'But what possible reason would she have—

Oh, it's too ridiculous to even think about,' she dismissed impatiently, shaking her head with disgust for even listening to such a lie.

'Is it?' Mark kept up his taunts.

'Of course it is,' she snapped.

He shrugged. 'This maid seems to think Suzie Forrester only stayed with her husband because she was so ill, that once she was cured she left him.'

'This maid sounds like she tells a very good fairy-story,' Merlyn scorned with finality.

'If she is telling the truth the film that we're making is a farce!'

'In that case *you* would no longer be needed, would you?' she returned forcefully.

A flush darkened his cheeks. 'If you can't stand to hear the truth . . .' He stood up. 'Enjoy your book,' he added mockingly before diving back into the warmth of the water.

The book she had been reading lay untouched across her bare waist as she tried to calm her chaotic thoughts. She was only partially successful.

Rand had lived like a virtual recluse since Suzie died. And he had told her himself that Anne's book was incomplete, that Suzie's notebooks hadn't told the whole picture. One thing she could be sure of, Rand had said that both he and Suzie were faithful during their marriage, and she believed him; if Suzie had left him it hadn't been for another man or because he was having an affair.

'You're giving the place a bad name,' James chided lightly as he joined her.

She forced a smile. 'I am?'

He nodded as he sat down. 'We advertise this place as somewhere you can come to relax and enjoy yourself and forget all your outside worries, and you've been sitting there frowning for the last ten minutes,' he teased. 'Besides, as I'm sure your despot of a director would tell you, you'll get wrinkles!'

She grimaced. 'And goodness knows I can't afford to get any more of those!'

He grinned, those deep brown eyes as warm as usual. 'I wouldn't have minded meeting you BA.'

'BA?' she echoed curiously.

'Before Anne,' he said dryly. 'Since I met her other women have lost their appeal.'

Merlyn laughed softly. 'I think that's the way it's supposed to be.'

'Mm.' He stretched out in total relaxation. 'I was a confirmed bachelor until five years ago; I never realised marriage could be this good.'

It was a perfect opening, one she might never have again, and yet she was loath to take it. Anne and James had both been so kind to her, it wasn't fair to use that friendship to gain information about Rand. And yet she was only human after all.

She moistened her lips, staring out across the pool. 'Was Rand's marriage to Suzie really as happy as it seemed to be?' She put the question as casually as she could, wondering if she only imagined the way James seemed to tense.

If he did he recovered quickly. 'Are you asking as the actress playing the part of Suzie and trying to get a deeper insight into the character—or as

Brandon's lover?' He quirked dark brows. 'Don't worry,' he drawled at her embarrassment. 'I haven't been spying on the two of you or anything like that,' he assured her as she blushed. 'I've known from the very beginning.'

'What beginning?' she frowned, not sure she and Rand had ever had such a thing; they just seemed to have happened.

'Since you first called him Rand,' he told her quietly.

'But how?'

'It was Suzie's name for him when they were alone together, or occasionally in front of Anne and me,' he revealed huskily. 'I've never known anyone else but her to call him it.'

'But he asked me to call him that—' She swallowed hard. 'James, I don't understand!'

'No,' he acknowledged raggedly. 'Do you think Brandon does?'

'Do you?' she groaned, stunned by what he had just revealed. Of course she had noticed that everyone else called him Brandon, but she hadn't really paid that much attention to it, not when she had a brother who affectionately called her Lyn when no one else ever did. But that was exactly what Rand's name was too, a term of affection, and yet he had allowed her that privilege. 'Unless he just didn't want me to realise who he was,' she spoke out loud as the thought occurred to her, shrugging as James gave her a puzzled look. 'He never did introduce himself properly,' she explained. 'I think he wanted to be someone else that day. I only realised who he was when I accidentally saw a photograph of Suzie in the house.'

'Ah,' James said wonderingly.

She didn't tell him that the photograph had been in Rand's bedroom, or that later that night she had seen it destroyed on the fire. Although that did bring her back to her original question. '*Were* they happy, James?' she prompted again, huskily.

'As far as it goes, yes,' he replied. 'They—had their problems just like any other couple. No marriage is completely without its ups and downs, it would be boring if it was. Why do you ask?'

She chewed on her inner lip. 'He isn't an easy man to get to know.' Which was true; even though they were lovers she knew there was still a lot of himself he didn't allow her to see.

'Brandon is exactly what he seems,' James shrugged. 'He's a man who has survived, in his own way, in spite of the raw deals he's been handed most of his life. His parents were killed when he was four, and with no close relatives willing to take him he was placed in an orphanage. But at four he remembered his own parents too well to really be wanted by a childless couple, refused to have them replaced in his life. Until he met Suzie I don't think there was anyone he loved or who loved him. He adored her,' James said simply. 'And Suzie worshipped him in return. It was a complete marriage by itself, but they both wanted children, were naturally disappointed when it didn't happen. Although that never detracted from their love for each other, in fact I think it deepened because of it.'

But there had been a child, although Anne had obviously not revealed to her husband the slip she had made by telling Merlyn that.

'When he found out how ill Suzie was it almost killed him,' James continued with a frown. 'And he was right beside her when she fought to live. I think her recovery was like a miracle to him, one of the few he had ever known. And then she was killed in the accident.' He shook his head. 'She was given back to him from the clutches of death only to be taken away again. He isn't going to open himself up to that sort of pain again in a hurry.'

If at all, Merlyn realised despondently.

'If it's any consolation,' James said softly at her look of despair. 'You've got the closest to him of anyone since—Well, I can't tell you how pleased Anne was when the two of you came to dinner last night,' he amended as he realised he wasn't being tactful.

She had been thrilled too when Rand had told her about the invitation to the Bentons' and asked her if she would like to go. And although the evening had had its awkward moments she had thought it went quite well. Damn Mark for giving her these insecurities.

'You're right.' She gave James a rueful smile. 'I'm expecting too much too soon.'

He quirked dark brows. 'Did I say that?'

Merlyn's expression was wry. 'In your usually polite way, yes!'

'Is it too late to warn you that you could be hurt?' he prompted gently.

'Much too late,' she nodded. 'I think it was too late for that even before I met Rand,' she added slowly.

James gave a puzzled laugh. 'What's that supposed to mean?'

She could understand his reaction to the statement; her feelings for Rand didn't make much sense to her either. 'Do you believe in fate?'

'As in "meant to be"?'

She shook her head, chewing thoughtfully on the edge of her bottom lip. 'As in "has to be". Destined.'

'Explain to this slightly befuddled man who's been having to make two o'clock in the morning visits to the hotel kitchen to satisfy his pregnant wife's craving for strawberries and peanut butter!'

'Well I—Strawberries and *peanut butter*! Really?' Merlyn pulled a disgusted face.

'Really.' James shuddered at the admission. 'She sits up in bed eating the nauseating concoction like a cat with a saucer of cream while I literally go green!'

'I'm not surprised!'

'And she had the nerve to complain to Liza about my eating biscuits in bed!' He swallowed hard, starting to look a little ill now. 'I don't think we should talk about Anne's nocturnal habits any more! Besides, you're getting side-tracked.'

She knew exactly what she was doing, but when it actually came to putting it into words about her fatalistic feelings for Rand she felt a little stupid. All she really knew for certain was that when it came to Rand she had no choices; she loved him.

'Merlyn?' James prompted softly.

She sighed. 'I'm a theatre actress,' began

Merlyn forcefully. 'I really had no desire to go in to films, was enjoying what I was doing too much, playing different parts every few months or so.'

'But when the big screen beckoned you reluctantly jumped at the chance,' mocked James teasingly.

'That's just it.' She shook her head. 'I actually *badgered* Christopher Drake into auditioning me for the part.' She still sounded slightly dazed by her uncharacteristic behaviour—as indeed she was. 'I'd heard about Anne's book, although I'd never read it, and then I heard they were going to make a film, and I—Well, I was drawn to it.'

James shrugged. 'I can't see anything unusual about that.'

'But there is,' she protested, blushing at her own vehemence. 'Maybe if I explain a little about my family it will help you understand,' she sighed. 'My parents are both doctors, my older brother is a lawyer——'

'And you're the black sheep,' he sympathised.

'Professionally, yes,' Merlyn acknowledged with a frown. 'But emotionally—normally, I'm as reserved as they are. Although I prefer to think of it as being cautious,' she added ruefully. 'It doesn't make me sound as cold-blooded. All I'm trying to show you is that I wanted the part of Suzie so much that I turned down the offer of another year's contract at the theatre before Christopher had even decided to give me the part, let alone attempted to overcome Rand's prejudices. Can't you see that this just isn't me?'

'Who is it, then?' He looked confused.

'I don't know any more,' she sighed. 'I think

I'm still me, a less cautious me than I'm used to admittedly, but I'm still me. Most of the time,' she added with hesitation.

'Maybe you've just been working too hard,' he advised gently. 'It must be a strain having to be someone else for up to twelve hours a day.'

If that were all it was! But it wasn't. She was used to playing someone else, had never had any trouble shaking off a character before. Besides, this had begun before she even came here and started work, before she had even met Rand. Sometimes she felt as if her actions were controlled by someone else completely . . .

That evening she and Rand went out to dine, the intimately small restaurant serving a selection of both Italian and English cuisine, an elderly man hauntingly playing the violin moving among the tables.

But for the first time in days the atmosphere between Merlyn and Rand was strained. Much as she hated to admit it, Mark's conversation this morning had bothered her. If Suzie had left Rand, why had she? If she had . . .

Merlyn had known of the rumours circulating at the time, that because Suzie was in London and Rand was still at their house in the Lake District the couple were actually living apart. But like the majority of the general public she had believed Rand when he denied any estrangement, and that angle of the story was dropped by even the most persistent of reporters. But Mark had planted fresh seeds of doubt in her mind that just couldn't be denied. Much as she had tried.

Rand was very quiet too, and while they had never been carefree lovers telling each other their every thought, they *had* passed the stage where he sat in brooding silence while she tried to guess at his mood.

She sat forward to place her hand over his. 'What is it?' she prompted softly.

He looked up, focusing on her with effort, as if for a while he had forgotten she was even there. 'Sorry.' He forced a smile to the hardness of his mouth. 'I was miles away . . .'

Or years away. Suddenly, as she looked around at the exclusive restaurant, remembered the way the maitre d' had seemed to greet Rand as if he knew him, she understood. 'You used to come here with Suzie!'

Rand's gaze was instantly watchful, his expression guarded. 'Yes, I did.'

There was challenge in his voice, as if he expected her to object. And she did, felt as if he were carrying out some sort of experiment. And she was the guinea-pig! 'And?' she returned that challenge.

He drew a ragged breath. 'And I can still see her sitting there with a white rose in her hair,' he rasped harshly.

All the colour drained from Merlyn's face. 'A white rose . . . ?'

He nodded abruptly. 'They were her favourite flowers; I always made sure the house was full of them.'

They were her favourite flowers too. But they hadn't always been, she used to prefer yellow carnations to any other flower. What was *happening* to her!

She stood up abruptly. 'I think I'd like to leave now,' she told him tautly.

Rand nodded, throwing some money for their meal down on the table before escorting her to the door, waving aside the manager's concern that there had been something wrong with their meal, his expression grim as he helped Merlyn into the waiting car.

'I'm sorry,' he finally exclaimed, the BMW eating up the miles back to the hotel. 'For everything,' he added bitterly.

Merlyn turned in the darkness to look at him sharply. He sounded suspiciously final. She could feel herself beginning to panic at that realisation. 'It wasn't your fault,' she excused quickly. 'We can't continue to avoid all the places you went to with Suzie——'

'I took you there deliberately,' he put in abruptly, his face granite-hard in profile.

Her panic rose to desperation. 'It was a very nice restaurant——'

'I took you there to see if I could bear to be *anywhere* with you that I was with Suzie,' he cut in cruelly.

Merlyn swallowed hard. 'And?' she prompted as she had in the restaurant.

'And I can't bear it.' His reply was pained.

Merlyn swallowed hard, starting to feel dizzy. 'Rand, you——'

The coldness in his eyes as he glanced at her briefly instantly silenced her. 'Something James said to me today made me realise——'

'James?' She was instantly on her guard. But

surely James hadn't broken her confidence and revealed to Rand their conversation earlier today?

'Yes.' Rand's eyes had narrowed. 'He and Anne like you, and they're afraid I may be—using you.'

'Surely that is for me to decide?' she defended heatedly, realising that while James hadn't betrayed her confidence he had put doubts in Rand's mind.

'Do you feel used?'

Did she? Sometimes. But not as much as she had at first. She *loved* Rand, so it didn't matter. Most of the time. Tonight had been different because she had allowed Mark's comments to get to her.

But she could see that Rand had taken her silence as acquiescence, his expression grim. 'Rand, you've been married before, it's only natural that you——'

'I still love my wife, Merlyn,' he interrupted harshly. 'The other night when I asked why you put up with me you said it was because of sexual attraction. Were you telling the truth?'

She forced a dismissive laugh that somehow came out as a choked rasp. 'Haven't I proved how attracted I am to you?'

Rand sighed, his hands gripping the steering-wheel so tightly the knuckles showed white. 'You've always been very passionate, even the night I took your virginity.'

'*What?*' He couldn't have just said that, he *couldn't*!

His mouth was thinned so tautly a white ring of tension encircled his lips. 'When we—made love

that night I had no idea, it was only later that
I——'

'When?' she demanded emotionally.

He shook his head. 'I really didn't know that
night. I'd never been with a virgin before; Suzie
was living with someone when I met her, and the
women I'd known up until that time weren't the
type to—I *didn't* know that night,' he insisted
gruffly.

'*When?*' she demanded again, her voice shrill.

'As Anne pointed out, your—your lip was a
mess, and I'd assumed all the blood—After you
left with Anne I took another look. There was too
much—I couldn't believe what I was seeing,'
he groaned. 'It took me several days to get
up the nerve, but I came over to the hotel to
apologise——'

'No!' Merlyn gave a choked cry as she knew the
dream that had haunted her for so long hadn't
been a dream at all.

He breathed raggedly. 'Your door was unlocked, I just slipped inside to talk to you. You
were asleep, or at least you seemed asleep when I
first came in. You looked so young. I bent down
to smooth the hair back from your cheek,
and——'

'And then you made love to me!'

He shook his head. 'You put your arms up
about my neck, called my name. It was dark in the
room, I thought you were awake, that you
wanted me as I suddenly wanted you again,
so badly. It was only later, afterwards—You
seemed to be in some sort of delirium. I thought
you had wanted me too, and you didn't even

know what had happened!'

Oh, she had known, she just hadn't known *who*! 'Is that the reason you finally agreed to let me star in the film?' she slowly gasped. 'A guilty conscience!'

Colour darkened his cheeks. 'Drake had made it clear he intended making the film anyway, and I—I never meant to come near you again, and I wouldn't have done if something hadn't happened and I—I needed you. I realise that's no excuse, but——'

'You're right, it isn't.' She was hurt and confused by the admissions he had made, deliberately banishing from her mind the reason he had needed her that day. He had known she was a virgin that first night since the day after it had happened, and he had said *nothing*! And he had left her with the haunting memory of their lovemaking, not knowing if she had dreamt it or not. 'You implied that you thought Christopher was my lover,' she reminded him accusingly. 'Another salve for your conscience?'

'I realise I was wrong about his being your lover before you met me, but afterwards——'

'Afterwards?' she spat out. 'I was too stunned by having taken you as a lover to want another one! Promiscuity has never interested me——'

'When you came to me that first time you did it out of pity——'

'I did it out of *love*,' she defended her actions vehemently, her eyes flashing with green sparks. 'I loved you then, and I——'

'No!' His denial was an anguished cry, his face very pale in the moonlight. 'I don't want your love. I don't want any woman's love.'

'I know that,' Merlyn said with quiet dignity. 'But I can't turn the emotion off just because you don't want it. I love you, and tonight—tonight you've hurt me more badly than I ever dreamt possible.' He didn't want her, had made it clear she could never even marginally replace his wife. And worst of all, he had only agreed to let her star in the film as a salve to *his* conscience. All this time he had let her go on thinking he didn't believe her. And she would never forgive him for not revealing the truth about that day in her hotel room.

'I know just how much I've hurt you,' he acknowledged harshly. 'That's why this has to end.'

'"This" being our affair?' scorned Merlyn bitterly.

'Yes.'

Tears glazed her eyes, and she felt as if a knife had been thrust between her breasts, but she agreed with him; it had to end. She wasn't a masochist, and there was only so much she could do to fight a memory. Where once she had admired and respected Suzie Forrester she now thought she hated her.

'Consider it over,' Merlyn uttered brokenly.

Rand's eyes gleamed silver in the subdued lighting outside the hotel as he brought the car to a halt, leaving the engine running as he turned to look at her. 'Just like that?' he said gruffly.

She stiffened into a straight-backed position, conscious of his arm resting on the back of his seat as he turned sideways to look at her. 'My father is an orthopaedic surgeon, and he's always told me that a nice clean break is always best. I'm sure that must apply to hearts as well as bones,' she added, her voice bitter.

'Merlyn——'

'No—don't touch me!' She shied out of reach of his hands.

Rejected, they clenched into fists before dropping back to his sides. 'I never meant to hurt you, Merlyn.'

'Then why did you?' Her voice was flat, emotionless.

He shook his head. 'Probably because hurting people is what I do best!'

She looked at him probingly, suddenly concerned at how pale he was. 'Rand——'

He straightened in his seat with a finality that cut short her questioning. 'You only have another week of filming here,' he stated. 'I think it would be better for everyone if I were to go to London and stay there for that time.'

Better for him, because then he could forget he had ever known a little virgin named Merlyn Summers. And better for her because she wouldn't have to die a little each time she saw him. 'This is goodbye, then,' she said abruptly.

Rand's mouth tightened, a nerve pulsing in his jaw. 'Yes.'

She winced, her hands starting to shake as she held back the tears. 'No age-old platitudes now either?' she said self-derisively.

He drew in a harsh breath, his eyes pained. 'You are such a beautiful woman——'

'No more,' she requested shakily, the Summers sense of dignity she had drawn on so much

during her relationship with Rand once again
coming to her rescue. If Rand ever thought of her
she wanted him to remember the good times.
And there had been some of them, no matter how
much he might wish there hadn't. 'You'll turn my
head with your compliments,' she dismissed
lightly. 'I wish you luck in your future life, Rand.'
Her voice began to tremble emotionally. 'I'd wish
you happiness too, but I don't think you'll ever
find that when you're living your life with a
ghost!'

'Merlyn——'

'I'm not going to apologise for saying that,' she
warned him. 'You *are* living with a ghost.'

'Memories, Merlyn,' he corrected painfully.
'I'm haunted by them!'

She nodded abruptly. 'I understand.'

'I doubt it.' He looked sad. 'Maybe one
day——'

'Don't, Rand,' she choked. 'Don't give me
hope when you know there is none!'

His throat moved convulsively. 'Can I kiss you
one last time?'

Her eyes widened at the request. 'Do you want
to?'

'God, yes,' he said with feeling, but he made no
move to touch her as he tensely waited for her
answer.

This man had just said goodbye to her after
telling her he still loved his wife and yet she could
see that he did truly want to kiss her. She didn't
understand him, but that was nothing new. She
didn't understand herself either as she moved
into his arms.

Their mouths fused in heated longing, Rand drinking from her lips again and again as he curved her breasts against his chest, his very gentleness tearing her heart from her body. She sobbed low in her throat as she became even more his, wanting to beg him not to leave her, to plead with him to take her to London with him and just forget the rest of the world existed. But she didn't.

And so the kiss went on, until both of them were shaking with a need neither had any intention of assuaging.

Rand was finally the one to push her firmly away from him, unclasping her hands from about his neck. 'It really was good between us, Merlyn, and you are wonderful,' he told her gruffly. 'The problems all lie with me. I just wish—Wishing is for fools and children.' His voice hardened. 'Just keep away from Hillier, okay?' he prompted with concern.

She blinked up at him, still dazed by his kisses. 'Mark?'

His mouth tightened. 'I don't think his vindictiveness is over yet. And with me gone——'

She stiffened indignantly as she straightened in the seat. 'I took care of myself for twenty-six years and I'll continue to do so,' she snapped, pushing open the car door to climb out. 'Mark Hillier doesn't frighten me!' she scorned.

Rand leant over in the seat to look up at her. 'Nevertheless, take care.'

She slammed the car door forcefully in his face, turning on her heel to enter the hotel, nodding abruptly as several people she knew acknowledged her as they sat in the bar area, all the time conscious of the BMW accelerating away and taking Rand from her life once and for all.

She was shaking uncontrollably by the time she reached the sanctuary of her room. But she wouldn't cry, she told herself, refused to cry—as the tears streamed down her cheeks.

Rand didn't love her, couldn't love her, and she had known that all along. But she loved him more than ever. How could she go on without even the little he had been prepared to give? Did she even want to?

She knew what her mother's answer to that would be, one of those women who believed no man was worth the heartache they caused, only the fact that she was known as *Dr* Summers preventing her using the Ms that Merlyn had told Rand she hated so much. Oh yes, her mother would tell her to pull herself together and get on with her life, the way she had after Mark's treatment of her six years ago. But Rand wasn't Mark, and the thought of never seeing him again made her drop down on the bed in a state of emotional exhaustion, the tears still wet on her cheeks.

She dreamt of Rand, the bitter Rand, Rand the lover, and that other rare Rand, the happy Rand that she had glimpsed only fleetingly. And as she dreamt she cried and muttered in her sleep, calling him back to her, needing him, wanting his arms about her as they had been the last few nights. But he didn't come to her, and her despair deepened.

Just as suddenly her dream changed. She was on a desert island, and it was hot, so hot, her clothes stifling her, hindering the movements of her body. It was so hot she couldn't breathe. *She couldn't breathe . . . !*

She fought against the heat, against the sun beating down on her so brightly, wondering why, even in her dreams, Rand didn't come to her. The heat was becoming unbearable, taking the air from her lungs even as she gasped to retain it, hurting her eyes. She needed air, she *had* to have air.

She woke in a panic, sitting up on the bed, her breath catching in a choked sob as she saw the flames licking their way across the room towards the bed, the smoke making her cough with its density. The fire had been the heat and light in her dream, the smoke preventing her from breathing.

As she climbed out of the bed the flames made a path across the carpet towards her, her panicked gaze fixed on their yellow-orange glow, just the heat from them seemed to burn her.

The door suddenly appeared a very long way away, but it was her only chance of escape, she had to get to it. As she started to step past the flames, the fiery tongues reached out to her and Merlyn started to scream as she saw that the bottom of her nightdress had caught fire.

She beat at the flames, but they just kept burning, and she turned to run to the door, feeling the flames against the tender flesh of her legs, feeling herself starting to sink to the floor as the pain became unbearable, reaching out for the door handle, only to fall as she did so, the flames engulfing her as she hit the carpeted floor.

CHAPTER THIRTEEN

IT was the pain that woke her, the pain of cold air
on her legs, the legs that felt as if they were still on
fire. Oh God, the fire! She groaned as she became
fully conscious of her pain.

'It's all right, Merlyn,' her mother soothed.
'Don't try to move, darling.'

Her mother? It was her mother's voice, and yet
it didn't sound quite right. She must be dreaming
again, her mother had never sounded choked
with emotion in her life. No, she was dreaming,
there had been a lot of dreams lately, Rand saying
goodbye to her, the fire— It came back to her
again with a vengeance; the *fire*.

Was she dead? She had felt as if she were dying
as she was burnt alive.

'Does it hurt badly, darling?' Her mother was
speaking again. 'The burns aren't too serious,
but— Darling, shall I get you something for the
pain?' she asked anxiously as Merlyn groaned
again.

Pain. Yes, she was in pain. And if she were
dead she wouldn't be able feel pain.

Her lids flickered open, the lashes feeling as if
they were tangled together, the blazing light
making her flinch until she realised it was just the
sun shining through the window. What window?
It couldn't be her hotel room, she remembered
that had burnt.

Her mother was sitting beside the bed, an older version of Merlyn, although her hair was more auburn than red, her eyes more hazel than green. But that they were mother and daughter could never be doubted. Although her mother's usual beauty, despite her years, was marred by lines of worry and fatigue, her eyes anxiously searching Merlyn's face.

'Well, you gave us all a scare.' She recovered quickly from whatever softer emotions had beset her, talking with her usual brisk manner.

Merlyn's mouth quirked ruefully at her mother's reversion to character, although even that small facial movement gave her pain. It seemed as if her whole body hurt her.

'The burns to your legs are just superficial,' her mother told her reassuringly as she saw the panic in her daughter's questioning gaze. 'Although I'm sure they still hurt,' she added in a gentler tone. 'When I think of what could have happened . . . !' She couldn't hold back her shudder of horror. 'Your bedroom was completely gutted,' she revealed shakily. 'They only just managed to pull you out of the room before you were overcome by the smoke.'

'They?' Merlyn managed to croak, even that small effort making her cough.

'It's the smoke inhalation,' her mother supplied dismissively. 'It will go off eventually. And "they" were the hotel manager and another young man who happened to be passing and saw the smoke coming from under your door. James and Anne Benton have been beside themselves with worry.'

Her mother was definitely getting back to normal, making it sound as if it were all Merlyn's fault everyone had been put to the bother of worrying about her!

'Your father and Richard too, of course,' her mother added unnecessarily. 'Although I insisted they both go back to work today once we knew you were going to be all right. Margaret and the children stayed in London, of course; I can do without them under my feet.' Dr Summers effectively put out of her thoughts her son's wife and her two grandsons. 'I realise it's difficult for you to talk, Merlyn.' She looked at her daughter reprovingly. 'But aren't you going to say anything?'

Her mother was like a runaway express train when she got going, and anyone who dared to cross her path without being invited to was likely to get flattened, but when you were invited to join in the conversation it was in the nature of a royal command, and during the next half an hour Merlyn managed, by one-word questions, which were all her coughing fits would allow, to find out that she had been in hospital sixteen hours, that the Bentons, Liza and Christopher had been sitting with her when her family arrived to take over. Her mother didn't mention Rand, so she could only presume he had gone to London as planned and was still there.

She also learnt that her legs were burnt extensively but not deeply, although the mess they were in made her feel weak when she managed to persuade her mother to help her move her head so that she could look at them.

'It isn't pretty, I'll agree.' Her mother eased her back down on to the pillow. 'But you'll soon be back to your beautiful self again. And that should please that director of yours,' she added somewhat indignantly. 'He's done nothing but pace up and down the corridor demanding to know when you'll be well enough to resume work!'

Merlyn's chuckles turned to another fit of coughing—for which she was firmly reprimanded.

The next few days were some of the strangest she had ever known, cosseted by her mother to such a degree that her other visitors had to sneak into her room during the odd times Merlyn managed to persuade her to go back to the hotel for a rest or to have a meal.

'She soon put Christopher in his place,' Liza chuckled on Merlyn's third day in hospital, sitting on the edge of the bed with a complete disregard of the notices that said you weren't to sit on patients' beds. 'She told him you would be ready to work again when *she* said so and not before!'

'What did Christopher say to that?' Merlyn's voice was still a little quavery, although she no longer coughed every time she spoke.

'Well, he didn't say "yes, Dr Summers" or "no, Dr Summers" like everyone else around here has been.' The subject of their conversation strode into the room with his usual arrogance.

'No,' Liza acknowledged mockingly. 'He said "of course, Dr Summers"!' she taunted.

Christopher gave her a pained look, laying the

bouquet of roses he had brought down on the
table at the end of the bed, the white buds just in
bloom, putting the newspapers he carried down
beside them. 'Your mother really is a battleaxe,
Merlyn!'

She looked unconcerned by his plight. 'This is
the first time in my life she's been this protective
of me—and I'm loving every minute of it!'

'Well, no one else is,' Christopher muttered.
'She even has all the hotel staff jumping to her
smallest whim.'

'My mother doesn't have whims!' Merlyn
protested.

'You should have seen Mark's face when she
turned up at the hotel that first night.' Liza's eyes
glowed with merriment. 'I thought he was going
to pass out on the spot!'

Merlyn gave a rueful smile. 'The two of them
never did get on together.'

'I would say that's an understatement,'
Christopher drawled. 'Even I feel sorry for him!'

'Well I don't,' Liza dismissed. 'I quite enjoy
seeing him so subdued!'

Merlyn picked up the roses Christopher had
brought to gently touch the velvety buds. 'Thank
you, they're beautiful.' She gave him a winsome
smile; Rand hadn't even bothered to send her
flowers, although she had received several other
bouquets from well-wishers.

She had had quite a few visitors too the last few
days, Anne and James managing to pop in separ-
ately at some time during the day, and yet as far
as she was aware Rand hadn't even telephoned to
see how she was. Anne had to have told him

about the fire, and he hadn't cared about her enough to call her personally and see how she felt. Even crying still hurt her, but when she was alone at night she couldn't hold back the tears.

'I have to keep in your mother's good grace somehow,' Christopher answered her comment about the roses. 'Do you know she even has *Anne* organised into putting her feet up for an hour each day?' he scorned. 'You should have heard the telling off James got when she saw how hard Anne works in the hotel.' He shook his head in wonder. 'And she put your father back on the train to London so quickly after he visited you yesterday he probably still doesn't know where he is!'

'Don't you believe it.' She gave the ghost of a smile, doing her best to banish thoughts of Rand, although it wasn't easy. 'You get used to being organised by my mother after a while.'

Christopher still shook his head disbelievingly. 'They say if you want to see what the woman will look like in thirty years' time look at the mother; no wonder you're still single, Merlyn!'

'Dr Summers has her stirling qualities,' Liza was the one to defend. 'Her concern for Merlyn to name just one.'

'I'll never know how Merlyn had the nerve to go into acting,' Christopher drawled mockingly. 'And talking of acting,' he looked at Liza with narrowed eyes, 'don't you have a script to study?'

'I——'

'Or something?' he added softly, pointedly.

Liza raised her brows, standing up with a shrug. 'I can tell when I'm not wanted. Just remember that Dr Summers will be back in about half an hour or so,' she warned before kissing Merlyn on the cheeks and leaving.

'As if I'm likely to forget!'

Merlyn smiled at Christopher's shudder. 'She really isn't that bad.' She had come to realise that herself during the last few days, her mother's almost regimental style of organising all those about her usually done for the other person's good and not her own. Her mother was also a dedicated doctor, and while she might have resented the interruption to her career her daughter's birth had made twenty-six years ago she was certainly putting Merlyn and her welfare first now.

Christopher took Liza's place on the bed, picking up Merlyn's hand lightly in both of his. 'I saw the tears in your eyes just now; he hasn't come to see you, has he?' he probed gently.

Their clasped hands swam in front of her vision as the tears she had been holding back threatened to cascade down her cheeks. 'No,' she choked, making no pretence not to know who he was talking about. There was only one 'he' who had ignored the danger she had been in and the pain she had suffered since then.

'Never mind,' Christopher replied briskly, putting her hand down on the bed to turn and pick up the newspapers he had brought with him. 'Have you seen these?' He held them up excitedly.

She shook her head. 'The nurse hasn't brought mine in today yet.'

He lay the newspapers flat on the bed. 'You've

become famous overnight,' he told her as he held up the first paper in the pile.

Merlyn blinked as she recognised the blurred black and white photograph on the front page as being her. It was one of the photographs from her portfolio, very glamorous, making her look twice as attractive as she really was with the strategic lighting in the studio. The lurid headline read 'Actress almost perishes in mystery fire!'

She took the newspaper out of Christopher's hand to slowly read the story beneath the headline. Her expression was rueful as she looked up at Christopher. 'The film doesn't come out of it too badly publicity-wise either, does it?' she derided.

He shrugged. 'It's going to be a fantastic film,' he said immodestly.

She picked up the second newspaper, and then the third. She seemed to have made the headlines in all of them. 'So,' she sat back against the pillows, 'is this "dramatic" enough for you, Christopher?' She challenged the claim he had once made about the ending of the film not being dramatic enough for him.

He flushed angrily. 'What's that supposed to mean?'

She shrugged. 'Well, the public's interest in the film has been piqued now.'

'So?' He was very tense.

Her mouth twisted. 'So you no longer need your "dramatic end". Accident-prone-Annie's giving you all the publicity you need.'

Christopher stood up. 'I hope you aren't

implying I deliberately arranged those accidents to achieve that?'

Of course she wasn't, she was just so tense about Rand's lack of concern for her that she had hit out at the first person she could, unfortunately it had to be Christopher. She could see how much she had angered him. 'Of course not,' she sighed. 'I only——'

'You only *think* it!' he cried furiously. 'The police believe the maid left a smouldering cigarette in your bin by accident when she came in to turn down your bed. Do you think I arranged that, too?'

'Christopher——'

'That's a hell of an accusation to make, Merlyn.' His hands were clenched into fists at his sides, his eyes deeply blue in his pale face.

'Mr Drake!' Merlyn's shocked mother stood in the doorway observing them both. 'That is no way to talk to a sick woman.' Her indignation filled the room. 'You shouldn't be in here at all——'

'Don't worry,' he bit out icily. 'I'm going.' He shot Merlyn a narrow-eyed glance. 'I think your daughter is suffering from a delayed case of shock; she's certainly having hallucinations!' He stormed from the room.

'Well!' Her mother's stunned gaze followed his retreating back. 'What was all that about?'

Merlyn closed her eyes, wishing she could shut out the whole world. She had insulted and enraged Christopher because of her hurt and anger towards Rand; she wondered if he would ever forgive her for the things she had said—and the things she *hadn't* said.

'Merlyn?' her mother prompted gently as her daughter's eyes remained closed, muttering about unauthorised visitors as she assumed Merlyn had fallen into an exhausted sleep, removing the 'messy' newspapers from the coverlet before quietly arranging the roses into a vase.

Merlyn had known she couldn't keep up the pretence of sleep all afternoon and evening, but she managed to do so until her mother insisted on 'waking her up' to have her tea.

'You must keep up your fluid intake, darling,' she scolded.

Merlyn was feeling too disheartened to fight her mother's more wilful character, even more so after persuading her mother to let her use the telephone to call the hotel and Christopher, only to be told he wasn't there! She needed to talk to him, to apologise, to make him understand it hadn't been him she was angry with at all. She would have to live with her recriminations until he could be found.

Her mother stayed and had dinner with her, no one daring to tell the autocratic woman it wasn't the customary thing to do. Merlyn could perhaps have found the situation amusing if she hadn't felt so miserable.

'I think you have the wrong room——'

'No—no, I have the right room.'

Merlyn's lids flew wide open at the sound of that husky voice, turning her face towards the doorway where her mother was trying to see Rand out. He was looking past her mother straight at her, the silver eyes darkened with pain as the burns on her legs were still vividly visible.

She had been lying in a semi-asleep state as her mother read her articles from a magazine she had brought in with her, the sudden harsh tone of her voice telling Merlyn they were no longer alone. But she hadn't expected the intruder to be Rand.

She put up a self-conscious hand to her hair, aware that it had been singed shorter in places, although Sheila had come in and styled it so that this wasn't too noticeable. But her face was completely bare of make-up, and her legs were bared and unsightly. She looked a mess.

She drank in the sight of Rand with a thirst that was unquenchable. He looked tired, lines around his eyes, the dark suit and white shirt he wore slightly creased. But it was so *good* just to look at him!

'I think you're mistaken, young man,' her mother began again in a patronising tone. 'Merlyn is not receiving visitors just yet, and——'

Cold grey eyes the colour of the Irish sea in a storm levelled on her with silencing arrogance. 'I have made no mistake, madam,' he bit out with icy disdain. 'And I think Merlyn will see me.'

'It isn't a question of what Merlyn wants,' her mother attempted to bluster as she realised this man wasn't as impressed by her air of command as most other people were. 'Her doctors and I——'

'Mummy, it's all right,' Merlyn assured her huskily, her gaze still fixed on Rand. 'Really it is.'

Some of the tension seemed to leave Rand's body, the arrogance fading a little too as he looked at her mother with new eyes. 'I hope I haven't sounded disrespectful, Mrs Summers.' His voice had softened cajolingly. 'It's just that I only learnt this evening of Merlyn's accident and my concern for her made me forget my manners. I'm Brandon Carmichael.' He held out his hand in a gesture of friendship.

Her mother seemed dazed by this sudden change in him, so much so that she didn't even correct him about the way he addressed her as Mrs rather than Dr as she would have done most other people who had dared to make that mistake. 'Angela Summers,' she returned abruptly.

He held her hand in a firm grip before releasing it. 'I should have instantly realised who you were; the likeness between you and Merlyn is unmistakable.'

She gave an acknowledging inclination of her head. 'As my daughter is very beautiful I'll take that as a compliment.'

'Please do,' he invited gruffly. 'It was meant as one.'

She did something then that she probably hadn't done for years; she blushed. 'Thank you. But I really must insist that Merlyn is not up to visitors, especially this time of night,' she added reprovingly. 'You should have——'

'Please, Mummy.' Merlyn's gaze hadn't left Rand's face even for a moment, her interest quickening as he told her mother he had known nothing about her accident until today. It seemed impossible to believe—but oh, how she wanted to believe it! The fact that he was here now filled her with hope. 'Rand and I are—old friends,' she explained softly.

Auburn brows rose over hazel eyes. 'I see,' her mother said slowly, looking at Rand with new eyes too now before picking up her jacket from the back of the chair she had been sitting in. 'Well, he's certainly an improvement on Mark Hillier,' she announced haughtily before nodding coolly to Rand and kissing Merlyn goodbye. 'See you tomorrow, darling.'

For a moment after her departure Rand continued to stand just outside the room, then he gave a rueful shrug. 'She isn't quite what I was expecting.' He stood beside the bed now. 'She was like an eagle protecting her young!'

'I've been surprised by her behaviour the last few days too,' Merlyn nodded. 'Maybe I've always misjudged her or maybe she's just mellowed. Whatever the reason, we seem to be friends for a change. Did you mean it?' She probed abruptly.

Rand's expression was suddenly wary. 'What?'

'About not knowing I was in hospital.' Merlyn's breathing was shallow as she waited for his answer.

'I only read about it in the newspaper tonight,' he replied without hesitation.

'But——'

'When I left you that night I did intend going to London and staying there,' he declared heavily. 'But once I got there I couldn't settle, and so I got on a plane the next morning. To the States.'

'But Anne must have——'

'She had no idea where I was,' he sighed heavily. 'I just went. I didn't tell her or anyone else where I was going. I needed time to think, without interruptions. But it didn't solve anything, and when I got into the airport earlier the first thing I saw was your photograph on the front page of the newspapers!' His expression was grim. 'I went straight to see Anne when I got back, and apparently she hadn't told you she couldn't reach me because she didn't want to worry you.' He shook his head. 'You must have thought me a callous bastard not to have even come and seen you!'

'Not callous——'

'Then a bastard,' he declared. 'My God, Merlyn,' he grated harshly. 'I didn't know what to think when they said you had been seriously burnt.'

'Well, as you can see,' she dismissed lightly, warmed by his genuine concern, 'the newspapers exaggerated—as usual.'

His darkened gaze moved slowly down the length of her exposed legs. 'I don't think they exaggerated at all,' he rasped. 'And if James hadn't found you when he did . . . !'

'Please!' Merlyn shuddered as he spoke of the realisation she herself had made, and that had haunted her, ever since she regained consciousness.

'I'm sorry for reminding you of it,' he groaned, sitting on the edge of her bed to clasp her hands.

'You're the third person to do that today, and it's against the rules,' she mocked, a catch in her voice.

'What is?' He tilted his head enquiringly.

'Sitting on the bed,' she told him huskily, very conscious of her hand in his, of the roughened palms and gentle fingers. 'Liza and Christopher both did it earlier when they visited.'

He raised dark brows. 'Together?'

'Briefly,' she nodded, her eyes becoming shadowed as she remembered how she had upset Christopher. 'They managed to sneak in while my mother was having her lunch,' she added lightly.

Rand released her hand to stand up abruptly and move away from her. 'She is pretty formidable.'

'Yes.' Merlyn watched him anxiously, sensing he had more on his mind than the fire that had burnt her.

He turned suddenly, his expression bleak. 'I think it's only fair that I tell you now that my time away changed nothing; I still believe I have nothing to give you!'

What little hope she had nurtured because of his visit tonight died a sad death. She had hoped, just because he *had* come to her— But they had been lovers, and he was gentleman enough to acknowledge that relationship by a courtesy visit to make sure she was all right after her ordeal.

'One thing did become apparent, though,' he revealed. 'I think—I *know* I owe you more of an explanation than the one I gave you the other night.'

She swallowed hard. 'Still being in love with your wife isn't enough?'

'No,' he bit out. 'You said that you love me,

and—I owe you the whole truth so that you'll hate me as much as I hate myself.' He put his hand into the breast pocket of his jacket to take out a small blue book. 'It's the last notebook Suzie wrote,' he grated, a nerve pulsing in his cheek. 'The one I *didn't* give to Anne,' he clarified. 'I want you to take it, and I want you to read it.'

Her eyes widened as he held it out to her. 'I couldn't do that, it's too personal.' She shook her head, her hands remaining clasped in front of her.

'I want you to,' he nodded, dropping the book down on to the bed. 'Then you'll know everything and you won't love me any more.'

She looked down at the small blue book warily, wondering what it could possibly contain that could turn her feelings for Rand around completely. Details of his infidelity, perhaps? If that were what Suzie believed she had been wrong, Rand had told her he was always faithful to his wife, and she believed him. There was *nothing* that Suzie could have written that would make her stop loving Rand.

'It doesn't matter what's in this book, Rand.' She sat forward earnestly. 'Can't you understand that it isn't important?'

'Oh, it's important,' he breathed heavily. 'And if I could tell you myself and know that you hate me I would, but I—' He ran a shaking hand across his brow. 'I have trouble living with it; I can't actually put into words the horror of what I did!'

Merlyn gave a pained frown at his self-hatred. 'Does Anne know?'

He drew in a rasping breath. 'Some of it,' he revealed gruffly. 'But not all.'

'But she doesn't hate you.' She shook her head. 'She loves you too.'

'I told you, she doesn't know it all,' he sighed, his hands thrust into his pockets. 'Suzie's gone, and I can't have you, but I need some people that care in my life. Read the book, Merlyn, and send it back to me when you've finished it. I can assure you, you won't want to see me again yourself.' The last was added bitterly.

Merlyn couldn't imagine anything she was told or read making that true. 'Rand——'

'Do you think Hillier had anything to do with the fire?' he cut in abruptly, the subject of the notebook closed as far as he was concerned; she *would* read it.

'Mark?' she echoed dazedly, momentarily thrown off balance.

'Anne said the fire was contained to one suite.' His eyes were narrowed. 'Yours.'

'Apparently the police have decided a smouldering cigarette started it,' she dismissed, the subject of the fire still a traumatic one for her.

'Left by the maid,' Rand nodded. 'Anne told me. But she checked, the maid didn't smoke,' he explained softly. 'Although obviously the person who did leave the cigarette in your bin didn't realise there was a different maid on duty that evening.'

Mark was friendly with one of the maids, he had said so when he repeated that gossip to her by the pool, but even so she couldn't believe he could have set the fire. He didn't like her, and he enjoyed watching her squirm, but she didn't think he actually wanted to kill her. That would be just too weird.

'I think you're wrong about Mark being involved, Rand.' She gave a shake of her head. 'It was just an accident——'

'There have been too many accidents lately concerning you,' said Rand grimly.

'Yes, but——'

'Don't be surprised if the police actually decide to pay you another visit some time soon——'

'The police?' Merlyn questioned disbelievingly. 'But I've already spoken to them, the day after the fire, they didn't seem to think there was anything suspicious about it—carelessness, perhaps, but not intent.'

'I don't happen to agree,' Rand told her arrogantly. 'And I'm going to make sure they reopen their investigation.'

'Rand, I think you're being a bit extreme about this,' she chided.

'I don't,' he said with finality. 'The next time something like this happens you might not be so lucky. If almost drowning and then being burnt to death can be classed as lucky!' His expression was harshly forbidding, his eyes narrowed.

'Drowning?' Merlyn repeated blankly, her expression clearing as she realised he meant that night by the gazebo. 'But that *was* an accident, the planking had rotted away——'

'I went over the next morning and checked.' He shook his head. 'I couldn't be sure but there was a possibility that the planks had been cut, the wood was certainly sound. I was going to have it checked by someone who knows what they're looking for later that day, but it was repaired before I could get back to it and the wood thrown away. But after the coincidence of the fire only being in your room, I have a feeling my suspicions about that planking having been cut may have been right.'

'But *why?*'

He shrugged. 'Hillier has a perfect motive— revenge.'

'I can't believe that,' she disagreed. 'It's too fantastic!'

'I can think of better ways of describing it,' Rand drawled.

'But anyone could have fallen through the planking if it had been cut as you say you think it could have been,' she reasoned.

'It wasn't just anyone who was scheduled to step out of the boat on to that very spot the next day,' he reminded her grimly. 'Obviously, with all those people about there was no actual chance of your drowning, but it would have shaken you up pretty badly.'

It did sound feasible when he explained it like that. But could it be true? Could Mark have done that to her? 'My mother said James and a "young man" helped me out of my room the other night.' She swallowed hard, very pale. 'Who was it?'

'Hillier,' Rand revealed gruffly—as Merlyn had known he would.

'Oh, Rand . . . !' The room swayed dizzily and she was grateful for the solidity of his arms as they came about her. 'I just can't believe *anyone* would want to do this to me. It can't be true, can it?'

'I'm hoping not! I've tried not to believe it.'

She looked up at him searchingly, sure she had heard more than just concern for a friend in his voice. A shutter came down over his emotions as he put her firmly away from him.

'I have to go,' he told her abruptly. 'And you should get some rest, otherwise your mother might decide I'm not an improvement on anyone,' he added lightly.

'But——'

'Read the notebook, Merlyn,' he rasped. 'It's the last month of Suzie's life.'

She fell back against the pillows. The last *month* of Suzie's life?

Long after Rand had gone she stared at the small blue notebook. Rand said it would make her hate him as he deserved to be hated. And she didn't want to hate him!

She picked up the book to push it into the drawer in her bedside unit, closing it again firmly, turning her face away from it as she tried to go to sleep.

It was a very long night.

CHAPTER FOURTEEN

'You should have seen Mark's face as they carted him away,' Liza giggled.

'Oh yes, it was very funny,' Christopher snarled from the other side of the room as he glowered at the two women: Merlyn lying on the bed, Liza sitting on a chair at her side. 'My female star is in hospital,' he strode forcefully into the room, 'and my male star is "helping the police with their enquiries" because she's *in* hospital!'

Liza gave a disgusted sniff. 'I was just sorry they didn't take him away in handcuffs!'

Christopher scowled at her as he helped himself to one of the grapes from the bag that lay on the bed. 'The publicity is going to kill this film before it's even made,' he groaned.

'Better that than Merlyn,' Liza reminded him hardly. 'Besides, you know damn well everyone will want to see the film now.'

He looked at her coldly. 'I've always thought it very unladylike to hear a woman swear.'

She shrugged unconcernedly. 'Then it's as well I didn't ask for your approval, isn't it?'

Merlyn thought it was time she intervened in the exchange, before the two of them actually came to blows. 'I'm so pleased to see you, Christopher,' she told him with genuine warmth.

He shrugged. 'I received a message that you wanted to talk to me.'

She had tried twice this morning to reach him at the hotel, once before the police came to talk to her, and once again afterwards, finally leaving a message for him to call her. Since Liza had arrived and told her of the furore at the hotel this morning after Merlyn had spoken to the police, Mark accompanying them down to the station so that they might question him further about her 'accidents', she hadn't expected Christopher to answer her calls personally, sure he would be very busy handling the press.

Liza grimaced. 'Is this my cue to say I have a script to study?' she observed wryly.

'I shouldn't bother,' muttered a disgruntled Christopher. 'In the circumstances it would be a waste of time. This is all your friend Carmichael's doing, you know,' he told Merlyn accusingly.

'He isn't my friend.' Her cheeks were flushed.

'Lover, then. He——'

'Not that either,' she refuted sharply.

'It's finally over then?' Christopher raised dark blond brows.

'That's no one's business but my own!'

'Well, he's certainly stirred up a hornets' nest,' Christopher muttered. 'My schedule has gone to pot!'

'Heaven forbid you should put him through the inconvenience of almost being burnt to death because of someone's maliciousness!' Liza raised her eyes heavenwards before giving Christopher a disgusted look. 'You're inhuman!'

'So I've been told,' he drawled, raising his brows at her pointedly.

'All right.' She stood up indignantly. 'I'm

going. Just don't upset her, her mother said she needs to rest today. Anne and James said to tell you they would be in tomorrow when you're feeling a little better,' she smiled encouragingly at Merlyn.

'Thanks for the grapes,' she called after her.

'My plea—Stop that!' Liza slapped Christopher's hand as he would have reached for another one from the bag. 'If you're ever in hospital I'll send you a pet scorpion; you'll be good company for each other!' she told him sweetly, giving Merlyn a triumphant smile as she went out the door.

'I somehow get the feeling she doesn't like me,' Christopher commented before putting another grape into his mouth.

'Too much of a challenge for you?' she teased.

'No challenge at all,' he dismissed dryly. 'If she hates me, she hates me. Besides, she has something going with Greg,' he shrugged.

Merlyn sobered. 'I've been trying to contact you since yesterday so that I could apologise for my behaviour then.' She looked at him regretfully. 'I said some very unkind things to you, and——'

'Please don't apologise,' Christopher sighed. 'With my male star as good as arrested I'm beginning to wish I had been the one to do it for the publicity!'

She couldn't help smiling at his cynicism. 'A bastard to the end,' she said without rancour.

He smiled. 'I mustn't step too much out of character, now must I?'

'I didn't realise you had ever done it!'

'I haven't,' he drawled unabashedly. 'And I can't quite see Carmichael as the Knight in Shining Armour either!'

'Rand is just concerned about me——'

'He wasn't concerned for three days, so why now?'

She bristled indignantly at his scepticism. 'He didn't know about the fire——'

'Most places in the world can be reached by telephone now, Merlyn.' Christopher's voice was scornful.

Her cheeks were fiery-red. 'I wanted to see you today so that I could apologise for yesterday, not argue with you again!'

'Can I help it if I think you're making a fool of yourself over a man who doesn't deserve you?' he answered harshly.

'Just because he's interrupted your precious schedule for filming——'

'Damn the film,' he ground out. 'It's you we're talking about now!'

'I can take care of myself, thank you!' Merlyn's eyes flashed warningly, remembering the last time she had claimed that, to Rand, and the fact that she had almost burnt to death hours later.

'I'm only trying to point out to you that Carmichael has as much reason for wanting you out of the way as Hillier does. More—because without you we can't go on filming!'

'*What* did you just say about Rand?' she gasped disbelievingly.

Christopher gave an impatient. sigh. 'Carmichael never wanted this film made, Merlyn. And your portrayal of Suzie must be bringing back memories he would rather forget. I'm only pointing out the possibility that he——'

'Get out of here,' she ordered shakily.

'Merlyn, try and see past your blind love for the man——'

'I said *get out*,' she repeated shrilly. 'I don't want to listen to any more of your lies! You——'

'Merlyn,' her mother cut in authoritatively. 'Calm yourself this instant. Mr Drake——'

'I know,' he declared harshly. 'Leave. Maybe you could try and talk some sense into your daughter,' he told the older woman disgustedly as she escorted him to the door.

'I don't know why you let that young man in here,' Merlyn's mother fussed around her tidying the bed. 'Every time he comes here he upsets you. And that isn't good for the baby. No more visitors today, I think. And you had better have a sleep now so that——'

'Baby?' Merlyn recovered enough to murmur. 'What baby?'

'Why yours of course, darling.' Her mother removed the bag of grapes from the bed with a delicate wrinkle of her nose. 'You've had enough trauma during the first few weeks already, without that young man——'

'Mother, *what* baby?' Merlyn exploded, her body stiff with tension.

Auburn brows rose in hurt surprise at the aggressive outburst. 'You always did have a temper.' Merlyn was rebuked. 'Even as a child— Merlyn, surely you realised you're pregnant?' her mother said impatiently as Merlyn looked ready to give another angry exclamation.

Pregnant? A *baby*? Well of course she was expecting a baby, the part of her that was still sane retaliated, that's what happened when you were pregnant.

She just hadn't realised she *was* pregnant. But usually as regular as four following three she realised she had missed a period over three weeks ago. That first time with Rand . . . ?

'Mummy, are you sure?' she voiced uncertainly.

Her mother looked affronted. 'I didn't do all those years of training not to be able to tell a woman when she's pregnant,' she informed Merlyn haughtily. 'Even if it is my own daughter!'

'I—But you don't seem—shocked?' Merlyn was, breathlessly so! Of course she hadn't come to the Lake District with the intention of having an affair with anyone, and so the question of precautions hadn't arisen. But even so . . . !

'I'm not,' her mother dismissed. 'I was a little disappointed you hadn't chosen to tell me about it yourself, but as you now say you didn't even know—!'

'I had no idea,' Merlyn confirmed dazedly.

'As long as you can assure me that the unpleasant young man that just left isn't the father I think I'm even quite happy at the prospect of being a grandmother again.' Her mother looked at her hopefully.

'Christopher isn't the father——'

'Thank goodness,' Merlyn was answered with obvious relief.

'But Brandon Carmichael is,' she told her in a hushed voice, still unable to fully take in the prospect of motherhood herself. She didn't *feel* pregnant. Of course she didn't, that sane voice mocked her again, she could only be five weeks along at the most. It just didn't seem possible that in approximately thirty-five weeks' time she would hold Rand's child in her arms. *Rand's* child. She had to tell him about it. After the tragedy of the loss of his other child he deserved to know about this one.

'I thought as much when he arrived here last night,' her mother nodded. 'I like a man who's decisive enough to know what he wants, even if he has to go through me to get it,' she added ruefully.

Another thought had occurred to Merlyn, would Rand want to know about *her* baby? That other baby, the one he had lost, had been Suzie's child too. Would he want to know about the child *they* had conceived, not through love—at least, not on Rand's side—but through blinding need? The question was really irrelevant, whether Rand wanted the baby or not she intended telling him about it.

But it suddenly became important that she read that notebook of Suzie's. It could never make her hate Rand, as he had claimed it would, but it might help her to understand him a little better.

'I think I would like to rest after all, Mummy,' she settled back on the pillows. 'Do you mind?'

'Not at all, darling. I'm just glad you've decided to be sensible.' Her aristocratic features softened as she bent over Merlyn. 'I know I haven't been the best mother in the world to you and Richard, but I am pleased about your baby.'

'There's very little chance that Rand will want to marry me,' she told her gently.

'I didn't raise a daughter who couldn't meet a challenge,' her mother told her encouragingly.

'Single parenthood is more than a challenge, Mummy——'

'Nonsense! You want the baby, don't you?' She looked at Merlyn frowningly.

'Oh yes.' Her eyes glowed like emeralds.

Her mother nodded, as if she had never doubted what Merlyn's answer would be. 'Then it will all work out, you'll see. Your father and I intend helping you all that we can, and——'

'Daddy knows too——? He didn't do all those years of training either, not to be able to tell when a woman is pregnant,' she said dryly at her mother's raised eyebrows.

'Exactly,' her mother confirmed with satisfaction. 'And you are not to worry about a thing. Your father and I have discussed it, and by the time the baby is old enough for you to want to resume your career I'll be thinking of retirement, and——'

'I'm sure there will be no need for you to do that,' Merlyn cut in with shocked dismay; she knew that her mother had *never* thought of retirement, and she wasn't going to let her make that sacrifice for her. 'As you said, I'm sure it will all work out, without your having to make such a drastic step,' she said lightly. 'And I'm sure Rand will want to help out financially.'

'Do you want that?' Her mother frowned at the strain Merlyn displayed at this last comment.

'I want my baby to know its father,' she

decided firmly. 'And Rand is the type of man to want to recognise and take on his responsibilities.' The last was added a little bitterly as she realised Rand would probably never love her child.

'Oh, darling . . . !' Her mother squeezed her hand comfortingly, tears glistening in her hazel eyes.

'I'll be all right, Mummy.' Merlyn gave an overbright smile. 'I'm your daughter, remember?'

'You certainly are.' Her mother straightened. 'I never realised how much until today.'

She had never heard that proud tone in her mother's voice before, had always felt she was something of a disappointment to her parents, refusing the opportunity to go to university in favour of becoming an actress. And probably a lot of parents would feel disappointed with a daughter who was pregnant and had received no proposal to marry the father. She suddenly realised she was proud of her mother too.

Her hands trembled slightly as she took out the notebook from the drawer beside her. The last month of Suzie Forrester's life. What had Rand done to induce the self-hatred he felt? God, how she dreaded reading about it.

The notebook was obviously different from those others that Suzie had written as a way of expressing her feelings, a way of venting her emotions during the terrible months of her illness. This book had been written by a woman broken spiritually and emotionally, and as Merlyn read page after page she realised why Suzie had been filled with a rage that had made her hate Rand for what he had done to her.

Suzie hadn't miscarried her baby at all, Merlyn learnt during those first anguished pages, but had been persuaded by Rand and her doctor that to receive the treatment she needed the baby would have to be sacrificed. Or she would die.

There would be other babies, once she was well, Rand had told her, persuaded her. And with a breaking heart Suzie had sacrificed the baby she had waited so many years to conceive.

Tears streamed down Merlyn's cheeks as she read of the terrible loss that had haunted Suzie through all the months that had followed, her only consolation—although even that hadn't seemed as important as the loss of her baby—had been that she did seem to be getting better. Although it hadn't been the doctor's treatment that had done that but the self-help she had found, and she had wondered time and time again whether the doctors could also have been wrong about the baby. She had never once blamed Rand, knew that he had wanted children as much as she did, if not more, and that he had suffered too.

And then a week before her death Rand had told her there could never be another baby, that when they had taken her child from her they had found it necessary to perform a small operation that meant she would never be able to conceive again.

Suzie had left Rand, gone to London, hating him with every fibre of her being for the death of her child.

Those days in London had been a nightmare,

Suzie reliving again and again the loss of her child and her inability to have any more.

The last entry in the book had been written on the morning she died. She had made her decision, she wrote, couldn't change the past, that had gone, but she could, and would, change her future.

By eight o'clock that night she had been dead.

At her own hand? Had she driven into that tree deliberately, with the intention of 'changing her future'? The police had reported that no other vehicle had been involved, and the road had shown no signs of oil or grease where she had swerved off it, and no mechanical or structural damage to the car other than that incurred by the accident had been reported either.

Rand certainly believed that Suzie had taken her own life because he had lied to her. She knew now that was the reason he hated himself and wanted her to hate him too.

Only she didn't. Her heart ached for the pain Suzie had known, but it also ached for Rand, for the agony he must have gone through mentally and kept hidden from Suzie all those months after their baby had died, for the decision he alone had had to make, knowing that once Suzie was told the truth she would hate him. As she had.

He believed he was responsible for the death of his child and then his wife, when all he had wanted to do was keep Suzie alive.

Rand was wrong about Merlyn completely, she did still love him, and she wanted to see him again, if only to tell him that her feelings for him hadn't changed and that they never would. Even if he could never love again he deserved to know that.

God, she had let one night and day already pass letting him believe she had read the book and despised him as much as he had thought she would. She wasn't going to let another night pass the same way. He had *had* no choice but to want Suzie alive.

She swung her legs over the side of the high hospital bed, feeling a little dizzy as she attempted to stand for the first time in four days, wishing the floor didn't seem quite so far away. Her legs felt sore too, where the burns were still healing. But if she could just get some clothes on she could ring for a taxi to take her to Rand's home.

'I just came to—What are you doing?' An astounded Christopher came to a halt in the doorway as he witnessed her struggles to get out of bed.

'What am *I* doing?' She reminded him that it was only six-thirty, too early for visiting hours.

He looked abashed. 'I came back to apologise for my behaviour earlier,' he muttered.

'*You* did?' she mocked.

His cheeks flushed angrily. 'There's no need to rub my contrition in my face,' he bit out tautly. 'All we ever seem to do lately is argue. We're going to have another argument right now if you don't tell me what you're doing?' He frowned as she finally managed to get her feet to the floor. 'You're in no condition to be out of bed,' he scowled as he came forward to steady her. 'Where are you going?' he prompted impatiently.

'Be a dear and get my clothes out of the closet over there.' She indicated the cupboard as she sat down weakly on the bedside chair.

'But——'

'Please do it, Christopher,' she asked wearily. 'You said you didn't want to argue any more,' she reminded him.

He strode angrily over to the closet, taking out the clothes Liza had got ready and her mother had brought in to hang in there ready for her discharge in a few days' time. 'I don't know what wild-goose chase you're on, but—What's this?' he frowned as he picked up the notebook that still lay on her bed.

'Nothing.' She unsuccessfully attempted to snatch the book out of his hand. 'Christopher, don't!' she cried desperately as he moved out of her reach to begin flicking through the pages. 'You can't use any of that in your film,' she told him stubbornly as he whistled softly through his teeth at what he was reading. 'Satisfied?' she glared at him resentfully as he silently handed her back the book.

'Where did you get that from?' he asked quietly.

'Rand. Who else?' she challenged, angry with him for his blatant invasion of privacy.

'I presume you're on your way to see him now?'

'Yes.' Once again she sounded defiant. He had had no right to read that notebook, no right at all!

'I'll drive you,' he told her softly.

Merlyn's eyes widened. 'You will?' she said uncertainly.

He nodded abruptly. 'I can't persuade you not to go?' He quirked his brows.

'No!'

'Then I may as well make sure you get there safely,' he shrugged.

This unexpected display of kindness from Christopher brought tears to her eyes. 'Thank you!' Merlyn gave him a shaky smile.

'Don't thank me,' he muttered. 'I still think you're making the biggest mistake of your life——'

'Oh don't,' she laughingly silenced him. 'Don't go and spoil it!'

He gave a terse inclination of his head. 'Do you need any help getting dressed?'

Colour highlighted her cheeks. 'I'll manage,' she mumbled awkwardly. Although she wasn't quite sure how; she already felt stiff all over, and as weak as a newborn kitten.

Christopher turned in the doorway to observe her laboured movements. 'Sure, you'll manage,' he drawled. 'Give me a call if you get into difficulties.'

'Into difficulties' in no way described the next ten minutes as she tried to dress herself, omitting the silky nylons Liza seemed to have put in; her mother would have realised she couldn't bear anything on her legs just yet. But through contortions and sheer will-power she managed to zip on the brown skirt and pull on the matching jacket over a cream blouse.

'Well,' Christopher surveyed her when she

appeared in the doorway, swaying a little, her expression one of triumph because of her achievement, 'the most I can say about you is that you're decent. Almost.' He straightened her blouse in the waistband of her skirt, undoing several of the buttons on her blouse and refastening them where she had matched them up incorrectly with the holes. 'You wouldn't win any prizes in a beauty contest.' His hand beneath her elbow helped support her as they began the slow walk down the corridor to the exit. 'But I suppose you'll have to do.'

'Thanks!'

He shrugged. 'I've never believed in giving false compliments.'

'I can tell that!' she spoke between gritted teeth, each step an agony.

'Well I——'

'Miss Summers, where do you think you're going?'

Merlyn rolled her eyes expressively at Christopher before leaning back on the wall to turn and face the young nurse who eyed her scandalously as she bore down on them in the hollow-sounding corridor.

'Mr Drake is just taking me——'

'He isn't "taking you" anywhere,' she was informed briskly. 'You shouldn't be out of bed. And you certainly shouldn't be dressed.' She gave Christopher a disapproving glare, knowing he had to have helped Merlyn get as far as she had. 'I know for a fact that you haven't been discharged——'

'I'm only going out for a short time,' Merlyn

protested. 'I'll be back.'

'This isn't a hotel, Miss Summers. We do not allow patients to come and go as they please——'

'She is a private patient, and she doesn't need anyone's permission to take herself out for a few hours,' Christopher was the one to tell the young woman with cool disdain.

The nurse bristled indignantly. 'Nevertheless, there are certain rules that still have to be adhered to——'

'Then you adhere to them,' Christopher said, taking a firm hold of Merlyn's arm to start walking towards the exit again. 'You would have made a perfect prison warden,' he added disparagingly.

'I'm sorry.' Merlyn turned to give the other woman a sympathetic grimace as she gasped her outrage at his insulting tone. 'He doesn't really mean to be rude——'

'Don't I?' he grated, turning to face the gaping nurse while swinging the door open for Merlyn at the same time. 'We're leaving now,' he challenged. 'Both of us!'

The nurse was galvanised into action. 'If Miss Summers is choosing to discharge herself there are certain papers that have to be signed, and——'

'I told you, I'll be back,' Merlyn called out to the other woman as the door swung shut behind them. 'You were a little hard on her, Christopher,' she scolded as he helped her into the passenger seat of his car. 'She was only trying to do her job——'

'She was trying to prevent you from leaving

when you've chosen to go!' The car engine only had time to roar into life before he pressed his foot down on the accelerator, the red sports car speeding away with a grinding of stones beneath its wheels.

'Christopher!' Merlyn complained as she was thrown back in her seat.

'Sorry,' he muttered. 'I've just never been able to stand that kind of restraint being put on my actions.'

She rested her head on the back of the seat, the effort of dressing and walking exhausting her more than she had realised. But she had to go to Rand, had to assure him that he had made the only decision that he could, that he was still worthy of receiving love, that *she* loved him.

'Are you all right?' Christopher was looking at her concernedly when she opened her eyes to turn to him.

'Fine.' She gave him a weak smile of reassurance. 'Just tired.'

He nodded. 'Lie back and rest for a while,' he advised huskily.

The idea did sound tempting, and she put her head back with a sigh.

She hadn't meant to fall asleep, but as she came awake with a start she realised she had done exactly that. Although it could only have been for a matter of minutes; they were still driving.

She opened her eyes with effort, instantly dazzled by the lights of oncoming traffic on the opposite side of the motorway. But there *was* no motorway between the hospital and Rand's house!

She sat up awkwardly, turning to Christopher, his gaze intent on the road ahead. 'Christopher——'

'Ah good, you're awake.' He glanced at her, his expression gentle. 'Feel better?'

'Yes. But——'

'You've had a good sleep,' he said with satisfaction.

She didn't understand, it had still been daylight when they left the hospital and yet now it was very dark away from the lights of the motorway. They couldn't possibly have been driving to Rand's house all this time.

'Christopher,' she voiced uncertainly. 'How long have I been asleep?'

'Several hours,' he told her lightly. 'We should be there soon.'

Several hours! 'Where are we now?' she demanded dazedly.

'Watford.'

'*Watford!* But why on earth—! Christopher, you were supposed to be taking me to see Rand, not back to London,' she protested.

'I don't want to talk about Brandon Carmichael,' he snarled.

'I know you've never approved of my relationship with him, but——'

'You don't need him!'

'I appreciate your concern, Christopher,' she began slowly. 'But now I would like it if you would drive me back——'

'To Rand!' he finished harshly. 'I told you, you

don't need him now, you have me.'

Confusion darkened her eyes. 'We've become friends the last——'

'Friends!' He repeated the description contemptuously, his eyes glittering angrily. 'I never wanted just friendship from you, I made that clear from the beginning.'

She shook her head. 'You flirted with me, yes, but it was nothing more than that——'

'That's a lie,' he hissed harshly. 'I told you how I felt the first time we worked together, but you just laughed it off by telling me you were married, that you were in love with your husband.'

'But I'm not married, Christopher,' she said desperately. 'You know that.' She frowned at the furious contortion of his features. 'I want to go back to the Lake District, Christopher,' she declared firmly.

'I told you last time I wouldn't let you go back to him. You don't love him.' His voice softened. 'You don't love him, it's me you love.'

Gone was the arrogant director she was used to, the self-confident despot, and in his place was—She didn't know. This was a Christopher she had never seen before. And he frightened her.

'Christopher, it is Rand I love,' she told him gently. 'I wish I didn't sometimes, but it's a love I can't stop.'

'You aren't going to him this time,' he shouted furiously. 'Dismissing me like a naughty schoolboy come to confess his infatuation while all the time intending to return to the man who hurt you. I couldn't let you go back to him last time, and I won't let you go this time either. I killed you last time rather than let him have you!'

Merlyn didn't feel as if she were breathing at all, feeling her heart begin to pound as panic rose within her, the realisation of what he was actually saying horrifying her.

She moistened her lips. 'But I'm not dead, Christopher,' she pointed out breathlessly, her fingernails digging into her palms as she fought to stay in control, even though hysteria threatened to engulf her.

For a moment he looked very youthful as confusion washed over him, and then he smiled, and it was unlike any other smile Merlyn had ever seen, a mixture of childlike innocence—and evil intent. 'Because you've come back to me,' he said happily. 'My Suzie has come back to me!'

CHAPTER FIFTEEN

CHRISTOPHER had killed Suzie.

Merlyn didn't know how he had done it, but she knew he had killed the other woman rather than let her return to Rand as she had intended doing. For *that* had been the decision Suzie came to that day, to go back to the man who loved her enough to do anything to keep her alive, the man she loved in return.

But Christopher had stopped her from reaching Rand. And now he intended doing it a second time, believing in his warped mind that *she* was Suzie.

This sort of thing always looked so easy to deal with on the stage or screen, talking the murderer out of his plan to murder again. But the victim never seemed particularly panicked in those works of fiction; probably because they knew the script and were aware of the outcome. But this was all too real, and she was alone in a car with a man who was completely unstable!

And no one knew where she had gone. No one knew she had gone *anywhere* except one rather indignant nurse who had probably reported her self-discharge before going off duty and forgetting all about it. None of her family, or Rand, would probably get to hear of her disappearance until tomorrow when one of them tried to visit her. And tomorrow was a long way off.

It was difficult to believe Christopher's self-admission of murder, although that smile he had given a few minutes ago told her he was perfectly capable of it.

She swallowed hard. 'Where are we going in London?' She deliberately made her voice light; after all he believed her to be Suzie, and that she had chosen him this time.

'My apartment,' he supplied easily. 'Rand won't be able to find you there,' he added with satisfaction. 'I know it was his possessiveness that kept you from me last time.'

That was what he had wanted to believe, hadn't been able to accept that Suzie really did love her husband. Poor Suzie. Poor Rand . . . She had no way of knowing what Christopher intended doing with her, if he was going to realise as suddenly as he began believing it that she wasn't Suzie, and hit out at her in impotent rage. But if she didn't get out of this alive Rand was always going to believe Suzie had killed herself because of him, would have no idea Christopher was responsible.

If she got out of this alive . . . ! Her mother said she had raised a daughter who could meet challenge; this was the biggest challenge she was ever likely to meet. She didn't intend dying.

'Why did you try to harm me again, Christopher, if you love me?' she asked softly, sure now that Mark hadn't been the one they were seeking at all, that it had to be Christopher who had arranged those 'accidents'.

He blinked, once again looking confused. 'I didn't try to hurt you——'

'But the cut planks, the fire . . . ?'

'That was Merlyn, not you,' he dismissed lightly. 'She was the one your husband was having an affair with. You see, Suzie, he hasn't been faithful to you, so why should you be faithful to him?'

'But why did you want to hurt—Merlyn?' she prompted gruffly.

'To punish him, of course. He cares about her, you know, and I knew he was hurting you. So I hurt him back,' he shrugged.

Merlyn didn't understand his logic, she doubted he did either, and yet she knew that in his mind she had become two women, the Suzie whom he loved, and the new woman in Rand's life whom he could use to hurt him for keeping Suzie from him.

Merlyn moistened stiff lips, vaguely aware that her nails had gone through the flesh of her palms and drawn blood, feeling the stickiness against her fingers. 'You're right.' She forced herself to smile, feeling as if a part of her stood away from herself watching. 'He's been unfaithful to me, he doesn't deserve my love.'

Christopher shook his head. 'I saw them together in her hotel room. I wasn't sure about them when she went to the Lake District to see him, but I had my suspicions. But that first afternoon on location they were in her bed together. That night too. I stood outside her room and listened to them both times!'

Merlyn felt sick as she imagined Christopher as the prowler outside her window listening to her and Rand in bed together. Christopher had been so determined that Rand should continue his affair with Merlyn that every time they had a disagreement or agreed not to see each other again he had somehow contrived to get them back together again, so that he could have 'his Suzie'.

And all the time he had continued to punish Rand because Suzie had loved him, refusing to let Merlyn wear a wig for her part and insisting she actually have her hair coloured and styled like the other woman's so that she would be a constant reminder to Rand of the woman he had lost. Had that also been the time Christopher himself got the two personalities confused in his mind?

All this time she had felt as if someone other than herself governed her actions, had wondered if Suzie . . . Christopher had manipulated them all, and somewhere in the midst of his plans he had become entangled in his own cruelty, now actually believed her to *be* Suzie.

'That was a little naughty of you,' she scolded.

'I had to be sure, don't you see?' he said vehemently. 'So that you were free to come to me!'

'You've loved me for a very long time, haven't you,' she said sadly.

'Ever since that first picture together,' Christopher remembered tautly. 'But you could never see anyone but your precious Rand. I loved you anyway, I knew one day you would come to me, that you would realise no one could love you as much as I do.'

He had loved Suzie so much he had killed her rather than let anyone else have her.

'I tried to tell you how I felt that day in London when I came to your apartment. I'd heard you were staying there, and I had to see for myself that you were completely well. It almost killed me not being about to see you during that time, the white roses I sent you every week just weren't enough.'

Merlyn remembered the bouquet he had brought to her in hospital yesterday. Would Rand see them, read the card that had accompanied them, and realise—? No, he wouldn't give them a second glance, she was just clutching at straws.

'As soon as I arrived you told me I'd only just caught you,' he rasped. 'That you were on your way back home. You thanked me for caring but told me you were still in love with your husband!'

'And so you followed me,' Merlyn prompted.

'Yes,' he confided scornfully. 'You were so wrapped up in thoughts of your precious Rand that you didn't even see me drive up beside you until the last moment, and by then it was too late. You turned off the road instinctively. I stopped my car and walked back to look at you. There was blood trickling down your beautiful face. But you still looked so beautiful!'

Merlyn didn't know how much longer she could ward off the hysteria and continue to humour this man. She feared what this strain was doing to her baby. Oh God, she couldn't die now, not when she carried Rand's child inside her!

'What?' Christopher gave her an irritated frown.

She brought herself under control as she realised it had been her choked sob that had angered

him. He believed that she loved him, that at last
Suzie had come to him; he had to go on believing
that if she were to remain alive. He had killed
once, and she knew he wouldn't hesitate to do it
again.

'Nothing.' She could feel her lips trembling as
she smiled at him. 'Maybe we could go out to
dinner to celebrate the fact that we're together at
last?'

'I want to be alone with you,' he declared.

'Well, of course, Christopher,' she instantly
humoured him. 'If that would please you.'

'I made them suffer for betraying you,' he told
her with satisfaction. 'I even signed Merlyn's
fiancé to play the part of Brandon instead of Gary
Parker so that Rand would know what it feels
like to only receive crumbs from the woman
you love. Gary Parker wasn't too happy about
being replaced, I can tell you,' he chuckled
maliciously.

The power Christopher had wielded over all
their lives the last few months was absolutely
terrifying. He had pulled their strings and they
had all danced to his insane tune.

'You've been very clever,' she said shakily.

'Of course,' he accepted with arrogance.

They were actually in London now, would
soon reach his apartment. And once they did that
there would be no help for her!

The anticipation in his eyes as he locked the car
in the parking area beneath his apartment building filled her with nausea. But his fingers on her
arm were like talons, making escape impossible,
and as was usual in these underground parking

areas, it was deserted except for the two of them. The lift a short distance away would take them straight up to his floor, to his apartment, and no one would even see her. She couldn't let that happen!

'You're hurting my arm, Christopher,' she complained, pushing at his fingers, all the time keeping a smile on her lips, even if her eyes did reflect her panic. If she could just persuade him to let her go for a minute . . .

'You're still very weak.' He kept a firm hold of her.

'Yes, but——'

'What do you think you're doing with her, Drake?'

Merlyn's legs buckled beneath her at the hollow sound of Rand's voice, Christopher's grip on her preventing her from falling as she desperately searched the car park for Rand. And then she saw him, standing motionless beside the lift that would take her up to Christopher's apartment. 'Rand!' she cried thankfully, not knowing how he came to be here before them or how he had known where to find them, just glad to see him as she attempted to go to him.

'No!' Christopher gave a feral growl. 'You're mine now. He betrayed you, remember?' All of a sudden Christopher held a gun in his other hand, that hand quite steady as he pointed the weapon at Rand.

The relief that had flowed through Merlyn at the first sound of Rand's voice was instantly replaced with the chilling horror of what Christopher could do to Rand with that gun. She had no doubt that it was real, and that it was loaded. She put her hand testingly on Christopher's arm, snatching it away again as he recoiled angrily.

'There's no need for this, Christopher,' she cajoled. 'As you said, I'm yours now.' She looked beseechingly at Rand for his silence as he gave a furious snarl. 'Suzie has come back to *you*, remember?' she prompted Christopher, moistening her lips as she realised how grey Rand had suddenly become.

God, surely Rand hadn't come here alone; hadn't he brought help with him?

'I've forgiven you for forcing me off the road that night when I mistakenly wanted to return to Rand,' she conveyed that message to Rand in the only way that was open to her, unable to see his reaction now as she concentrated on Christopher exclusively. 'I was a fool not to realise it was you I loved all along.'

'If you love me then it won't matter if I kill him,' he reasoned calmly, aiming the gun at Rand still.

'But if he's dead you'll never know whether I stayed with you because I loved you or because Rand was no longer alive,' she pointed out desperately.

'I'll take that risk,' he told her coldly.

He was going to shoot, she could see that he intended going through with it. And there was no way she was going to allow him to kill Rand.

'Merlyn, no!' Rand shouted as she made a lung for the gun, a shot sounding loudly in the hollowness.

Merlyn was aware of a scuffling sound behind

her, and then the pain in her arm covered everything in darkness.

This time she knew it was a hospital bed in which she lay, recognised the impersonality of the cream decor, the stark walls, the smell of antiseptic in the air.

Her left shoulder ached, pain shooting down the length of her arm as she tried to move it.

Then she remembered Christopher; insane Christopher who had convinced himself that Suzie lived again, in her, his cruel punishment of Rand because he was the one Suzie loved backfiring on him in a way he hadn't conceived. She wondered when it had begun—with the sudden possessiveness he had begun to display when they first arrived in the Lake District? Certainly he had allowed himself to believe it was the real Suzie he made love to the day he took over from Mark in the gazebo. She shivered with revulsion as she remembered the passion she had believed to have been pretence, but which had been very real to Christopher. He had killed Suzie, the woman he loved, so that she shouldn't return to Rand!

Rand! Where was he? The last time she had seen him he had been at the receiving end of Christopher's gun. From the pain she was in she would say the bullet hit her first, but where had it gone after that?

She made a move to sit up, the pain that racked her body making her sway weakly. 'Please,' she gasped, her head turned towards the door. 'Can someone help me?' The last was a choked cry.

'Merlyn!'

Her aching body protested strongly as she swung round at the sound of that voice. Rand sat beside the bed, a Rand who had obviously been dozing in the chair as he waited for her to wake, a Rand haggard with grief and worry, his face grey, a dark stubble on his tautly clenched jaw.

'I'm so sorry.' Tears filled her eyes at the suffering he had known the last two years, at the needless death of the woman he had loved so deeply.

'You were the one who got shot.' He clasped her hands tightly in his as he sat forward. 'How do you feel?'

'Like I've been shot,' she answered wryly. 'But that wasn't what I was sorry about.' She looked at him anxiously. 'You do realise what I was trying to tell you about Suzie, don't you?'

Naked pain showed in the darkness of his eyes. 'Drake killed her.'

'Because he knew she had accepted and come to terms with the decision the two of you had made, that she loved you,' Merlyn prompted forcefully.

'He said he did it because he loved her.' Rand shook his head disbelievingly, tears in his eyes, his face ravaged. 'That isn't love, it's obsession!'

Merlyn wasn't as successful in holding her tears in check, her body moving convulsively as she watched him stand up to pace the room.

'The irony of it is,' he continued, seeming to be talking to himself, 'I'm sure Suzie wasn't even aware of his feelings until—until that last day. She told me he always flirted with her when they worked together,' he said dazedly. 'But it was never anything demanding.'

'Christopher was always demanding of his leading ladies,' Merlyn said with remembered pain. 'He either gave them hell or had an affair with them.'

Rand frowned. 'Suzie always said he was very kind to her——'

'Christopher was never kind,' Merlyn exclaimed, vividly remembering his humiliating cruelty to her the first morning they worked together. 'Rand, how did you find me? How long have I been here?' Daylight streamed through the tall windows.

'They arrested Drake yesterday, you've been unconscious since then. They had to operate to get the bullet out of your shoulder.' He drew in a ragged breath. 'We might not have discovered you were missing until today if Hillier hadn't kept insisting he'd had nothing to do with your so-called accidents, demanding to know why the police didn't talk to Drake and me as we were the two having affairs with you!'

Merlyn gasped. 'That isn't true, there was only ever you!'

'I know that, but Hillier insisted he had seen Drake coming out of your suite a couple of times. He assumed you were playing us off, one against the other.'

She swallowed hard. 'Christopher never came to my suite.'

'Not when you were in it, no,' Rand acknowledged huskily, his profile harsh in the brightness of daylight. 'He came in a couple of times when you weren't there though, and Hillier saw him.'

'What's happened to Mark now?' she frowned, feeling guilty about her own suspicions of him, knowing he must be furious at being held at a police station 'for questioning'. It wouldn't do his precious career much good!

Rand's mouth twisted. 'He's probably being consoled in Jenny's waiting arms.' He sighed. 'Thank God the police decided to check into his story on Drake, otherwise we might never have realised you had left the hospital with him. As it was, a young nurse had reported you had checked yourself out voluntarily——'

'I did leave voluntarily, I was coming to see you,' Merlyn explained. 'I'd read the notebook that afternoon——'

'Only that afternoon?' Rand looked puzzled.

She shrugged. 'It took me a while to get up the courage to read it. And after I had I—I knew I had to see you, to talk to you. Christopher offered to drive me,' she rushed on as she saw Rand retreat from what she was obviously trying to tell him; that she still loved him. 'I fell asleep on the drive, and when I woke up we were almost at London and he was calling me Suzie . . .'

Rand breathed raggedly. 'I knew there was something wrong when Anne telephoned me to say you had discharged yourself. I went to the hospital myself, I just didn't believe you could have been in any condition to go anywhere. And then I saw the roses.' He shook his head. 'I told the police I believed Drake had you, and I flew down with them to try and get here before the two of you did. Suzie used to get a bouquet of white roses every week.' His expression softened. 'I used to tease her about having a secret admirer she didn't want to tell me about. He sent them to her, didn't he?' he groaned.

Merlyn nodded. 'He had convinced himself that Suzie didn't really love you, that she only stayed with you because you were so possessive you wouldn't let her leave. I know,' she soothed at Rand's angry protest. 'You aren't in the least possessive. But Christopher had to explain Suzie's staying with you to himself somehow; he just couldn't accept that she genuinely loved you.'

Rand's hands were clenched into fists at his sides. 'A madman's obsession robbed me of the woman I loved!'

'Yes.' What else could she say, it was the truth. Suzie had survived a serious illness, the loss of her child, the knowledge that there would never be another one, had come to terms with all those things, only to be destroyed by another man's obsessive love. *Rand* was going to need time to come to terms with the way Suzie had died.

'He would have killed you too if you had opposed him,' he realised raggedly.

Merlyn had discovered exactly how dangerous Christopher was, but she couldn't help wondering how Rand would really have felt if Christopher had harmed her.

He seemed to become aware of that question the same time that she did. 'Merlyn——'

'It's all right,' she told him huskily. 'I've never

asked you for anything, and I'm not going to start now.'

'All this has—I can't comprehend——'

'Of course you can't,' she soothed, knowing that even their baby would have to wait for the shock to wear off before Rand was told of its existence; he just couldn't handle any more pressure just now, especially emotional pressure. She was going to have to wait for him to come to her. If he ever did.

'I do care for you, Merlyn.' His eyes were silver. 'More than I ever wanted to. I'm just not sure it's enough. For you.'

She held back the tears stinging her eyes. 'Shouldn't you let the police know I've regained consciousness?' she prompted lightly. 'I'm sure they must want to talk to me.'

'They do,' he nodded. 'I just—Have patience with me, Merlyn?' he requested gruffly.

She did have patience, but their child didn't, she thought ruefully as she received a painful kick against her rib-cage. At seven months she felt sure the baby was trying to kick its way out, not content to wait another two months to be born normally.

It had been a long six months for her, would have seemed even longer, she acknowledged, without the steady growth of her pregnancy and all that entailed to occupy her time. This morning, for instance, she and her mother had been out shopping for nursery furniture, which was probably why Merlyn felt so tired and the baby didn't!

Rand should have been here to share in the excitement of choosing their baby's furniture, should be lying on the bed with her now with his hand resting on the swell of her body as they both felt their child's impatient movements.

It had been an easy pregnancy so far, and she had received a lot of help from her family, and friends like Liza and Anne. James and Anne had been told about the baby early on in the pregnancy, had visited her in London a couple of times, but they, more than anyone else, knew that Rand mustn't be told about it just yet. It was through them that she learnt he was slowly coping with Suzie's death at the hands of a man who had been certified as insane.

But it had been six long months now, and Rand should be here!

He will be, a gentle voice assured her. *He's coming to you now. He loves you.*

Merlyn's eyes widened with shock as she slowly looked around the bedroom trying to locate that voice. She was alone, completely alone. And yet she had heard a voice. Hadn't she . . . ?

Take care of him, Merlyn—

'Who is this?' She sat up in alarm, her hands tightly gripping bunches of her quilt as she realised she was talking to herself.

She must have been on the edge of sleep, dreams often seeming more vivid then, chastising herself for her imaginings as she lay back on the bed.

Love him—Please, don't feel alarmed, that voice soothed as she once again sat up in a panic. *I mean you no harm*, that whispery voice comforted.

She wasn't dreaming at all, the voice was inside her head. She was going mad!

No, Merlyn, you're perfectly sane, that voice chided her. *Please, just listen to me.*

Merlyn lay on the bed stricken with terror now. If she wasn't going mad, then who— 'Suzie . . . ?' she whispered chokingly.

Yes . . . The voice sounded relieved. *Be good to Rand, Merlyn. And love the daughter you carry and the sons you have yet to come.*

She had to be dreaming this, Merlyn realised as a curious calm settled over her. She would wake up in a minute, these naps never lasted long.

'I'm having a son,' she told that dream dismissively.

It's a girl, Merlyn. Rand will love you both so much. So much . . .

Only she and Suzie had ever called him Rand! But it was a dream, that calm reminded her, and dreams could do anything they wanted to.

I'm no dream, Merlyn, that voice spoke softly. *I just want you to know he's all yours now, that he loves you completely. There will be no more ghosts now that I can leave him with you, as I always intended I should . . .*

'Suzie, I—Suzie?' She half sat up on the bed, turning her head from one side to the other. But not even the voice was there now.

Merlyn was trembling all over as she got up unsteadily. *Had* she imagined it or—? The doorbell rang to interrupt the question she was frightened to find an answer to anyway. Because if she accepted that Suzie had come to her just now she had to accept that Suzie *had* been the one guiding her from the moment she attempted to get that part in the film.

Her movements were necessarily slow as she moved to the door, her slender body bearing the added weight of her child with an ungainly gait that made her appear slightly front-heavy.

'Who is it?' she called through the closed door, still slightly shaken from the vividness of that dream.

'Special delivery for Miss Summers,' came back the muffled reply.

She gave an irritated frown; surely by some miracle of organisation the shop hadn't managed to deliver the furniture on the same day? Her mother! She could organise anything she chose to, was taking great delight in preparing for the advent of her third grandchild.

'Just a minute,' she called out as she unlocked the door, frowning as, instead of meeting someone's gaze on eye-level she stared at fresh air. A small squeaking noise at her feet made her look down, giving a small gasp of pleasure at the sight of the two kittens in the box that looked back at her, a pure black one, and a long-haired tortoiseshell.

'Where did you come from?' She looked up and down the corridor but there was no one in sight. Someone must have just dumped them on her doorstep and run. 'You poor little things,' she crooned as she picked them both up out of the box. 'Doesn't anybody want—' Her stunned gaze was fixed on the label attached to the red ribbon about the tiny black neck, 'MISSY not Ms' it read.

She turned quickly to the tortoiseshell, the small brown body squirming as she tried to read the label on the green ribbon, 'BISCUIT'. Rand!

Her heart began to beat faster than ever. 'Rand . . . ?' she called uncertainly. Suzie had said he was coming. . . And who else could know the significance of the kittens' names? 'Rand!' she called again, more desperately this time.

He stepped out from the corridor that adjoined hers, thinner, but with none of the bitterness in his face that she had always associated with him. 'I thought we could have two kittens to start with, and as they are a male and female I'm sure they will soon solve the problem of the "houseful", although one of them might have to change his name! The rain seems to be something we can't stop falling this year, and Mrs Sutton has baked enough burnt biscuits to—My God.' His stunned gaze lowered to the swell of her body, his throat moving convulsively. 'No one told me you were pregnant!'

'*We're* pregnant,' she corrected, her throat full with emotion, putting the kittens back in their box as they drooped against her tiredly. 'We've been waiting for you.'

He didn't touch her, just came to stand in front of her. 'I love you, Merlyn Summers. I began to love you that first night you came to me, but I felt guilty for allowing myself to feel again.' His silver gaze held hers. 'I felt responsible for Suzie killing herself, and that I didn't deserve to be happy again. Finding out that she was killed doesn't change the fact that I made her unhappy, and now that you're carrying my child I don't know how you feel about what I did——'

She put silencing fingertips over his lips. 'The same way I always have; that you made the right decision.'

'A part of me will always love and remember Suzie, but she's my past, and if you'll have me, you're my future!' His beautiful eyes looked down at her anxiously.

'You have to be sure, Rand,' she told him earnestly. 'You said you couldn't bear to be anywhere with me that you went with her——'

'Because being with you blocked out the memories I had with her.' His hands clasped her hands. 'And at the time I didn't want to forget——'

'Are you sure you do now?' She was still wary, couldn't take anything less than total commitment this time. 'It's been six months.'

'I can see that.' He looked indulgently at the swell of her body that was his child. 'But I wouldn't have come to you now if I wasn't sure the past is behind me, that I'm not offering you less that you deserve.'

'And you?' she looked at him anxiously. 'What do you deserve?'

'You,' he answered simply. 'As my wife. As the mother of my children.'

'As far as I'm aware there's only one in there!' she teased him, a slight catch in her throat.

'I'm hoping there will be others,' he said huskily. 'That other child——'

'Rand, I knew before reading Suzie's notebook that you and she had lost a child,' she told him gently. 'Anne told me accidentally one day. And at the time I was glad she had; it explained your uncharacteristic aggression that first afternoon you came to my hotel room—before you made such exquisite love to me.'

Rand shook his head. 'I couldn't believe the things I said to you that day!'

She understood him well enough to know aggression with a woman was totally alien to him. And in the end it had been the gentler side of him that made love to her. 'I knew you didn't really mean them,' she assured him. 'And really there was no need for force; I was only too willing!' She looked down at the tangible evidence of that willingness she had had to belong to him from the very first moment she saw him.

Rand's expression was agonised. 'Don't you hate me for what I did to Suzie?'

She was shaking her head even as he voiced the question. 'I told you that nothing I read in that notebook changed my feelings for you, and it still hasn't. You did what you had to do, and I'm sure that if you had to make that choice again you would make the same one.'

'I would,' he acknowledged flatly. 'There really was no choice.'

She looked up at him with all of her love in her eyes. 'I'm sure Suzie knew that—and accepted it. She was just hurt and confused when she realised you had lied to her.'

'She would have insisted on putting the baby first if I hadn't!'

'I know that.' Merlyn smoothed the lines from between his eyes. 'And so did Suzie. More than anything else she knew she loved you, and that's why she was coming back to you. Suzie will always be a part of *our* lives, my darling, because she was the one to bring us together.' She believed that now in a way she could never tell Rand, knew that he *had* put his life with Suzie behind him, and that today Suzie had relinquished her hold on his heart.

'She would have liked you,' Rand said with certainty. 'When she was so ill she told me that she—that when she was gone, she wanted me to find someone else to love, to be happy with them. I told her that would never happen, and at the time I believed it. But Suzie was so much wiser than me, and I began to realise how right she had been the first time I made love to you.' He framed Merlyn's face with loving hands. 'I do love you, so much, and you make me so happy. I'd like to hold you, to love you, but I don't want to hurt you or the baby.' Rand looked uncertain.

'You won't hurt me,' she assured him huskily. 'And I think the baby would like it too!'

'Would you have told me if I hadn't come here tonight?' He looked so vulnerable. 'I'd understand if you weren't going to——'

'Of course I was going to tell you about our child,' Merlyn admonished, knowing he still found it difficult to believe there *was* a child. 'My mother has strict instructions to call you as soon as I go into labour!'

'What a shock that would have been,' he said ruefully.

'Not much more than it is now,' she derided. 'Pregnant women aren't very glamorous——'

'You're talking about the woman I love, adore,

worship,' he punctuated each endearment with a kiss, each more lingering that the last. 'Desire,' he added shakily. 'Do you think we might go into your flat for our lovemaking?' he remarked candidly, the evidence of his desire moving impatiently against her. 'I think we might be a little conspicuous out here!'

His teasing lightened the mood between them. They smiled idiotically at each other as Rand carried the box with the kittens into the flat and closed the door. But their smiles quickly became sensual pleasure, their shared love deepening their love for each other.

It was some time later, their love expressed in the most fundamental way possible as Rand made love to her with a tenderness bordering on reverence, that they returned to anything resembling rational conversation, the kittens both fast asleep in the box beside the bed.

'I've seen a preview of the film.' Rand caressed the hair at her temples. 'You were absolutely beautiful in it.'

After much confusion and indecision the film company had finally decided to go ahead and make the film under a totally new director, and it had been completed several months ago, before Merlyn's pregnancy was apparent to any but the most discerning eye. It was due for general release very shortly, and while Merlyn knew it lacked Christopher's obsessive genius, it was a more accurate account of Suzie's story.

'Anne and James send their love, and of course Daniel Brandon does too,' he added.

The Bentons' son had been born only a few

months ago, and while Merlyn hadn't seen him yet she had been assured by his parents that he was the most beautiful baby in the world. As he had partly been named after his uncle, she didn't doubt it for a moment!

'I think we should start thinking about arranging our wedding before *our* son decides to put in an appearance!' Rand still looked slightly in awe of the child he had felt move beneath him, his hand even now resting possessively on the squirming body.

'Daughter,' Merlyn corrected softly.

He raised dark brows at her certainty. 'You sound very sure about that, have you had one of those tests done to establish the sex?'

'No,' she smiled, loving each rugged inch of his face, even the past that had put the lines there. 'But I do have it on good authority,' she said huskily.

'Merlyn's magic?' he teased.

'Not exactly.' She caressed his beautiful face, knowing that Suzie hadn't meant for her to tell Rand of their conversation. Conversation? It still seemed slightly unreal, and yet Rand was here as Suzie had said he would be. It had happened. Hadn't it . . . ? 'It will be a daughter, you'll see,' she said with renewed certainty.

'If you say so.' The love in his eyes almost blinded her as he bent his head and his mouth claimed hers.

Angela Suzanne Carmichael was born exactly six weeks later.